The Winter Swimmers' Club

by

Sheila G. Bardas

ISBN: 978-1-8380929-7-9

Published By: -

i2i
PUBLISHING

i2i Publishing. Manchester.

www.i2ipublishing.co.uk

To Christos, Gordon and Helen.

Acknowledgements

I would like to thank all family and friends for their encouragement over the years.

Also, I must mention the members of the Phidias Writers Group and thank them for their support.

Finally, I am thankful to Lionel Ross at i2i Publishing, Mark Cripps, his senior editor and Dino Caruana, his cover designer, for their help and support in the final stages of the project taking the book to publication.

Season 1

Troubled Waters

Characters

Julia – Former society lady. Well-groomed, and now in her late sixties. Energetic winter swimmer.

Pavlos - Julia's taxi driver. Chain smoker and world-weary. In his mid-forties.

Betty – Cafe proprietor. In her early fifties, a bubbly and friendly person who organises everyone.

Lt Michael Mavromatis - Retired from service in Alexandropoulos and Cyprus. Always dapper, complete with army beret, medals and worry beads. In his early seventies, likes to be in control and provide a moral compass for others. Accomplished dancer.

Barbara - His wife and son Andreas are both deceased.

Dimitris – Mild mannered, eighty-year-old. Retired accountant and grandfather of Marina.

Marina - Sociology graduate. In her early twenties with a unique, soft punk style. Assistant to Betty in the cafe.

Alexi - In his early seventies. Part time animal shelter worker. Scruffy individual who changes to win over Julia.

Caesar – Alexi's large lovable dog.

Antonis – In his late twenties. Mountain bike enthusiast and anarchist. Gay.

Petroula - In her late twenties. Tall, blonde Hungarian. One-time pole dancer, now a housekeeper.

Tom – Petroula's son by Panos. Cute six-year-old with a stammer and some learning difficulties.

Bartholomew - In his fifties. Unemployed banker. Sings in the church. Always a very smart dresser.

Poppy - In her early thirties with a cascade of red curls and a shapely figure. Opinionated, hard-working English teacher.

Kyriakos - First unsuitable boyfriend of Poppy. In his mid-twenties. Pathetic, mothers-boy type.

Nikos – A shy, lean, and weather-beaten farmer. In his late twenties, his clothes are clean if eclectic, in choice.

Matthew – Handsome, charismatic, and gay. In his mid-twenties. Rides a large motor bike and works as a riot control policeman.

George - Rather overweight factory worker. Generous and jovial. Victim of economic problems. Now in his early sixties.

Roula - His wife. Parent to Maria and Antigoni.

Kalim - West African refugee in his mid-twenties. Athletic and good looking. Dreams of playing football but runs an escort agency.

Nadeen – In her twenties. Works for Kalim, then becomes his girlfriend. Has survived unimaginable horrors in her own country. She blossoms into a confident, independent, woman.

Illias K. - In his mid-sixties. Stocky and mean looking. The ex-boss of George.

Markos - Second unsuitable boyfriend of Poppy. Spoilt egotist in his mid-thirties.

Jacob - Son of Betty. Ex-army and now suffering from depression. In his early twenties, goes from hippie style to hipster. His twin brother Jannis is now deceased.

Philipos - Third unsuitable boyfriend of Poppy. Spaced-out alcoholic in his early forties.

Kitso - Cousin of Nikos. Electrician and clarinet player. Boyfriend of Poppy.

Others:

Louli - Brindled, friendly, female cat who lives in the cafe.

Commander Sideris – Ignorant and authoritarian.

Jannis – Sideris' driver, who acted with courage and showed a healthy disregard for the commanders orders.

Prologue

A Secret Crime

Athens shimmered and sweltered in the oppressive, unrelenting heat of late summer. It was a Saturday afternoon. The sky was grey and the air gritty with dirt and dust. The glare and heat bounced off the concrete walls of housing blocks and factories alike. Most residents were now inside waiting for the relative cool of evening. George had been manoeuvring building supplies around on a forklift all day. His shift was now over, and he slumped over the handlebars of his Vespa, exhausted and despondent. He cursed his weight as sweat soaked his tight shirt. He could not face going home yet, so he drove off through the noise of the traffic down the coast road towards his favourite beach to cool off and have a drink or two in the café there.

He finished his beer and looked outside. The sky was opaque and windless. Suddenly overcome with fatigue, he decided to go outside and have a rest on the bench. He belched and rubbed his distended paunch, regretting drinking the beers, although they had taken the edge off the perpetual ache in his right arm which dogged him on most days. He lay down and stared up into the green canopy of the plane tree above and sighed, "I hope I live long enough to see my pension." Louli sauntered over, then jumped up and curled into him purring, so he cuddled her. "You don't have to worry much, do you puss?" he said, as he dozed off, imagining his daughter's wedding, the kind he knew she dreamt of. I'm sorry Maria, I just can't afford it, he thought to himself, as he wiped away a tear. "I'm becoming sentimental these days," he said out loud, before his eyes closed.

In the café window, a candle in the lantern twinkled. The beach was empty save for a hippie-looking character collecting rubbish and putting it into a plastic bag. He was followed by three smallish, hairy dogs, tails wagging, tongues lolling out happily. On his bench, George began to stir, the sun was sinking, and it was cooler. The noise of car tires crunching on the pebbles outside the café had woken him. He opened his eyes, dazed after a deep afternoon's sleep. Everyone seemed to have gone home. He rubbed his arm which was now stiff and a bit painful.

He began to think of more pressing matters: his wife Roula patiently resigned to living on a tight budget while his daughters, Maria and Antigoni could not hide the resentment in their eyes. In shame, he rubbed his face. How had it come to this? He remembered Maria as a little girl. "Daddy, one day I'll be the princess in the white dress," she had proclaimed to him. He was torturing himself. It was too hard for kids today with too much emphasis on having this or that, the latest smartphone, the designer labels, the school trips, and the teasing they get. It made him sick. He rubbed his head again.

"Don't get angry, you'll get your blood pressure up," he could hear his wife say, "It doesn't matter darling. We've got each other and the girls are healthy, and we're lucky compared to some, those desperate people queuing for food every day, most of them alcoholics or junkies. They can't live at home obviously, but no one seems to care much. It's like they're invisible."

George sat up, his head now clear and his senses alert. The car had stopped but he remained still and peered out. He could hear voices and in the front seat, a dark girl was checking her lipstick in the mirror. Then, she got out. She was wearing a tube dress in a burgundy colour. "Wow, she's cute!" he whispered. The girl turned to look at the tall good-looking African man in shorts who was helping, or rather pulling at, a short, white man, slumped in the back seat. He managed to support him with difficulty. The man leant heavily against him and his head lolled on the African's shoulder. Then together, they stood and stumbled down to the sea. The short one presumably was Greek, thought George, who noticed that he was wearing underwear and socks, which was odd for swimming. The black man virtually had to lift the other man up and together, they waded into the sea. Then smoothly, he swam away, towing the smaller man along. The light was fading; George could no longer see clearly. After some ten minutes, he heard splashing, the rhythm of a strong, experienced swimmer. The African had returned alone and walked back to the car. George automatically put his hand over his mouth in horror at the thought that he'd just witnessed a murder! Flustered and sweating, he scrabbled in his jacket pocket for his cell phone but in his panic, it dropped at his feet. Calm down, man, he told himself. Stay still. You don't want them to see you. His imagination was now running wild. Maybe I'll be next, he wondered.

Suddenly, the phone buzzed with an incoming call which he closed with his foot and froze. The couple glanced up towards the tree for a second and then continued talking. George listened to them in disbelief.

"Hey, Nadeen. Next time, hot stuff, don't bonk him to oblivion. I gotta clean up this mess. Looks bad for the business, you know. If word gets out, they gonna throw away the key on me."

"Kalim, you're joking, man. He no Viagra cucumber man, that one. Real floppy. He liked to talk dirty, nasty man, one humph and he done. His heart just stopped. I got scared, it ain't nice."

"I don't need the details, girl. Here, take his clothes down to the sand, neatly now and don't take anything."

"Ahh, no, I don't want no ghost to get me!"

"Get on with it. I want the police to think its suicide. I'm not going down for this one. I still got big dreams, one day I'll get picked for the team. Then, I can hold my head up again."

"Don't get ahead of yourself, Kalim. You got a business to run."

"Hey, don't burst my bubble. Take them clothes, careful now."

Nadeen tripped down the beach on impossibly high heels and left the clothes on the sand, as instructed. George watched as she smoothed down her tight dress and returned to the car, shook sand out of her high heels and slid into the front seat.

"Me never did like the beach. Sand gets where it shouldn't!" She laughed, a normal young woman again, not a professional working girl.

"Can you swim?"

"Afraid not … you gonna teach me?" She leant forward and crooked a finger at him provocatively.

"No, you'd drive me mad. Right, we're done here. Let's go … back to work."

Silence returned as the posh car pulled away into the dusk. The dust settled. George got up stiffly and walked down to the sand and looked at the sea. There was no sign of the body. He turned to look at the pile of clothes, a cheap suit, shirt, and shoes. "God forgive me," he whispered as he went through the pockets. Eventually, he found a wallet and took out the taftotita. He flicked his cigarette lighter on and the flame illuminated the photo and the name. George gasped. He was holding the ID card of his former boss, Ilias Kavouris, and crossed himself. "I don't believe it!" he said aloud. Then, he remembered the bastard and how he treated everyone: the overtime with no extra pay, the verbal abuse, the threats of the sack. Everyone would keep their heads down and their mouths shut so as not to lose their jobs, knowing full well they were being exploited. No help from the unions when the sod never paid you on time and owed you money, month after month … He opened the wallet, "God help me! There's a lot of cash in here!" he said. George stood still for some time. Then, without further hesitation, he took the money and replaced the ID and wallet unaware that eyes that had been watching him had disappeared into the shadows. George kick-started the bike and drove off in a swirl of dust. On his way home, he stopped at a kiosk and phoned the police to make an anonymous report of a suspected suicide. As he stood by the kiosk, he started to shake, "Get a grip, man!" he told himself. "If I tell Roula I got lucky on the lottery, she'll believe me, and Maria can have her fairy tale wedding."

Meanwhile, the current was gently pulling his late boss out to sea where the peaceful slosh of water and darkness engulfed him. In the distance, the flickering of a candle could be seen in the cafe window and a thin line of smoke was rising from an adjacent hut.

Little did he realise that the decision he had made that evening would touch the lives of all the winter swimmers who gathered on Sundays at Betty's beachside café.

Sunday 1

Home from Home

The following afternoon, from out of the dark recess of a deep-set doorway and into the breathless blinding glare, stepped a lady of a certain age. She adjusted her straw hat and large-rimmed sunglasses. "One must keep up appearances," she murmured. Light and heat engulfed her as she emerged from the shade. Her summer Chanel-type suit was courtesy of a well-known second-hand import emporium on Athinas Street, although you would never know it. The ensemble was completed with matching sandals and handbag, the latter a voluminous affair holding towel, swimsuit, kaftan, flip flops, sun creams, and other oddments. Around her neck, a thick row of artificial pearls, quite incongruous in this heat, were the necessary hallmark of fashion, for which she was moderately famous, together with immaculately manicured and varnished nails and well-cut grey bobbed hair. She waited a moment for effect and then hailed a taxi.

A few curtains twitched, noting the time of her departure. The neighbours never missed much; their eyes behind shutters squinted in instant analysis. In this city, anyone's timetable was often of daily concern to a host of others, so to avoid the slippery slope into paranoia, it was best to become immune. Better still, find someone else to keep an eye on, just for the fun of it! Anyway, being Sunday and still too hot to do more than move the fan, or take a shower, or sweat under the air conditioning, if you could afford it, most residents kept movement to a minimum, until sunset.

Beyond the church, even the incompatible blue flags, Greek and EU, flapped listlessly, never at ease, as if reflecting the current political mood of two incompatible systems relentlessly chafing each other raw. A priest in full black regalia strode along holding onto his hat with one hand and clutching a brief case and bottle of water with the other. On Sundays, at least. he had his work cut out.

"As I was saying, don't believe what they tell you on TV ... ever. It says thirty-five degrees which means forty or so. Like the banks won't close but they did." Julia waved her hand vaguely. "You know where to go." Her taxi driver, Pavlos, glanced in the mirror at her and acknowledged her comments, drew on his cigarette, took a sip of frappé through a straw, changed gear and glided away into the traffic. They've had this arrangement for years now. She phoned him in times of crisis, like hospital visits or trips to the vet with sickly cats. Nearly every Sunday in winter, he took her to the beach, as she proudly asserted that she was a winter swimmer.

"This particular summer has been interminable with the daily grind of opening and closing of one's shutters, trying to keep your rooms cool, living in the dimness. Then, along with the heat came the fires, the demonstrations, the economy, the taxes, the price increases, not to mention the annual angst of students waiting for university entrance exam results or foreign languages. Those exams cost a fortune now, but it could mean the difference between employment or not." Julia paused, as if to check if Pavlos was listening. He nodded on cue.

"It's been suffocating. I do have air conditioning in the lounge, but the filters need attention, so I don't bother anymore." She rolled down the window and caught a blast of hot air. "I didn't go away this year. The lady I stay with on Kos was renting all her rooms daily to unexpected visitors from Turkey and beyond. Everyone seems to be making money out of their misery ... I only hope they know what to expect. Life in northern Europe can be cold and indifferent ... Better than being bombed or shot at, I suppose?" Pavlos glanced up, eyebrows raised, he just nodded in agreement. He was, after all, a captive audience. "Anyway, the beach is sweltering. At my age, I keep well away."

Pavlos suddenly commented, "You know, I can't remember my last holiday. The wife and I had a few days in Serres, at my brother's wedding ... and it rained."

But Julia continued with her train of thought, "It's all family groups doing nothing but huddling together under an umbrella, eating peaches, or body beautiful types roasting themselves like lambs on a Paska spit, or kids throwing balls at each other in the water, or those enthusiasts playing rackets ... tick-tack, tick-tack, annoying everyone!"

"Chance would be a fine thing," Pavlos said aloud, but again, she ignored his comment.

"And those poor foreign vendors, laden with doughnuts, watches, plastic toys or whatever, padding patiently up and down in these withering temperatures with tiers of sunhats balanced precariously on their heads. I don't know how they do it. I bet they don't sell much these days ... No, it's noisy, crowded, and dirty. No thanks, I'll wait until the hoi polloi have got bored ... By late September, it'll be tolerable again."

The lights were at red. Pavlos glared at her. What a stupid old snob, he thought.

Oblivious to the criticism, she continued, "Is it just me or does everyone seem overweight these days? It's probably all this economic stress and cheap pork sold by McPukadees!" The traffic was moving again and Pavlos grunted. At last, some progress, but Julia kept on talking. He sighed wearily as she continued, "Even a few degrees cooler you know, and people can think straight again. You can make reasoned decisions. What was that nice young prime minister thinking? Talk about blackmail, those creeps in Brussels had him by the balls, excuse me! But I voted NO to austerity ... all the euphoria of change nearly within our grasp. I should know better at my age to indulge in hope!"

Pavlos wasn't sure whether to agree to this or not. Julia fell briefly silent. "As I was saying, even a few degrees cooler and people can be civil to each other again. Every year, relationships are ruined by hasty words brought on by near heat stroke." She waved an arm out of the window like a child. "Bliss, the breeze is a little cooler."

In early September, it is tradition to greet one's fellow Athenians with a cheerful kalo himona, regardless if it is raining, or ironically, if it is still sweltering. The prospect of a few drops of rain can make you giddy with relief. Pavlos was now sweating. "Winter, my arse, it's thirty-six outside, if not more." He swore as the driver ahead turned abruptly without signalling.

Along a central boulevard, they flashed past brutal high-rise blocks of concrete, glass and chrome, each jostling for a sea view. Architectural fantasies loomed over the crumbling summer houses of a century ago, testaments to an affluent era enjoyed by the elite or the corrupt, now stood like rotten teeth bedecked in senseless graffiti and piles of plastic rubbish bags. Even the homeless refused to sleep there.

"Apparently, my family had one of those houses once," Julia said, as if to herself. Roused, Pavlos showed interest. Over the years, he thought he'd heard it all, but he didn't know this one. "Yes, I remember going there as a young child. It was considered to be a bit of a palace in the wilds then, you know ... but it was sold to pay off my grandfather's debts ... then he ran off to America with the nanny," Julia explained.

Pavlos was now enthralled. "Really, the scandal, the disgrace it must have caused," he observed.

"Well, yes, I suppose so. At least I have relatives over there. In the sixties or seventies, I visited them. I was supposed to be doing a secretarial course. I even had a Carnegie grant." Pavlos regarded Julia seriously in the mirror. She looked back at him and smiled. "I was young once! We went on a road trip, hitchhiking, Route 66, San Francisco, doing the hippie dippy thing, dope and the music clubs."

"Well, I never," Pavlos exclaimed.

As they drove along one of the city coastal roads, on one side, it was lined with palms and a pavement full of bikers weaving around pushchairs, and on the other, with more architectural monstrosities. Julia indicated, "Now one of those has long since crushed my mother's cherished rose garden." She fell silent, remembering people and places from a long time ago. Pavlos was rather impressed. Well done lady, he thought.

Gradually, the traffic lessened, and the city faded into a shimmering memory, a mirage of itself. The air became cooler and sweeter. Roads began to narrow and wind by olive orchards, fields of grape vines past a neat marble yard with slabs of grey stone arranged in shape and size, and next, an abandoned rusty car was slumped down among tall weeds. Julia sighed, "I've always liked this place. A bit unfashionable, a bit out of the way and you have to try to get here and of course, you have to be careful about getting back. Those coastal buses are a shy and retiring species at the best of times." She giggled at her own joke.

The road became lined with oleander in deep pink and white and before long, there was a gated entrance to a bleak communist-inspired hotel, complete with honeycomb octagonal windows and a thousand tiny balconies. The Aqua Palace, once popular in the sixties and seventies, remained open thanks to a roaring eastern European trade organised by the Sunny Smile Travel Services who were now investigating the opportunities created by the burgeoning Chinese tourist trade. However, the tourists would hardly venture out to the city except on organized bus trips to carefully chosen locations. They had everything on site, restaurants, bars, shops, and the underpass to a private beach kept them off the road. Even the entertainment and cinema were in Russian or Bulgarian. These tourists weren't interested in the world outside their hotel. They have it all, sun, sea, sex, and sanctuary, plus booze. They could be on the moon for all they knew or cared.

Suddenly, they'd arrived. Pavlos swerved off the road past the bus stop and overflowing dustbin where, years ago, some wit had sprayed the word kalpi, Greek for ballot box. A thin young man was poking around the rubbish bags with a stick. His dogs barked and chased the taxi. Pavlos crossed himself. "God help him," he said.

The taxi crawled down a narrow stony lane, the dust blew up coating the car and he swore at the prospect of cleaning it. The lane led seawards where several wind-blown heat-battered palms, probably planted by the local council in the days when money was spent on such frivolities, swayed, and shimmered in the breeze. Next, there was a roadside shrine, a dusty, rusted tin box with a cross on top. But on closer inspection, you would find it clean inside, where there was a photo of a young boy standing by a red canoe, smiling proudly, and an oil light and wick that was lit every evening by unseen hands. Around the base, the same loving hands had tied on a bunch of plastic flowers, their colours long since drained by the sun.

After this, there was a small play park for children, popular, no doubt, with a pre-digital generation. It was hardly the most stimulating of places, with three squeaking swings and a circular concrete area with some undulating bumps designed for skateboarders.

The taxi ground to a halt. When the dust had settled, Julia clambered out, took a step forward, opened her arms and breathed deeply. Pavlos threw his cigarette away and headed to the café for a coffee and a game of tavli before the return journey. Julia would probably take the bus back. Every Sunday, he would have the thought, "This time I'll swim, too," but he kept putting it off. The wife would get suspicious, so anything for a quiet life!

When Julia slipped off her sandals, the wind blew her hair across her face, so she clamped on the large straw hat and walked down the coarse sand. She passed the clumps of sea holly and white iris that grew around the shower, a homemade old pipe-and-hose affair. Today, the sea was glistening and whispering, asleep or pretending to be.

Set back from the beach, there was a café. Over the years, it had had a variety of owners, names, and success. For the last eight years, it had been called *Barkayan* and presided over by Betty, where a few regulars hung around and a graduate student, who helped.

Under the trees, there was an array of multi-coloured wooden tables and chairs. Inside, a Russian stove and metal chimney occupied the central area, a blessing in winter. There was a kitchen at the back with more eclectic furniture. A collection of donated board games and books were piled up on a cupboard with antique crystal knobs which must be of value. Above this, hung a huge gilded mirror, although unfortunately, the damp had begun to speckle the surface with black mould. However, by way of contrast, high up on the opposite wall, a flat screen TV had been attached as a focal point which was usually on, in case something happened.

Geraniums adorned the windowsills in pots fashionably painted in the same colour as the sills. Around one of these was curled a brindled cat named Louli who was content to sleep her life away, except at mealtimes. She was a real hussy, gentle by nature and would tolerate being petted by anyone. No-one knew exactly when or how she became a fixture. She just arrived one day and stayed.

Over the years, generations of children brought the shells they had found and piled them up around the base of the white-washed tree trunks, one of which had a handmade notice pinned to it announcing 'Winter Swimmers Welcome', and the dates of races to be arranged. From the branches of another tree, hung a large bamboo wind chime that clonked softly in the breeze. At the far end an old wooden boat, or rather half of it, had been painted and filled with plants and flowers. Beyond this, stood a small insignificant hut, like those given to those unfortunates made homeless after the earthquake some years ago. It was set back against the cliff wall, half drowning in bougainvillea.

As an act of defiance, the end wall had been splattered with graffiti, notably 'Legalize it!' Then, there was a group of menacing looking Antifa characters proclaiming that 'The street belongs to us', alongside a number of anti-fascist slogans, then underneath the stencilled outline of a TV with a broken screen had the words 'Crashed Greek democracy' next to it. Surprisingly, to one side, there was a beautifully painted owl in blue and green with a neat sign saying 'LOAF'. The rest was just the usual angry scrawl of witty, if slanderous, political statements and anarchist slogans, all obscuring each other. At first sight, the hut appeared to be used for storage, but a chimney at one end indicated habitation. Who would want to live there, was a matter for speculation. Behind the parking area and half hidden in the shade of a plane tree, there was a bench, an excellent place for a snooze out of the sun after a swim or a drink or two, or for canoodling on!

Betty ran a tight ship; drinks, sandwiches on order, ice-cream and one cooked dish of the day, no choice, to be consumed at two o'clock, and by seven o'clock, she was ready to close up in the winter months. The regulars adored her. She was full of simple words of wisdom like, ''No-one should eat alone, it's a miserable experience, tuck in,'' and they did. She was fond of adding, ''When we had money, we ate out once a week. There were about ten of us, the whole family, it was a chance to exchange news and sort out any misunderstandings before they got blown out of proportion. Now, you're lucky to get some cryptic e-mail telling you what's going on.''

Yet at dusk, she always lit the candle in the lantern on a small windowsill facing the sea next to a surprisingly modern pair of high-tech binoculars. Julia had often wondered at this routine but never inquired, as sometimes, it was best not to delve into people's privacy.

Julia pushed open the screen door to the café. Pavlos and a tall, white-haired man in a smart blazer with some military badges and immaculate shirt and slacks were playing tavli. He clicked his worry beads rhythmically and his army beret rested on his knee. Another man sat smiling vacantly near the TV, with an upside-down newspaper in front of him. A young girl in her early twenties, in an assortment of soft punk clothes with a cascade of plaits down her back and coal-black eyes, was wiping the tabletops. In the kitchen, Betty was attending to the cooking, which smelt wonderful. An unkempt man with scruffy hair, dirty teeth, and crumpled clothes, jumped up, delighted to see her.

"Hello, gorgeous, did you miss me?" His dog, on cue, jumped up too and bounded across to her.

"Good afternoon, Alexi. Gentlemen." Lieutenant Michael Mavromatis and Dimitris both half-rose in greeting, the old-fashioned way. The dog jumped up at Julia, tail wagging. "For God's sake, man, call your brute off."

"He's harmless, just affectionate like me! Here, Caesar, down boy."

"No comment." Julia raised her eyes. "How's business at the animal shelter?"

"Sadly, busy as ever. People can't afford to keep their pets anymore, so they dump them. Apart from dogs and cats, someone left a donkey. He's all skin and bones, poor thing but he's doing all right now. We've even got one of those fancy tropical iguanas." He paused to scratch through his hair. Julia frowned, speculating what was causing the irritation. "It doesn't do much though. Would you like an iguana?"

"No, thank you," she confirmed.

"I've got a cage you can have," he offered. Julia shook her head and turned away.

"Betty, Marina, how are you today?"

"Fine, it's been a bit quiet, but these rogues keep me busy enough. Considering they don't do an honest day's work between them; they've got good appetites." Betty gently dusted the lantern, windowsill and binoculars and stared out to sea for a moment.

"Marina, how's life treating you?" Julia asked.

"Well, I graduated, and grandad managed to get to the ceremony, and we took some photos and went for coffee afterwards. It was quite an effort for him, but my friends made a fuss of him and he had a great time."

"Congratulations."

"Thanks," she replied ironically. "Yes, finding a proper job is impossible. The adverts ask for native speakers of Russian, French, and English, whatever. I'm thinking of doing Erasmus or trying to get a scholarship to study abroad, there's nothing going on here!"

"What about your grandfather, darling?" They glanced across at Dimitris, who was trying to fold the newspaper as best as he could with arthritic hands.

"That's it," she whispered. "How can I leave him?"

Julia decided to go and change for a swim and Pavlos nodded to everyone and left. When Julia emerged from the back of the café, she was wearing a royal blue swimsuit - this season's colour according to Vogue - the straw hat and kaftan all colour-coordinated, complemented by a good, shapely figure.

Alexi rose from his chair. "Ahh, a dream, a vision of beauty."

"Stop it, man!" scolded Lt Mavromatis. "She'll think you're an idiot, which you are." He clicked his beads around sharply.

Dimitris suddenly woke and looked up. "Yes, very nice!"

"See you later, gentlemen." She walked down the sand, dropped her bag and kaftan and without hesitation, waded in, dived and swam off. The three café regulars had long since given up swimming in winter and often found excuses not to in summer. Julia swam strongly, then dived deeper and swam along with her eyes open. Through her mask, she had become part of another world of greens and blues and silver bubbles, all reflection and refraction. It was a garden of delights, where the occasional flash of tiny fish in shoals flitted amongst the jagged rocks and yellow coral flowers. She surfaced, circled her arms slowly back and forth. She leant back to float; her eyes closed. The sea, this was the place to forget, to be at peace, a place where life and time stopped for a while. Age slipped away and she was a young woman again. She began to swim again with steady strokes, at one with her element.

While back on the beach, other winter swimmers were arriving. A young man in his mid-twenties, dressed in the uniform of jeans and black hoodie, boasting an elaborate tattoo on his arm, pedalled up on a mountain bike. He propped it against a tree and waved at everyone inside the café. He obviously felt at home here. He passed Lt Mavromatis, who had watered the plants and was now fussing around a broken artificial fountain, examining a blocked-up water filter which he began to clean. During

Antonis' army service, Lt Mavromatis had been his commander in Avlona.

"Sir." He gave him a half-hearted salute.

"Ah, Antonis, here for your swim. Jolly good, carry on." Antonis stripped off and dived in. "Good athlete, that boy," observed Lt Mavromatis, replacing the filter, and switching on the fountain which bubbled into life.

Along the lane from the bus stop, a tall, blonde lady was walking slowly. Petroula carried a bag in one hand and held the hand of her young son Tom with the other. Her little boy was wide-eyed with excitement. He stammered and pointed at the seagulls gliding overhead. They found a suitable spot, sat on the sand, and began to make a sandcastle using a plastic bucket and spade. His mother showed him patiently, again and again, how to fill it up and turn it over until he got it right. Then she coaxed him to the water's edge where they paddled but when the water reached his knees, Tom started to shake, and wail so she picked him up and carried him back to the sandcastles.

Meanwhile, a gleaming Volvo had drawn up. Out stepped Bartholomew decked out in smart casual attire, nothing too flashy - the operative word would be tasteful - matching shorts and top, reflecting status and success. After neatly folding his clothes, he nodded to the café regulars, snapped on his goggles, walked down to the sea, dived in smartly and swam away.

A stir of interest greeted a young woman with curly red hair, wearing faded jeans and an old tee shirt, who appeared carrying a pile of blue schoolbooks and a towel. She was accompanied by a man in white trousers and a tee shirt with an inappropriate slogan on. He looked about and started to complain. "There's no bar, no sun chairs, no music." The young teacher just ignored him and waved to Julia who called to her.

"Poppy, come on, the sea's warm." Poppy indicated that her friend should come too.

"No way! I only swim in a pool. The sea is filthy, and I saw some dogs over there, disgusting, and that kid is crying. God, what a place! I'm going to see if that café can make me a decent frappé that won't poison me," and with that, Kyriakos retreated. Poppy removed her clothes, piled her books onto her towel and shook out her hair over her shoulders. "Bye-bye, got rid of that one, hey Julia!" and she swam off to meet her.

As if from nowhere, Nikos emerged from behind the old boat full of flowers. He too, was obviously a regular but he greeted everyone shyly. Kyriakos ignored him. For a second, Nikos looked hurt by this snub. His checked shirt and jeans were clean, if well-worn and out of fashion. His boyish charm should have ensured him a lovely wife years ago, but lack of prospects and confidence had put paid to that. Now his face bore the lines of hard outdoor work and drink. He had a smallholding from which he made a living. From out of a plastic bag that he was carrying, he pulled some aubergines, peppers and tomatoes and took them to the kitchen. "From my own patch," he said proudly, as he gave them to Betty.

"You darling!" Nikos blushed. "Thank you so much. Organic vegetables cost a fortune in the shops these days." Caesar bounded up and Nikos patted him automatically.

"Shall I take him for a swim, Alexi?"

"Sure, just watch out for the fleas jumping ship!" Alexi winked.

Kyriakos winced and pulled a face. Nikos, thin and strong, left for the beach with Caesar bouncing around him.

It was not long before he noticed Petroula and heard Tom crying. Without a second thought, he walked over. Petroula looked up and smiled, interested. Would this be her knight in shining armour? Tom stopped crying and looked up too. "Hi! I'm Nikos. I come here every Sunday to swim. Why is your little boy crying?"

"I was trying to teach him to swim but he panicked."

"Don't worry. I was a lot older before I learnt to swim," Tom had forgotten his fear and was looking at Caesar who had flopped down on the sand. "I'm taking the dog for a walk along the beach, would your boy like to come too? I think he would enjoy playing with Caesar."

"M-m-mummy, p-p-please!" Tom jumped up and down enthusiastically. Petroula realized that Nikos was being straightforward, and this was not a pick-up line. It was difficult to refuse as Tom was already patting Caesar.

"Thank you! That would give me a few minutes peace. "I'm Petra but I prefer Petroula and this is my son Thomas; he's known as Tom. By the way, he has some problems: he stammers and he's afraid of the sea."

"Don't worry, we won't go far," he assured her. "Let's look for some shells, shall we, Tom?" She watched them walking along the water's edge. Tom was now happily splashing in the shallow water with the dog for company and Nikos was picking up stones and shells.

Around the bend, the growling noise of a large motor bike could be heard approaching. The man driving it was in his early thirties. He parked and casually removed his worn leather jacket revealing a body to die for. Surreptitiously, all the winter swimmers eyed up the newcomer. They saw charm, confidence, strength, control, and power, plus good looks. Both Poppy and Julia sighed, "Ahh." Petroula pretended not to be looking but smiled.

Betty said quietly, "I wish I was in my twenties again!" The three regulars laughed. Marina stared at him for a moment then said, "Relax, Betty, he's too good to be true, which means he's probably gay," and they all laughed. Both Bartholomew and Antonis had watched his arrival, Antonis nodded and growled, "Wow." Bartholomew frowned at him. Kyriakos, now sulking in a corner, just glared. However, our body beautiful hero with a tan to match had a nasty bruise on his left arm and leg. Undeterred by the attention, he dived in and swam towards the men where he introduced himself as Matthew.

Last of all to arrive was George on his clapped-out, groaning Vespa. A man of simple pleasures, who smoked, drank, and enjoyed his food, despite repeated warnings from his doctor about his weight. He had been coming winter swimming for years. Before the accident to his arm, he used to play beach tennis well. Now swimming provided exercise for an injury which usually ached all winter. "Hello, everyone," he waved cheerfully at the café regulars and went to the sea. He nodded at Nikos. "Have you found a new friend?" Nikos indicated to Petroula, now sunbathing in a bikini, "It's her son."

"You should be playing with her and not the kid!"

"I wish," said Nikos. Oblivious, Tom was happily splashing around with Caesar. George waded in and swam steadily away.

Winter swimmers as a rule, swam, really swam! No treading water or lolling in the shallows. Swimming had a purpose. For a while, the sea was their element. They were as one and free. But today, fate had other plans.

The gentle wind that had rustled the reeds and shook the palm leaves now blew fresh and the sea started to churn into angry white waves. The sky was changing colour and the sand blew in stinging gusts. On the horizon, menacing clouds were mounting up and distant rumbling could be heard. The beach dogs had vanished, which was always an ominous sign. Within minutes, the winter swimmers were wading out of the surf and heading for the café, wrapping towels and kaftans around themselves for the sake of warmth rather than modesty.

"As I was saying to Pavlos earlier, you can't trust what they say on TV, especially the weather forecast. Look at it," Julia commented. The sky was rapidly darkening. "I'll have a cappuccino, my dear, and a juice for the little boy, if that's okay?"

Petroula smiled, a little overcome at the unexpected kindness she had been shown.

Julia flopped onto the settee next to the banker.

"Ah, Madam, God moves in mysterious ways. Perhaps he sent the wind to stop over-exertion." He offered his hand. "Bartholomew, Deputy Manager at Beta Bank, Syntagma."

Julia surveyed the smart fifty-year old sceptically. "Really." She could barely hide her disdain, but they shook hands and she moved up a bit for Petroula and Tom to sit down.

"What's your name?" The boy looked down shyly.

"I'm Julia."

"Thanks for the juice ... Careful, Tom ... I'm Petroula and this is my son."

"Where are you from?" Julia asked with the natural open interest shown by most Greeks who can, within a few minutes, ascertain your life history.

"A very small village, outside Budapest."

"You're a long way from home. Do you ever visit?"

"No, I've never been back."

"What do you do?"

"I'm a housekeeper for Mr. Konstantinopolis. He's a lawyer in Piraeus."

Nikos brought up a chair. He was obviously taken with her. Tom turned suddenly, spilling some of his drink over Nikos. "Careful!" she said sharply, raising her hand as if to smack the child. Instinctively, Nikos put his arm out to protect him. "It doesn't matter, Petroula, it's only some juice."

"Sorry, he gets a bit nervous. The teachers say he'll grow out of it."

"Really, I don't have much faith in what teachers say." He looked at the boy, "How about a game of UNO?" Tom nodded. Poppy watched them sadly as Kyriakos scowled and raised his eyes in contempt.

"What's for lunch, Betty?" she asked, drying her mop of curls.

"Okra and potatoes with cheese."

"Mmm." Kyriakos was slumped down looking bored. "I want to go, let's go," he said.

"Why?"

"I'm not eating here."

"Why not?" Poppy was not amused. "Perhaps you'd better go home then!"

"No problem! Phone me." He left, slamming the door.

"In your dreams. Goodbye. What a rude jerk." Poppy looked around embarrassed.

"I'm hopeless. I can really pick the losers." The three regulars, Alexi, Lt Mavromatis and Dimitris shook their heads and gave the thumbs down sign. "Thank you, gentlemen, you're always right. I think I need some help!"

"That one was, if I may say so, my dear, one of the worst. Tied to his mother's apron strings. No experience, no discipline ... needs to do his army service." Something Lt Mavromatis regularly recommended to young men.

Alexi added, "No balls, that one." He winked at Poppy.

"I wouldn't know!" she fired back. "Maybe he couldn't swim, who knows?" and she started to mark her books. "Back to reality."

"Never mind, dear, there's plenty more fish in the sea, as they say," soothed Julia.

"I'm here, darling, just waiting," Alexi jumped in.

"Oh, give up, man or ... go get a decent haircut and see about your eyebrows and nose while you're there ... and teeth!"

"For you, anything," he bowed. "Well, nearly!" Caesar flopped onto Julia's feet, all sea-wet and sand, gazing up with big adoring eyes. Julia shook her head in despair.

As the café filled up, the room seemed smaller. The windows started to steam up as outside, grey clouds began gathering. The wind caused the wooden wind chimes to mournfully clonk and dong together.

Matthew and Antonis found themselves at the same table. They eyed each other up. It was Antonis who opened with, "You look familiar."

Matthew replied with "So do you."

"I can't place it. Do you hang out in Kolonaki or Exarchia?"

"Both. I spend a lot of time up there."

"Oh, me too." They fell silent, mutually suspicious.

Matthew tried again with, "Where are you from?"

"Stilida."

"You're joking! My dad is from Lamia."

Antonis continued, now quite animated, "It's a small world." He reached out to touch one of the nasty bruises. "Did you have an accident?"

"Sort of. I work out a lot, kickboxing, weights, etc. I must have been over-enthusiastic and caught myself on one of the machines at the gym."

George came in puffing, pulling on his track suit as he did so. "Is there room for me?" He rubbed his head with his towel and introduced himself to the newcomers. "I'm George. I'm a regular winter swimmer here. Betty makes the best galaktoboureko, although I'm not supposed to eat it, diabetes you know. The doctor keeps telling me I'm living dangerously. Stop smoking, stop drinking, no this, no that … Marina, my dear, I'll have a small beer and a packet of crisps, please."

"Are you sure? You had quite a bit to drink yesterday."

"Yes." George ignored her and surveyed the company. "Hey, I know you." He was addressing Bartholomew, who puffed himself up importantly.

"Yes, I'm Bartholomew, Deputy Manager at Beta Bank in Syntagma. Are you a customer, perhaps?"

George laughed and shook his head. "Hardly. I've had no money in the bank for three years now!" He stopped laughing, abruptly. "Those were the days when we had some savings. They've long gone," he sighed. "I know where I saw you. It was Paska, at Agios Dimitrios church, Philopappou. You were singing!"

At this, Bartholomew had visibly paled. All eyes were on him now. "Yes, you are correct."

George gushed, "You were marvellous. Didn't you know there were hundreds standing outside listening to you? In the end, everyone was singing along."

"I had no idea. It's small and stuffy inside there. It was my first Paska I was rather nervous ... and I hate fireworks."

"Well, you did a good job; your singing really lifted my spirits."

"Thank you very much," he said, humbly.

But George wasn't really listening. His attention had been caught by a large plastic bag by the door. He wondered if the clothes that had been left on the beach were inside. It would be typical of Betty to collect them up. George thought he'd better make a move, so he casually called across, "Shall I throw out the rubbish?"

"Oh no! Don't touch that!" she quickly replied. "It's some clothes that were found on the beach this morning and there was an ID card with them, so I phoned the police and they said they'd come around this afternoon to collect them and check it against missing persons."

A few heads turned to follow the conversation. "Clothes left on the beach, with an ID. Sounds suspicious to me," said Lt Mavromatis.

"Could just be a midnight swimmer," suggested Poppy.

"Or maybe some poor person committed suicide?" suggested Julia.

"Let's leave it up to the police, shall we?" said Matthew and with that, the subject was dropped.

George breathed a sigh of relief. "Well, I'd better be off now," he said cheerfully.

As the Vespa was bouncing along the lane, he swerved sharply to avoid an oncoming police car approaching at speed. Its occupants were worn out after a long hot day of dealing with a myriad of minor misdemeanours, and now, having to retrieve some clothes, all because of some hoax call about a suspected suicide, so no wonder their humour was wearing thin. Nearly colliding with this man on his bike was the last straw and they cursed him heartily. Suffice to say, they unceremoniously collected the bag and drove off to deal with more pressing matters, and the winter swimmers went their separate ways into the evening dusk.

Sunday 2

Helpful New Recruit

It was a heaven-sent September autumn day with a clear sky of pale blue with a hint of a cool breeze from the north which rustled the trees. Large, yellowed, plane tree leaves littered the ground whilst the bark from the eucalyptus had twisted and curled and fallen to earth to be kicked and crunched underfoot. The sea was warm and felt like silk. The sun, gentle in the morning, could burn by mid-afternoon. On the beach, three pale dogs barked happily at some imaginary enemy, watched over by the solitary thin young man holding a plastic rubbish bag who was leaning against the side of the hut smoking a joint and gazing out to sea.

The café was already open and occupied by the three regulars. On the outside door, there was a police notice about the death of one Ilias Kavouris, asking for information or witnesses. It was old news now and life had moved on. Inside, the TV was on and Marina was serving coffee and Betty was in the kitchen cooking.

Julia's taxi arrived and she entered with a flourish, sporting a new outfit, this time a mix-and-match ensemble in dark rose with black accessories, more suitable for an embassy garden party than the beach.

With arms wide open, Alexi rose to greet her, "Hello, beautiful!!"

"You never give up do you?" she replied.

"Never, my Aphrodite, my ..."

"Down, Caesar! Down! Call your dog off, will you?"

Both man and dog were becoming irritating.

"My vision! What about cocktails at the rooftop bar of the Grand Britannia Hotel? Later we could ..."

She examined him closely, as there had been some changes. "Nice haircut. Now what about those hands? You look like you've been potting plants for a week."

"Ah! If only you knew!" He smiled. His teeth were seriously discoloured.

"Please don't tell me, spare me the details ... err ... those teeth of yours could do with a polish. When was the last time you went to a dentist?"

"Umm, the year Marina started University ... I think."

"Good Lord, that's three or four years ago. Come on. Look after yourself!"

The beach was slowly filling up with the regular winter swimmers. Matthew roared up on his motor bike and parked next to Antonis' mountain bike. He waved to everyone, then went to sit next to Antonis, who had already been swimming. Julia carefully entered the water in a fetching polka dot swimsuit, then, with a splash, she was away, flippers leaving a trail of silver bubbles behind her. Bartholomew was sunning himself and Nikos was holding Tom's hand as the little boy jumped up and down in the shallows laughing. Petroula was relaxing, reading a magazine under the beach umbrella.

The peace was broken by the crunch of expensive car tires on the stones outside the café. All eyes turned to see who it was. Out of a fabulous sports car, all gold metallic paint and white leather interior, stepped Poppy with a pile of books in her arms. She was still dressed in clothes more suitable for a club than the beach and she was accompanied by a good-looking, obviously wealthy, young man whose loud voice oozed ostentation.

"But I prefer living in the Ekali house, the view is nice, and the pool is a decent size ... as I was saying ... I wasn't interested in school much, but daddy insisted I went to college in London to study business. What else is of any use really? After six months, I quit. It was so boring ... Then mummy got me out of the army service ... It's such a waste of time ... I spent a year in Australia at my uncle's place, now that was a blast."

"Really, Markos." Poppy was obviously bored. She yawned and stretched, then leant against the car gazing at the sparkling sea. Suddenly, she kicked off her high heels, removed her jewellery into her bag, got out a towel, then she pulled off her evening dress revealing matching burgundy underwear to which Markos seemed oblivious.

"... Then a friend of my brother pulled a few strings and now I'm working for a TV station. Life's good. What do you do again?" At last, he turned to look at her.

"I teach English in an evening school."

"Oh, that's nice. Let's swim. Did I tell you about the time I once fell into the Thames and had to be rescued?"

"Yes, you did." They walked down to the sea and swam away, as they passed by, Julia looked at Poppy questioningly. Poppy shook her head and mouthed, "Another dud."

The sun shone down, and the winter swimmers relaxed. Then, as if from nowhere, another car appeared moving slowly and stopped quietly. The swimmers raised their eyebrows in surprise. This was a first. A tall, handsome, black man got out of a white Mercedes. He was wearing orange reflective sunglasses and was dressed for the beach in designer shorts, showing off an athletic body, perhaps that of a runner. He sauntered across the sand and down to the sea, tested the water with his feet but did not swim. Instead, he looked casually around, as if to check out the place. He stood for a while and looked at the bench under the tree, then walked back to his car for a moment and smiled. He seemed to like what he saw. However, the blind in the window of the hut twitched; his arrival and activities had been noted. On returning to the café, he studied the police notice on the door, entered the café, ordered a drink, then settled down to wait, knowing Greek curiosity.

Alexi was the one to break the ice. "Where are you from?"

"Good morning, sir. I'm Kalim from West Africa," he said in near-perfect Greek.

Lt Mavromatis was impressed. "You speak good Greek. Have you been here long?"

"About three years now. I read that notice on the door, what happened?"

Alexi shrugged, "No idea, some clothes were found on the beach a few weeks ago."

"And the body of a man in his early seventies was found five kilometres away down the coast opposite the little island. The police said it was suicide … Poor man!" added Lt Mavromatis.

"Po, po," said Betty emerging from the kitchen covered with flour and wiping her hands on a cloth. "I think there's more to it."

Kalim swallowed, "Really," He sat down close to Dimitris snoozing in front of the TV, who woke up and smiled at everyone.

"Hello, Grandad. Do you want a drink?" Marina smoothed his hair down.

"Yes, dear, just some water,"

"Where's Martha, has she gone shopping? She should be back by now."

"No, Gran has been gone four years now, remember?"

"Oh, I thought I heard the door."

"Let's watch the TV. The news is coming on soon." Kalim looked sad. "My grandfather went the same way, eventually. He couldn't remember the family names or how many cattle or wives he had."

"Ah, man, wives, you say?" asked Alexi, intrigued.

"Oh, yes, it is tradition, but it can lead to a lot of confusion and jealousy ... So many birthdays to remember."

"One wife is enough for any man; takes too long to train another one!" Marina glared at Lt Mavromatis. "Only joking. How on earth did you end up here?"

"Well, if you've got time, I'll tell you." So, they settled down, the ancient ceiling fan whirred around and at the back, Bartholomew slipped in to listen. "I was born on a farm near Bouake in the Ivory Coast into a large family. My father was a headman, like your mayor. He was a traditional man, fair, but sometimes hard. I think he loved his cattle more than his kids! Anyway, times changed. The army came into power and they took what they wanted, land, animals, women, and the youngsters for the army. Father was angry. He wouldn't keep his mouth shut. There's no democracy, like here, people shouting about whatever they like, you don't know how lucky you are. Then one day, an army truck arrived, and men jumped out with clubs and guns. They burnt our houses, my school, the gardens, the cattle were stolen and some of my family were killed."

"Po, po, child! What happened next?"

"Well, Father went funny. He just switched off. I was arrested and beaten up."

"Dear God!"

"It's common, but I was a good student, I have a gift for languages. By the time I was fourteen, I could already speak French and English as well as our local tongues. My relatives got together and paid some money to a man on the coast who said he would take me to Europe. So, I left. He said I would go to Paris and start university and I'd get the football scholarship I'd been promised. Then I could get a good job and send money home ..."

"And did you?"

Kalim shrugged resignedly, "No, it was a ruse, a trick, all lies. I ended up in Turkey. More money had to be paid for a way to Europe. I was lucky. The boat I was on was intercepted by a Greek coastal patrol. To be honest, I don't think that boat would have lasted the night. They don't put enough fuel in and there's too many people in the boat and most of them can't swim and they panic easily. The kids were crying, the women shaking in fear. I'll never forget it."

"Ah, man, that's awful. I've seen it on TV."

"There were not so many refugees when I came, things were easier. I was taken to Kos, but the local people didn't know what to do with us. One old lady came up to us with some bread and grapes and water, God bless her. Others were scared of us, and I'm not surprised. We must have looked and smelt awful, I'm sure."

The regulars were all looking sad now.

"Eventually, I ended up in Omonia Square. I looked for my own people, some were selling handbags for the Chinese and sleeping in flats in Kypseli. We had no work or papers, but it was better than being forced into the army or killed in my own country. So here I am. I started my own business, you know ... err ... an employment agency.

"Really?" Bartholomew raised his eyebrows.

"The girls don't stay long. When they have some money, they want to go north ... more opportunities. Not quite the life I'd imagined as a student of sports technology or being a footballer, eh?"

"No. What's next?" inquired Lt Mavromatis.

"Don't know, I'm still waiting for my papers. I'm training on my own, maybe a football scout will spot me one day ... before I'm too old,"

"And do you ever send money home?" asked Betty being practical.

"Of course! I don't do such work for fun!" he laughed. "Those girls cause me a load of trouble." At the back of the room, Bartholomew crossed himself.

"There for the Grace of God go I!" he said.

"Amen to that," added Lt Mavromatis.

The atmosphere was broken by Poppy and Markos who had come into the café. She was rubbing her wet hair and he had a towel around himself. He carelessly knocked over a chair and ignored it, so Poppy picked it up.

"As I was saying, the skiing in the Pyrenees is much superior to the Dolomites ..."

"Were you? What's for lunch, Betty?"

"Welcome! Today's speciality is red beef stew with rice."

"Great!" said Poppy. "I'm starving."

"Oh, I know a lovely place not far from here. It does amazing lobster. I want to eat there."

"Look, why don't you go and eat there then? I want to stay here." Her Greek was deteriorating rapidly.

"Right, I get the message," he said, as he stalked out, slamming the door petulantly as he went. He revved up the sports car and roared off.

Poppy laid her books down. "I'm sorry about that. Another disaster!" The three regulars all looked at her and gave the thumbs down sign. Again.

"Thanks, boys." She started marking. Louli jumped up onto the table and walked over her books. "At least you love me. Let me give you a cuddle." The cat had no problem with this offer and purred loudly. Poppy was still angry though. She looked up and threw down her red pen. "It makes me crazy! These rich, lazy types. Everything falls into their laps just because they know people or were born with money. It makes me sick!"

The regulars were now watching her closely. She was rarely angry or spoke Greek, so everyone was listening. She blushed at the attention and turned to Kalim. "Do you know why I live here?"

"No," he said, knowing it could hardly be the same as his reason.

"It's because we had the same economic mess in England as we have here today. There were so many people out of work, especially in the north. They didn't know what had hit them. In those days, boys worked where their dads did; engineering, textiles, mining, fishing, whatever. So, thanks to the new economic policies of the conservatives, the whole social structure was upended. It was sink or swim." She paused for breath, remembering that she had been one of those who had sunk.

"I had to leave. I couldn't pay the rent or eat properly. Any teaching work was on a temporary contract basis. So, after a few months, when you'd just got to know the kids and had them under control, the council money ran out and you had to leave the school. Any jobs advertised had been filled long before. To be honest, I don't have any sentimental feelings about my country now. A lot of my generation feel betrayed: Seven years of studying, for what? Nothing."

"Is life really any better here?" Marina asked.

"Now we have the recession here, things are difficult, but at least I have a job, a place to live in and a few friends, so the basics are taken care of, and I can swim all year round!"

"They say there's lots of work in London."

"Yes, Marina, there is, but the cost of living is terrible."

"I'd love to go, just to try but I can't leave grandad now.

Kalim, who had been listening carefully, spoke to Poppy in English. "London, by what I hear, is all that glitters is not gold."

"Indeed, you speak good English."

"Thank you. Was it easy for you here?"

"Mostly, but some landlords won't rent you a place or rip you off just because you're foreign."

"You're telling me. Try being black!" They laughed loudly. "I once had a flat at the top of a tall building. I called it Cockroach Kingdom! The heat was awful in summer and in winter, the cold was worse. The landlady kept two dogs on the flat roof. Unwanted pets, I suppose."

"Disgraceful," Alexi commented.

"She lived miles away and left out a bag of dry food for them once a week. The pigeons would flock down and eat most of it. Those poor animals were half starved. I used to throw them scraps when I had any leftovers. Their water dish was always drying up, so she left the tap on the roof open ... drip, drip, drip ..."

Alexi was now simmering, "I could strangle the woman!"

"Well, I nearly did, man! When dog shit and water started to ooze down the wall of the kitchen, I flipped out!"

"That's disgusting. What happened?"

"Things didn't end well. I went away for a few days and when I came back, the neighbours told me that the dogs had died, and the smell had been so bad that the police had been called. As you understand," he lowered his voice and leant towards Alexi. "In my line of work, it's best to keep a low profile, so I did a flit, just moved out."

"I don't blame you," said Alexi, shaking his head. "What about the wretched woman?"

"Ah, my dear landlady put it about that I'd killed her beloved dogs and threatened to press charges against me."

"Unbelievable! Don't worry, I think it will blow over," added Betty.

Poppy continued, "No, being foreign isn't easy anywhere, I suspect. Then there are those awful neo-fascists. I saw a march once by accident. I was shopping on Athinas Street. They were banging about, shouting obscenities, and knocking over foreigners and tourists. People were stunned and scared. I ran into a candle shop for cover. It was like being in an old film of the black shirts in Nazi Germany!"

"I remember that, you were not the only one running for cover!" They laughed again.

"What really happens to your girls, Kalim?" Lt Mavromatis inquired gently.

"It's true that most leave and try to get to northern Europe. They become cleaners, kitchen staff, nurses, and many marry. Look, this work is just a job, a means to an end."

"Humph," said Bartholomew sceptically.

"Oh, get off your high horse, man, it's the oldest profession in the world," Alexi pointed a finger at him. "Didn't your father send you off to the 'lady behind the curtain'?"

"Certainly not!" Bartholomew replied indignantly, "Everything in good time: You shouldn't force a boy when he's not ready!"

"Well, you're lucky, mine did!" Everyone was shocked.

"You!" He looked at Lt Mavromatis.

"Why are you surprised? It was the thing to do in those days. It was supposed to 'make a man of you.' To be honest, it was not a memorable experience ... the lady in question was, let's say, had seen better times! I don't dwell on it. Enough."

Petroula, Nikos and Tom returned from the beach, Tom was looking happy. He was carrying some shells which he gave to Dimitris as a present.

"F-f-for you," he said.

"Thank you very much," replied Dimitris gracefully, as if receiving a precious gift and arranged them on the table in front of him. "Come here, my child, and tell me about your day."

"Nik-Nik-Nikos showed me a st-st-starfish and a s-s-snail with a funny hat on and we saw a black c-c-cormorant bird flying low across the sea and a goat was coming down the rocks and a m-m-man with some dogs was s-s-sitting on the sand. He looked sad."

"All in one morning! Well done, boy." He stroked his head fondly.

Petroula glanced across at Kalim and he acknowledged her. She casually walked across. "This doesn't seem like your kind of place or are you looking for business?" She said icily, all the time smiling.

"I'm just hanging out," came the smooth reply.

"Just keep out of my way," she said, between clenched teeth.

Nikos missed this as he was setting up a game of UNO with Tom and Dimitris. However, Julia hadn't. She was now dressed in hat and flowery kaftan where upon Alex offered her his chair with a flourish. She thanked him and sat down. Outside, Matthew and Antonis were examining the big bike, engrossed in each other's company. "They seem to have hit it off! Petroula, would you and Tom like to have some dinner with me? My treat."

"Thank you, Julia that would be nice." The plates arrived and Marina organized Tom, who started to eat hungrily. Julia looked at Petroula and then at Kalim.

"Do you know that young man?"

"I'm not sure. For a moment, I thought we'd met somewhere. It's a small world."

In fact, Petroula clearly remembered going for a job interview at his employment agency when she'd desperately needed a job. She had been offered a live-in cleaning job for a wealthy family which she couldn't take because of Tom or there was a client who required someone for housework every afternoon. This had sounded suitable. However, she quickly learnt that this would entail a lot more than she'd expected. She shuddered as she remembered the creep had come up behind her in the kitchen with only his underwear on and had pinned her against the sink while she was washing up. She had escaped by threatening him with a frying pan. Her eyes hardened. She loathed men like Kalim who exploited women for profit. She turned her back on him. Kalim, who didn't want any confrontation, retreated to a table by the window.

"Indeed." Julia sounded unconvinced but she changed tack. "I remember you said you came from Hungary. What was it like?"

"Ha! My village was tiny … One central road, with wooden houses down either side, a church at one end and a school at the other. We had a large garden with a well. We had chickens and a cow. We grew vegetables and had fruit trees. My grandmother made the bread once a week. There was no supermarket when I was a kid, so we just had to manage. A lot of the men left to work in the city factories, my dad and brother went off together. We were lucky, they would send money home and visit regularly. Many men just disappeared."

"How did you end up in Greece?" Having heard this story before and as he'd finished his lunch, Tom slipped off his chair and under the table to play with Louli who, after a few minutes of rough handling, zig-zagged between the tables and made for the door, pursued by Tom on all fours. The big people's voices receded into the distance as he followed the cat into unknown terrain.

"When I was young, I found village life very claustrophobic. Sometimes, a lorry would stop, and the drivers would sweet-talk the girls … into you know what … In return, they gave them whatever was on the lorry, mostly electrical stuff like hair dryers or food mixers, which weren't much good actually because the power supply was quite irregular!" Julia nodded. By now, the others were all listening. "I didn't dare go near the lorries. My mother had a heavy hand and kept an eye on me. Then one day, a respectable couple with church connections came around the village, saying there were opportunities for young women in a computer company that was opening up. They said that training would be given and showed us photos of the company building. My mother thought it was a good idea and sent me off with three older girls. Ha, computers! I never learnt how to use a computer until three years ago!"

Everyone was silent, fearing the worst.

"The rest is history. After a long, dark train journey, we ended up in a dingy house and our papers were taken away. Next day, a woman came to teach us all kinds of stuff. Luckily, I was fairly athletic, so I was sent to learn pole dancing. After a week, I was given an outfit and started work. Six hours a night. You had to be pretty fit. The men in the clubs knew the rules ... Look but don't touch ... No sexy stuff ... or the bouncers threw them out. The man I had to give my money to was called Panos. He didn't seem to be interested in me, just in what I could earn."

Julia glared at the men who were now all leaning forward to hear the story. They pretended not to be listening and immediately started to examine their fingernails, shoes, the ceiling, or the sea.

"Then one night, as I said I was young and inexperienced, and Panos was irresponsible ... now you see Tom. "She said bluntly.

Julia leant forward and touched her shoulder sympathetically. "You poor girl!"

Louli didn't want to play and had disappeared under the hut, so Tom wandered off followed by Caesar. He climbed up on the rocks and watched the dreaded sea sloshing and sucking in and out below. "How could people swim in such cold unpredictable stuff that stung your eyes and gagged your throat?" he wondered. "Everyone seemed to be able to swim, most of the kids in his class said they could, just like they could read and speak properly and remember their times tables, why can't I?" Hot tears of frustration squeezed from his eyes. Inside the café, the big people were listening to his mum.

"Panos wasn't such a bad man. He brought me to Greece to have the baby. Actually, his father came to see me in hospital. He seemed kind. He told me that Panos was the black sheep of the family, useless with business and careless with relationships, but his mother refused to see us. Then, he held Tom up, blessed him, emptied his pockets of whatever money he had and got the nurse to write his name and address down. I don't think he could read or write very well. Then he left."

"What a nice man."

"Yes, he was lovely, but he died not long afterwards. Such a pity, he would have made a good grandfather for Tom."

"What about your parents?"

"I haven't told them yet."

"How did you find work?"

"After Tom was born, I made friends with a girl from Bulgaria called Joanna. She's got two children back home and her mother is bringing them up. She also had connections to Panos, although goodness knows what business he was into then! We shared a place in Piraeus. She knew Panos better than me … if you see what I mean! Joanna's not the sentimental type. She told me that he was just a cheap crook with a sunny personality, which is attractive if you're down in your luck. But for all his posh clothes, gold jewellery and red sports car, he was just out to make a quick buck and didn't care who was made a victim. I heard he borrowed money from his friends for each 'investment'. He wasn't exactly a trafficker, more of a middleman; his businesses have all failed. The last I heard; he was working as a waiter. He's a dreamer and he's had girlfriends galore."

The men leant forward again for the details. Julia glared at them but this time they were too engrossed to move.

"They're mostly bimbo types. Ironically, he fell in love with one of his Russian imports. He even married her and had more kids. I think they're divorced now. I've never known him pay tax. He just coasts along under the legal radar. He thinks he's somebody, a self-made man, but he is just a pathetic con man. But, you know, it's himself he's conning. Like so many men. Yet, I must admit, he's a bit of a charmer!" She glanced at Kalim, who blushed and looked down ... surprisingly, so did Bartholomew. "So, there we were in Piraeus. Joanna helped me with Tom and then she got a job making things for weddings and baptisms, putting cream coloured sugar-coated almonds into little bags etc. Panos had a shop selling such things. Then, I saw a job advertised in a newspaper and I started work as a housekeeper-cum-nurse in a large house belonging to a lawyer who is quite poorly and needs a lot of help. He is a decent man who pays me on time, and I get Sunday off, so Tom and I come to the beach." She looked up, suddenly embarrassed. "Sorry, I talk too much." She looked around for the boy.

"Finish your lunch, my dear, it's getting cold," Julia said gently.

Kalim had only been half listening as he was far more concerned with what might happen if the truth about Illias Kovouris untimely death ever got out. He absentmindedly gazed out of the window and realised he could see the boy standing on the rocks watching the waves. The child had bent down as if to pick something up and then he was gone, and the dog was barking furiously. Kalim alone realised what had happened and dashed for the door shouting, "The boy, the boy!"

Peroula stifled a scream, as he sprinted down the beach, dived in and swam around to where he'd last seen Tom. By now, Petroula and Nikos were watching helplessly from the shore and the others were crowded around the windows of the café. It seemed like an eternity as Kalim swam in and out of the rocky gorges and inlets and searched through the swathes of long undulating underwater sea grass. As he surfaced, he saw the child's legs dangling in the water. When Tom had slipped, his shorts had snagged on a jagged rock, suspending him above the water. Kalim approached slowly. "Hey, kid, it's me. You got stuck eh? Let's get you free and back to your mum."

Kalim carried Tom back to Petroula. He was soaked, wide eyed, pale and shaking with fear." M-M Mummy, M-M-Mummy!" he wailed as Kalim put him into her arms. Later, when Tom was cradled in her lap and the situation had calmed down, Petroula looked at Kalim with different eyes.

"Thank you and sorry, I misjudged you."

"We all do what we can to get by. I'm just glad the kid's okay."

George bustled in oblivious to what had gone on. "You're late," said Betty.

"Yes, Yes, I've been busy, busy. Got a wedding to plan, lots to do!"

"Congratulations, who's getting married?"

All eyes were on George now as he opened his arms wide joyfully, "My beautiful Maria and you're all invited." He stopped abruptly when he caught sight of Kalim. Luckily, no-one noticed because Julia was clapping her hands.

"That's wonderful, George! Any excuse to dress up," Petroula was looking wistful. She said quietly, "I'm not sure if I can go; I've nothing suitable to wear."

"We'll see about that," replied Julia.

"Bravo, George!" Nikos said, and then unwittingly to Poppy, "Where did your young man go?" The three regulars responded with thumbs down sign. "Oh, I see, not suitable."

"No, he was awful; self-absorbed, rich, spoilt and rude. I can really pick them."

"All you need is a little help," explained Nikos. "My aunty, who lives in Stupa, had four sons. She married three of them off to girls she thought were suitable. The other married a girl he'd met on holiday from Crete. They were crazy about each other, yet they were the only ones to get divorced."

"Wow! What about you, Nikos?" He glanced at Petroula.

"I wasn't so lucky. Come on, Tom, let's find that old kaleidoscope and look at the patterns."

Poppy sighed, "Life!"

"Life can be cheap," said Kalim quietly to no one in particular.

"You shouldn't be so glib young man! Considering what just happened to Tom!" Julia replied sharply.

"Madam, I meant no offence!"

"I know, I know. It's just that recently a young man from Bangladesh who lived in my area was murdered on his way to work last week."

"No!" said Betty. "I never heard about that. Was it on the TV news?"

"I doubt it. He was deliberately knocked off his bike by two neo-fascist types on a large motor bike and he died immediately."

"Did they arrest the men?"

"Yes, they did and surprisingly quickly. A taxi driver had witnessed the whole thing and reported it straightaway."

"Poor boy, so far from home," Betty said, wistfully.

"Well, the next evening the locals put small candles on their windowsills to mark his passing. We're not all barbarians! Sorry, it really upset me."

"Let's just be thankful that nothing happened to Tom, shall we?" Betty concluded.

The evening was drawing in and the winter swimmers and the regulars started to leave. Betty lit the lantern and looked seaward as the sun set, casting a golden glow across the sea like a pathway, "It's so beautiful," she whispered into the emptiness. "And yet so many lives are filled with sadness and difficulties. I wonder how they cope."

Another Sunday was over. Louli twisted herself around her legs and purred lovingly.

Sunday 3

Beachcombing

It was a silent, misty, grey day. Leaves hung motionless and the sea undulated in a slow swell, as if coated in oil. The air was sticky, heavy with unfallen rain and the scent of fig and pine. Julia's taxi approached the cafe and passed two boys who were skateboarding in the park. They were taking it seriously, up, down, around, up, twisting in mid-air and down again. She was impressed. "What I'd give to ski again," she whispered.

"What's that?" asked Pavlos.

"Nothing dear, just thinking aloud: Those boys were good."

"It looks dangerous to me."

Walking along the shoreline were Nikos and the strange boy who lived in the hut. He had his rubbish bag in one hand and a metal detector in the other. His dogs scampered about, tails wagging, splashing in and out of the shallows. He swayed from side-to-side moving the detector from left to right methodically.

"How are you doing Jacob?" Nikos asked. They walked for a while, silent with the easy manner of old friends.

"Okay, I'm sleeping a bit better. The headaches come and go though sometimes I feel so angry. Mum wants me to see a psychologist."

"It might help, a lot of people do, I hear."

"Like your teachers?"

"Point taken." They fell silent again. Jacob was thin and pale, his eyes haunted and lost looking. They stopped again while he rolled a joint and smoked it, then he offered it to Nikos who took it and they sat on the sand to watch the sea. Nikos was also slim but was quite good looking and healthy in comparison, despite the lines from working outside and drinking, which added character.

"How's the farm?"

"Ha, twenty acres of corn doesn't make that much, and a fox got my chickens last year. I tried geese this year but the noise they make is enough to drive you mad." They laughed. "Wait until Christmas, I'll get my own back." They started giggling.

"I couldn't kill anything I'd looked after."

"Chickens and rabbits are one thing but if I'd hand fed a lamb, then come Paska, I couldn't do it, I know." They stood up and smoked and looked out to sea. Then Nikos said seriously, "You've been holed up in that hut since the army. It's been six months now. You don't even watch TV. You're losing it ... too much smoke, you'll get paranoid."

"Yes, but, but ..."

"Look, no more excuses. Come in from the cold. There're some nice girls at the café on Sunday."

"Sure, look at me, Prince Charming!" They cracked up laughing again.

"Yeh, and me."

The metal detector started to beep. "Where's the treasure?" asked Nikos, still giggling. Jacob fell to his knees on the sand and started to dig down, much to the interest of his dogs who tried to join in the fun. After a few minutes, he pulled an old spoon out of the mud. It was obviously handmade and had a cross on top of it.

"See, treasure!" He wiped it and stuck it into his shirt pocket.

"So much for finding a diamond ring! I've got my land tax to pay. They even charged me for the chicken coop, for God's sake. It's a large wooden box. Damn it, I don't know why they bother with me. I'm nobody. Why don't they tax those big Chinese companies? I bet they don't pay tax. Last month was difficult although my cousin left me some groceries by the back door. He says it wasn't him, but I saw him sneaking away."

"I saw something too …" but Jacob stopped because the beeper had sprung to life again. He bent down and unearthed a two-euro coin. "More treasure, here take it, every little helps."

"I'm going to get fat on that, aren't I?" he said, and they started giggling again. The winter swimmers were starting to arrive and when Jacob saw them, he became distracted. "Got to go, bye," and he whistled for his dogs and disappeared into his hut.

Nikos watched sadly as his young friend retreat into the safety of his hut, then he went into the café to greet everyone. He put a bag of fresh vegetables on the kitchen counter.

"Thanks," said Betty. "You're very kind. Did you get through to Jacob?"

"Not really, I think he's got stuck."

"I know. I'm at a loss what to do."

"Was his army service so bad? I was on Limnos, It was hard and boring and hot, but we had a few laughs, like catching those camel spiders! I just don't know. It hurt his soul for some reason." Suddenly, two F16's, flying very low, screamed overhead. "Listen to that, it's enough to break your nerves!" Little Tom jumped up and down and waved.

"J-j-jets!" He stretched out his arms and pretended to fly.

"It was different in my day," announced Lt Mavromatis. "None of this counselling or questioning or answering back. The army made a man of you." He looked at Antonis. "He was one of my men, 'salt of the earth'." Antonis was, in fact, busy rubbing sun-tan oil onto Matthew's back, which was a bit odd seeing as it was such a dull day!

Betty raised her eyebrows, "Really!" She asked Marina to help her prepare some salad and they went off into the kitchen giggling, leaving Lt Mavromatis looking a little confused, so he started to click his worry beads.

Julia made an entrance in yet another outfit. Today, it was a beige trouser suit and heels and the usual accessories of beads and large framed glasses complete with wraparound scarf in autumnal colours. She had already had her swim.

"Ah, my angel!" Alexi greeted her, holding out scrubbed hands to show her.

"Well done."

"Now I'll take you to lunch on the roof garden of the GB!"

"Really, I'll think about that, in those clothes, I presume?"

"Aw, they're my favourites." These were an old corduroy jacket, with patches of leather on the elbows, a green tee shirt with a picture of Che Guevara on the front and a pair of jeans held up by a belt. "I thought this was fashionable," he exclaimed. Julia just looked dismayed.

"Caesar, for goodness sake, down boy!" but the dog continued to lick her legs adoringly.

Poppy walked in holding her books as usual, accompanied by yet another young man. Philippos was wearing his clothes from the night before and looked a mess. He even kept his sunglasses on inside, as he was obviously hung over. He removed his glasses, swayed a bit, and held on to a nearby chair. "Yeh, it's bright in here, yeh, I like the sea, yeh, I can swim … where's the bar? I need a drink."

Poppy looked at him aghast and shook her mop of red curls. "He seemed such fun last night and he's a really good dancer, but this morning, he's a wreck. What shall I do?" she whispered.

Betty came to the rescue, "Philippos, shall I order a taxi for you?"

"Yeh, good idea. I need some sleep. Where's the bar again? I mean bathroom, I feel a bit sick." Betty bundled him out.

"I'm so sorry." Poppy looked at Dimitris, Alexi, and Lt Mavromatis. They all gave the thumbs down sign and shook their heads in unison. Betty returned, "Got rid of that one quickly and quietly!"

"Never, never, again. I give up. No more," Poppy sat down with her head in her hands.

"Don't say that," said Nikos suddenly. "I've got a decent cousin. I'll introduce you one Sunday … the old-fashioned way!"

Poppy opened her books. "Okay, I've nothing to lose, have I? I'll just mark these compositions before I swim," then she closed her books and laughed, "Damn it, I'll swim first!"

"That's my girl! "said Dimitris. "One day, I'd like to swim again."

"Really, do you think you're up to it?" asked Marina.

"Why not?"

George came forward, "I'll help you." Marina looked doubtful and then Kalim appeared.

"Together, we can manage," For a moment, George looked shocked, then recovered and smiled.

"Yes, we can."

So, wearing a rather baggy pair of shorts, Dimitris was escorted down the beach by George and Kalim. The weather was not nice, but the sea was calm and warm. Tom led the way blowing a whistle enthusiastically while Alexi and Lt Mavromatis followed behind carrying a plastic chair and towel. Gently, they guided him into the sea, where he began to move his arms and legs against the force of the water. He smiled blissfully.

"Thank you, gentlemen. You've made my day." With Kalim in attendance, Dimitris started to float, and then he turned over and slowly swam about, while Marina kept watch anxiously out of the café window. After a while, George helped him out of the sea and sat him on the chair and wrapped a towel around him.

"I remember being able to swim across to the island and back not so long ago … Martha was a better swimmer then … Every Sunday, we'd come here when I first retired." Then, he fell silent, as memories became stronger than reality.

"Let's take him back, "suggested Kalim and slowly they returned up the beach and the café.

"Well done, Grandad. Did you enjoy that?"

"Lovely, fresh, your gran is such a good swimmer …" Her eyes filled with tears.

"Thanks, gentlemen. Let's go and get dry and dressed shall we, Grandad?"

Lt Mavromatis sat down heavily and exhaled in relief. "I never thought he'd make it!" Then, he glared at Tom, "Let's get rid of that whistle. It's enough to warrant a Turkish invasion."

"We used to get up to all kinds of things a few years ago," said Alexi, "We're getting soft."

"And all kinds of trouble," said Betty quietly.

Poppy, who had returned from her swim, sat correcting homework. Her hair was dripping onto her dry clothes. She was not really interested in it and was, in fact, casting a professional eye over Tom, who was trying to show a piece of seaweed to Dimitris, who had fallen asleep.

"Come here Tom, can you help me with this?" She drew a picture of a donkey. "Can you colour this in for me?" Felt pens emerged from her bag. Louli jumped up immediately and sat next to the book to watch what was going on. Poppy gently pushed the cat onto the floor. The colouring was not going very well. Next, she wrote some letters, "Can you copy these for me?" He tried, but they all came out backwards, so she guided his hand over her writing, p, b, m, "You try now." Very carefully, he copied the letters. "Bravo!" She turned to Petroula who had been watching, "I think he's a bit dyslexic."

"Can it be cured?"

"It can be helped. He needs a special teacher though."

"How do I get one? He's so behind at school and he doesn't understand why."

"I'll try and find out for you." Nikos who had been watching intently, said quietly, "I wish someone had helped me." Then from his pocket, he produced a plastic dinosaur for Tom to play with. The boy's eyes lit up. Poppy looked at Nikos and gently asked, "What was it?"

"I'm left-handed, but in those days, it was seen as a sign of the devil or some religious crap. In short, they hit you until you put the pencil in your right hand."

"Good God!"

"I wasn't very smart at school. To be honest, I couldn't understand what the teacher said. It was like listening to a foreign language."

"I can sympathize with that one."

"Some of the teachers tried but others yelled at me and were sarcastic, so in the end, I made up excuses not to go to school … and the more lessons I missed, the farther behind I got. I had to repeat a year once."

"Why didn't your parents encourage you?"

"Ha, that's another story, Poppy."

"I have all day," she fixed him with blue-eyed attention.

"To begin with, my real parents and brothers and sisters lived next door."

"Huh?"

"You see, my aunty and uncle, in whose house I was brought up, couldn't have kids, so my real parents who had six, gave me to them."

"Is that legal?"

"In those days, there weren't any questions asked. I didn't find out until I was ten or so."

"Were they okay with you?"

"Yes, fine. As long as I turned up at mealtimes and didn't destroy my shoes! They didn't bother with me much. There weren't many books in the house. To be honest, I'm not sure if they could read or write very well because the eldest girl Nancy, who was my sister, would come around from next door and read any letters or fill in any papers they got. She always used to cuddle me when she left. She married a local man and never left the village. I often stay with her at Christmas or Paska; she's always been my favourite."

"Nikos, why didn't you ever marry? You're good looking and so kind and generous." He blushed. "Well, there was Vaso and Katia and Cassandra, all good girls. But when their parents found out about my situation - no family connections, a small-time farmer who didn't finish school - they wouldn't even consider giving their consent. Maybe, one day." He glanced at Petroula again without realising it.

"What was life like in your village?" Poppy asked.

"Pretty good. A lot better than kids today, stuck in their rooms with the air conditioning on, playing endless computer games or getting bullied online. No wonder so many get depressed. My cousin Kitso and I played hide and seek in the corn and we'd run under the irrigation plumes to keep cool. We kept rabbits. We were a bit rough I suppose. We'd steal cherries from Mr Andrea's orchard and if he caught us, he'd chase us waving a brush in one hand and an old gun in the other. We'd run for it, dripping with purple juice. Yes, I think we were happy. Ha, we'd hide our shoes in the shed with the horse, so they didn't get ruined." She smiled encouragingly, so he continued.

"Once we borrowed a bike. Kitso peddled and I clung on. We went to the sea; I learnt to swim that day. Then, on the way back, we went to the well where they stored the watermelons to keep cool and helped ourselves! Sometimes, we'd sneak into the cafenion to watch cartoons on TV and later, we'd wait outside Natasha's house to watch her getting washed at the pump. Her father would run out, take off his belt and snap it at us until we ran off."

"It sounds idyllic!"

"It wasn't really, those were the good times. Things were tight; we often scavenged for newspapers, and then cut them up into squares for toilet paper!" He paused, lost in thought.

"And school was a nightmare and if you missed church, the priest came around to the house. There was a lot of prejudice and bullying. Villagers have long memories, sometimes it was like the civil war had never ended. We often didn't have much to eat and many teachers hit you with wooden rulers ... yet, I remember our shirts were always clean and ironed stiff." He turned to Poppy, "If you meet Kitso, he'll tell you more. Betty, I need a drink after so much talking. I'll have a beer, please."

Betty served him, as if nothing has been said because for him to talk so much was a minor miracle. Little did she know that he had been smoking a joint earlier!

Quietly, Julia came across and sat down next to Petroula. "I hope you won't be offended, but I came across this the other day." She reached down into her voluminous bag and pulled out a beautiful designer dress. "It's a KK original. I thought you'd look good in it, for Maria's wedding, perhaps?" Petroula gasped and stood up and held it against herself. Julia cast a professional eye over her. "Perfect!"

"It's very generous of you but I can't take this."

"Please, it's nothing. Enjoy it. I like to look nice, just to spite those two witches who live down my street, Lydia and Litsa. All these years and not a kind word. They look at me as if I'm dog dirt! 'Po this and Po that,' the way I dress, the company I keep, you'd think I was twenty-five, the way they go on!"

"Maybe they are jealous of you?"

"Who knows, they've got no sense of fun or adventure and nothing positive to say. We live in such a beautiful place with so much going on. I call them the black witches," she whispered.

"Shh, careful," said Petroula. "They'll put the evil eye on you."

"Please, be sensible!"

"Maybe, they had hard lives then?"

"Hardly, I know for a fact that they inherited property."

"Well, it just proves that money doesn't make you happy."

"True, my dear. I sound such an old snob, but I get so annoyed at them for acting poor, all those black clothes and the smell of moth balls wafting after them. As women, we should keep up appearances, not for men but for ourselves."

I've had my fair share of nasty comments too, Julia. It's best to ignore it all and hold your head up."

"We have to, don't we my dear?" they laughed.

Tom and Nikos were now sitting together looking at a comic. He pointed to the characters and got Tom to repeat the names slowly. "Mickey."

"M-M-Mickey."

"Pluto."

"P-P-Pluto."

"Goofy."

"G-G-Goofy."

"Donald."

"D-D-Donald."

"Bravo!" There was a small round of applause.

The rain was starting. Large, wet drops were falling at random but gathering momentum. In the distance, a black band of cloud hung menacingly across the horizon, the winter swimmers gathered at the window to watch in amazement as above the black cloud, a white one emerged and then cascaded over the other like an enormous waterfall or tsunami wave and rolled forward over itself. As the rain came clattering down, everyone crowded inside the café. Antonis and Matthew were sitting at a table together deep in conversation, looking at each other seriously. As their voices rose, everyone turned to listen. Antonis was now banging his fist into his hand, "You can't trust any of them. They all eat from the same pot. I hope they choke!"

"Fair enough," replied Matthew calmly, "but the system is out-dated, all these public servants, bored to death and paid for life. They can't be fired, so there is no incentive. Things aren't working properly."

"And it can't work at all, if people have no money to spend."

"Bah! I see plenty of people still with money to spend."

"We have to stop chewing on this. There's no answer. It's ordinary decent people who will no doubt have to suffer. So, let's agree to disagree on politics, eh?"

"We'll have to."

As if to defuse the situation, Antonis commented that Matthew had another nasty bruise on his arm again to which he explained casually had come about by him being a bit careless during kickboxing practice.

Bartholomew, George, Petroula and Kalim started a game of cards as the rain pattered against the windowpanes, while Nikos and Tom continued to pronounce words from the comic and Poppy marked her books with Louli watching her. Alexi just gazed at Julia and

Dimitris, who wanting to watch TV, was fiddling with the controls. He unintentionally hit a music channel, and everyone looked up.

"Switch it up man," ordered Lt Mavromatis. "I like this one." He pushed his chair back. "Miss Marina, may I have this dance?"

"Certainly." She left a tray full of dirty plates on a table and joined him. They did a swing number, followed by a rock and roll classic and there was a round of applause. The next track was slower.

"Barbara and I used to go dancing every Friday night for years. She passed away a year after our son died." The café went silent and everyone froze as few knew about this. Marina continued to dance with him. Lt Mavromatis looked into the distance ..." Stephanos died just after his fourth birthday. He had pneumonia. The doctors thought he'd recovered and took him out of the ventilator but two hours later, he just died. The child in the next bed died too. Something about a virus or inaccurate blood tests. It hardly matters now. It was sheer incompetence. He would have been thirty-three this year."

"Did you get to see him?" Marina coaxed as they dance on oblivious of their surroundings.

"Ha, my commander was a bit of a bastard. Commander Sideris said that kids got colds all the time and wouldn't give me leave. But his driver Yannis had balls. When Sideris went to inspect another camp, the driver turned up with a jeep and some passes and he drove me all night to Athens. We got there at dawn. I was too late."

Antonis was standing now, holding his chair tightly. "With respect, sir, I never knew. That's awful."

"It was a long time ago."

"Did you and Yannis get punished?"

"No. Actually, we didn't. When we got back, everyone already knew. The Commander couldn't face me. He was moved to Limnos shortly afterwards. Come, my dear, one more dance. As they say, let's dance the blues away." They danced to *Summertime Sadness*, which was quite fitting. Marina with her soft punk clothes and Lt Mavromatis in his smart outfit, all differences in outlook, generation or style ceased to matter.

The evening was coming on early, the rain had stopped, the sky was grey and the air cool. "At least, I won't have to water the plants tonight," said Nikos, as he left. Betty began to light her lantern as the card players packed up. George looked at Kalim and for a moment, thought, it's not what we say but more what we don't that gives you away. We all have secrets my friend. Then, he looked at Bartholomew, still the embodiment of success. I suspect you too have a story to tell. You're too good to be true!

Along the lane, the dust encrusted old yucca plants had been washed clean and had sprouted spires of flowers that fluttered like white butterflies. These usually appeared with the first rain and died about a week later, a glorious if brief life. Alexi walked down the lane kicking a stone and whistling. Caesar was snuffling about in the bushes. The kids who were skateboarding earlier had long gone. Caesar barked and scrabbled at something, when Alexi went to investigate. He found a skateboard lying abandoned in the ditch. Without hesitation, Alexi picked it up and smiled mischievously. He placed it on the ground and stood on it gingerly, then with his arms open wide for balance, pushed off. He wobbled across the concrete circle, turned and, imitating a surfer, returned at speed. He jumped off and raised his fist in the air and shouted in joy!

Sunday 4

Fire Alert

The weather had changed yet again. A southern wind had been blowing hard for days. Now, it was hot, far too hot for this time of year. Dried leaves swirled and danced like dervishes, reeds bent and thrashed, the poplar trees blew white and the cicadas that once squabbled and scolded each other had fallen silent. Most fields were parched dry. Flocks of sparrows spiralled up and down feeding. On the telephone lines, young swallows gathered twittering impatiently, waiting the ancient call to migrate. The fig trees were surrounded by windfalls and a rotting sweetness filled the air. Up on the hills, dark spires of Cyprus penetrated the chaos of oak and thorn. Lower down, paler olive orchards were broken by some squares of ploughed land. Whilst high in the sky, the tell-tale clouds of yellow could be seen, which meant that there was either a sandstorm coming or there was a fire somewhere. Above the café, the ominous drone of a sea plane could be heard approaching.

The winter swimmers, in various stages of undress, were standing on the beach watching the sky, while inside the café, the regulars were watching the TV, in case the fires spread closer. Matthew, thinking ahead, asked Betty if there were any hose pipes, buckets or brushes available and she went to check. Then, he made a phone call to a friend of his in the fire brigade and then announced to everyone that there was no need to worry, as the fires were in another area.

Julia appeared in yet another outfit. Today, it was a straight dress in navy and white stripes, plus heels and the usual accessories. She patted her hair and checked her lipstick.

"Sorry, I'm a bit late. There was a diversion because of the fire," she said, well aware that Alexi had been waiting for her.

"My eyes, what a nautical delight!" he responded, saluting her.

"Thank you." She looked at the sea, but he wouldn't be ignored, so he bowed with aplomb.

"Do you approve of my attire, Madame?" She surveyed him seeing white shirt, faun slacks and battered trainers, where a toe could be seen trying to push through.

"Passable, what about those shoes?"

"Aww, they're comfy!" Caesar flopped down next to him, and lovingly licked his toe.

"Indeed." She pursed her lips disapprovingly.

"I'll take you to the moon and back," he crooned, opening his arms wide. "What about going bowling or to a film, then pizza?"

"Sounds interesting. What happened to the Grand Britannia roof garden bar?"

He looked sheepish. "Temporary cash flow problems. My stockbroker is on holiday and I've had trouble with the private jet!" Julia couldn't help but laugh at this. Poppy smiled at her, "He's shaping up nicely."

"Yes, he is." Julia was smiling happily.

"Ah, where is my knight in shining armour on his white horse?"

"Trust me, a decent man on a donkey is much better!"

"You're probably right," She walked to the sea, dived in and swam away, her red hair floating out behind her like a mermaid's. In the shallows, Matthew and Antonis were having a mock fight, more 'slap down' wrestling, all noise and splash, rather than hurting each other. George and Bartholomew were swimming together with strong and slow strokes. Meanwhile, Petroula and Nikos were trying to get Tom to use a float and kick his legs, but he was still unsure of the water.

Everyone paused to watch, when Kalim arrived with a honey-coloured girl on his arm. She had a soft sweetness about her. When she lay down on the beach, she seemed a little awkward and self-conscious, almost modest about being on a beach half naked in front of strangers, despite looking lovely in her swimsuit.

"You look great girl. Relax, what's your problem? Not used to showing a bit of skin?"

"Don't be mean, Kalim. Things are different now. I feel a bit shy."

"No need to be, these all good folk. This is Nadeen everyone," he announced. George, of course, recognized her immediately and hoped that she had not seen him on that fateful night. Under the umbrella, Julia and Poppy were giggling over some article in a glossy magazine.

Petroula swam up to Bartholomew." I heard you singing in Church last week. You were marvellous."

"Really? Thank you. I didn't know you were a churchgoer."

"Yes, at home, we were Catholics, but Tom is going to be baptized Orthodox soon."

"Bravo, but why?"

"His new school is putting pressure on me and if it helps him fit in and be accepted, then why not?" Bartholomew was not sure about this but said nothing.

George swam up to Bartholomew. "You know, I've come into some money recently. I won a bit on the lottery. Do you think I could open another account or get some advice on short term investments?" Quick as a flash, Bartholomew switched on.

"Wonderful, certainly. I'm only middle management but someone on the front desk will help you." He lay back to float and collect his thoughts. "Security, dear God, how I long for some security." The water gently surrounded him, offering him his only security.

"Dear God, help me," he said aloud, like a thousand times before. His head pounded. "So much for my career. A job in the bank was supposed to be for life, safe, secure, boring, take it steady, be careful, don't make any mistakes, smile and be polite … I did it all. God, why, why me?" He recalled those heartless words, "Thank you for your service. We regret the cutbacks. Take an early pension."

He dived down and swam under water. Without goggles, his vision was distorted and blurred, like his life, he thought, but his head was still on fire. His pension had been calculated. What a joke. He wondered if he would ever be able to pay off the mortgage on his house now. "Dear God, the pretence." His wife had no idea. For eight months, he had got up, dressed, and left for work as normal. Please God, she mustn't know nor our son, who was away from home studying. I miss him, but I couldn't bear the shame; me unemployed and helping at the church food bank or singing for a few Euros and a bag of groceries. Dear God, forgive my vanity, he thought He surfaced and turned to swim away with hot tears burning his face. Why, God, why? I'll get about two thirds of what I'd expected. Why have my dreams been crushed because of the greed of others? I always paid my taxes. I never stole anything. I'm a good man, why punish me? He took off his goggles.

"Are you okay?" asked George.

"Not really. I saw something the other day which upset me."

"Yeh, what?"

"You probably heard about it on the news; an elderly man hung himself in Syntagma Park."

"I know."

"I saw him. I was on my way to w ... err ... I was just walking by and saw a group of people standing around in dismay. Then, the police came and told us to move away."

"Dear God!"

"I heard someone in the crowd said that about five-thousand people have taken their lives because of economic problems over the last few years. It's awful that it should come to this." This was a red rag to a bull. George bellowed and charged in.

"I think nearly everyone has been affected. You hear people talking about the situation and most believe that those in power don't understand what we are going through. Those in Belgium or Germany see the tourist islands, the villas, the clubs, the coffee shops, the sun, and the sea and think this is how we all live! It's ridiculous! We haven't eaten out in nearly a year and as for new clothes or shoes, ha!"

He paused for breath, and then continued. "It seems like Germany is holding the purse strings of Europe tight, like a miser. What I don't understand is how a nation that caused so much devastation in Europe twice in a hundred years can be in such a position of power again? It's an economic occupation if you ask me. They want to slap us around in order to keep the rest of them in line so they can protect their own interests." George was now exhausted. His heart was racing, and he was short of breath.

"Cheer up! Think positively, George. When we are dead and gone, I think that EU will fall apart. We are all too different. It looks like the Brits are about to leave."

Julia swam up, "If you don't like things the way they are, go to the rally next week and shout for an end to this austerity. I'm going. I'm sick of being poor. I know everything is relative, but many of my friends are being wiped out and they are educated middle class types, and they're really struggling. Everyone is borrowing money to keep afloat. One of my neighbours gives most of his pension to his married son because he and his wife lost their jobs. They were both graduates with decent jobs and they've got two kids, it's terrible."

George was becoming exasperated, "Julia, do you really think it's worth the effort to go and shout yourself hoarse? You might as well shout into the wind. These EU types in Brussels will shit on us, wait and see."

There was an impasse here, so they treaded water slowly as the sea glittered around them. "Well, I'd rather try something. Surely, they'll respect democracy?" she added, naively.

"I'm not so sure. These politicians have degrees in double talk and manipulation. Economics makes me sick, partly because I don't understand it and I feel I'm being blamed for something I didn't do!" George was puffing and gasping now. Bartholomew intervened, "Relax man, you'll get ill. You must watch your blood pressure. Too much adrenaline can kill you."

So, they all swam slowly to the shore, the joy of swimming had been rather spoilt now and they sat on the sand together. "I come here every Sunday to get away from such matters but now it seems there's no escape." George continued, "It's difficult to get by unless you've got family money to rely on. When I was first unemployed, we lived off the money my wife's father left her. You know, she's never complained, God bless her, going to the food bank or to the church when supplies were low. There's nothing extra for the kids which is hard on them too!"

"Don't I know it? My boy is at university in Thessaloniki and he works as a packer in a warehouse three nights a week for his pocket money. Every bit helps."

"I thought you had a good job, Bartholomew?"

"Well, err ..." he faltered. "As I said, every bit helps."

"If it wasn't for my fashion blog and editorial work for the magazine, I'd be sunk! My dear deceased drunk of a husband, who was a journalist, was useless with money and his pension hardly covers the rent. Now, there are grown men chasing jobs usually done by students. It's crazy, does anyone care anymore? I can't watch TV anymore. All the media spin showing images of what they want us to believe. Those EU types kissing and laughing and pointing to someone in the crowd who they recognize. Bah, it's all pretence. They spend more on a night in a hotel than I live on in a month and don't ask me about the bonuses those corporate bankers receive ..."

They sat in silence on the sandy beach. The sea sucked in and out around their legs soothingly, but each was lost in their own thoughts.

In the café, Dimitris was in his chair snoozing, an unread newspaper lay open in front of him and Louli curled on his lap was purring happily. In the kitchen, Betty and Marina were banging about preparing lunch. While everyone was otherwise occupied, Alexi beaconed to Lt Mavromatis.

"Come here, man," he whispered. Betty looked up suspiciously. Lt Mavromatis looked up from his crossword puzzle. "Come on, man. Outside, I've something to show you. Come on, let's live a bit."

"What have you in mind? At my age, I'm not up for much."

"Rubbish, come on." They went outside and Alexi pulled out the skateboard which had hidden behind the café.

"What have you got there?"

"It's a skateboard, idiot. One of the kids left it near the park, the other Sunday."

"What do you intend to do with it?"

"Skate, ride, do tricks. It's like snowboarding or surfing. I've always wanted to have a go. I've seen it on TV."

"Are you mad? You'll break every bone in your body or worse, crack your head."

"Don't spoil the moment." He leant forward, and their heads touched. "What happened to Commando Mavro? Tough man, knife in his teeth, gun at the ready, a regular Rambo you were. You showed them in Cyprus!"

Straightening his blazer and putting on his beret, he reminded Alexi, "That was a very long time ago." Regardless of this, they sneaked off to the park, with the skateboard between them. They both looked down, considering the next move.

"Come on, look, its easy. Hold my hand," instructed Alexi.

He took it wondering, "Is it clean?" Caesar jumped about with his tail wagging. Alexi balanced on the board and started to roll along. When they reached the concrete circle and slope, they stopped. "Now what?"

Alexi had big ideas. "I want to glide across, up the edge over there, the one like a teacup, then flick the board around and jump on and come back again, easy."

"Okay, off you go, I'll be phoning for an ambulance!" Alexi scoffed at this and pushed off. He glided across and climbed the edge at an ever-increasing speed but instead of a flick-back, he disappeared over the edge and could be seen rolling away down the slope, arms flailing like a windmill. Lt Mavromatis ran after him with Caesar in pursuit, barking wildly.

"Where's the brake?" Alexi yelled.

"Jump off or use your heel, man!" Alexi put down his foot and ground to a halt, destroying what was left of the sole of his trainer.

"That was brilliant. Your turn, mate." He coughed with the exertion and spat.

"Not likely, next week, maybe." They walked back to the café as casually as possible, grinning like naughty schoolboys.

"Would you like some water, gentlemen?" Betty and Marina burst out laughing, as they had witnessed the whole thing. "Well done boys. It's a pity I didn't catch all that and put it on YouTube. We'd have had a million hits and gone viral!" Alexi looked confused.

"What's she on about?" He looked at Dimitris, who just shrugged his shoulders.

Poppy was sitting at a table with a pile of papers, red pen poised for the attack. "Only sixteen compositions this weekend, here goes. "As she picked up the first paper, Nikos approached her, accompanied by another man.

"Have you got a moment?" She looked up, her face framed by a mass of red curls, with astute blue eyes and a sprinkling of freckles across her nose. She was wearing a printed cotton dress with a pair of black leggings, which was not exactly the height of fashion. "This is my cousin Kitso, I was telling you about ... remember, stealing cherries?"

Everyone looked up. The three regulars especially showed interest and they exchanged glances of tight-lipped approval. Kitso was a stronger version of Nikos, a bit younger but with the same unruly hair. He was wearing cut-off jean shorts, doubtlessly homemade and a plain white tee shirt.

"Yes, I remember. How do you do?" They shook hands. There were nods of approval from the regulars.

"Okay," he answered.

"What do you do?" she asked.

"Pizza delivery by night, electrician by day. Before that, I was at university in Milan for one glorious year, but it was too expensive for my family, so bye, bye, archaeology."

"That's rough."

"That's life. But at least I can speak some Italian and English now and I got to see the sights. To be honest, I partied a bit hard as well."

"We're going swimming, Poppy, do you want to come?" asked Nikos.

"Yes, that would be nice. Anything is better than marking this lot," she replied.

As they left, the three regulars looked at each other and slowly gave the thumbs up sign. "At last," said Dimitris. "They'll make beautiful children,"

"Grandad! They've just met!" scolded Marina.

On the beach, Antonis and Matthew were playing ball with wooden rackets, tick, tack, tick, tack, back and forth, equally matched. Julia was sunbathing as Nikos,

Petroula, Kitso and Poppy started their swim. George looked around nonchalantly and wandered up to the cafe for a forbidden snack, leaving Kalim and Nadeen to play with Tom, making pictures from shells and pebbles on the sand. Bartholomew was now sitting alone, nursing his pain.

He dug his feet into the sand remembering that last Friday when he had been stopped by a camera crew. They had asked him about the economic crisis and how it had affected him. Without thinking, he had told the world that he had been made unemployed eight months ago and that his pension had been cut and how he was working for the church. He'd said that the country was in a disgraceful state due to corruption and mismanagement. Then, it was over. Thank you, next. He'd been pushed aside in favour of some simpering blonde in a tight top with a voice to cut glass with, another insult! Unfortunately, he had not waited to hear what she had to say, which was a pity because she had been quite coherent in comparison to his emotional outburst. He had yet to learn that appearances can be deceiving. He had almost forgotten the whole incident.

He put his head into his hands, "I never realized just how much you define yourself by what you do, your name, where are you from, it's the same the world over. For twenty-three years, I was someone, respected and respectful. Now, I'm no-one, nothing, invisible ..." George, who was walking by with a sandwich in his hand, saw he was distressed.

"What are you muttering about? Come on, don't let things get you down. Let's go to the café and have a beer."

"Thanks, I think I will. Why not?" They walked up to the café together. Inside, the TV was on showing some current affairs programme. Nobody was paying much attention to it, so George and Bartholomew sipped their beer companionably.

Suddenly, the announcer said, "Now for some reaction on the street to the current political and economic situation gripping our city and its citizens ..." The dramatic introduction drew all eyes to the screen... and there was Bartholomew, telling his story. Everyone watched and listened. At last, the blonde came on and Betty lowered the volume. Bartholomew held his head down in disgrace. Betty approached him, with her hands on her hips, clearly not amused.

"You should have told your wife and son. Imagine how they will feel seeing that on TV. People will be phoning, asking questions. Shame on you! She'll be feeling awful."

Bartholomew just cringed, "You're right. I just couldn't face it. It's disgraceful. I'm supposed to have a job and provide for my family. When I was very young, my father couldn't cope and three of us ended up in church school. It was that or starve."

George leant forward. "It's not a disgrace man, it's the fucking economic crisis. You are not to blame here!" He yelled, "I was made unemployed by some unscrupulous bastard after eleven years of hard work and abuse. His damn faulty machinery nearly took off my arm, look!" He pointed to a nasty scar. "At least, you went out with a bit of dignity."

"No, I'm finished. I'm washed up. I'll never work again." He wallowed in self-pity.

Betty gently held his shoulder. "You never know what the future holds. We are your friends here, so stop feeling sorry for yourself. You have a gift of your voice. I've

heard you sing in church too. I'm sure you will find work."
Bartholomew just hung his head.

"I think I had better go home and talk to my wife."

"That's a good idea." She patted his back, as if
comforting a distraught child and he slid out, still with his
head down. In fact, neither his wife nor son had seen the
TV clip and were unaware of his deceit. The regulars all
watched him go sadly.

The TV was now reporting on the fires that had swept
over different parts of Greece, showing pictures of burning
fields, trees and even houses where bystanders tried
beating out the flames with branches or throwing buckets
of water at the fires with heart-breaking futility. Sheep and
goats huddled together on the roadsides, lost, and
confused.

By late afternoon, with the light fading, the wind had
disappeared, but it was still hot. On the beach, Nikos was
teaching Tom to swim with a plastic ring around his
middle. They were laughing and splashing about. Kitso
was lying on the beach, not too close to Poppy though,
fiddling with something.

"For you," and he gave her a little cuttlefish boat with
a stick for a mast and a leaf for a sail. She accepted the gift
with a sweet smile. The three regulars, who were watching
events from the café window, smiled. "Love is in the air,"
hummed Dimitris.

As they watched, a white paper lantern could be seen
floating overhead with a flickering candle inside. Nadeen
squealed, "What is that?"

"Just a UFO or aliens, maybe spy drones," teased
Kalim. "Don't panic woman, take it easy." But Julia lifted
Tom onto her knee and Caesar came to lie at her feet, then
Louli jumped up to cuddle in too.

"Look, there are some more," Nadeen pointed to the sky. Everyone looked up as more floated overhead. "Aren't they lovely?"

"Oh! My God!" said Matthew. "Quick, Antonis, get that hose pipe ready and make sure there is water pressure. Betty, where are those brushes and buckets?" For once, lost for words, she just pointed. By now, three lanterns had landed. One was near the park, another on the roof of the hut and one on the beach. Matthew sprang into action. First, he wrapped a damp towel around himself, then started organising everyone. "Petroula, take that bucket fill it with sea water and put out the lantern that landed on the sand. Antonis, try and get the hose pipe to reach the hut. Kalim, you too. Poppy, when they get there, turn on the water slowly and keep the pressure steady."

White smoke was now billowing up towards the cafe. "Niko, Kitso, let's get down to the park," They ran with the brushes and buckets of water and started to beat out the burning grass and bushes near to the swings only to be engulfed by clouds of smoke. Lt Mavromatis, George and Alexi turned up carrying more buckets of water. George threw his water onto the side of the road as new flames and sparks shot up. The men beat and stamped at the fires spreading under their feet, then poured water onto the smouldering ground, shouting encouragement at each other when returning to get more water. After a while, the fires were out. They all stood around dazed and grubby with smoke. "That was a bit close," coughed Alexi. By now, Matthew was standing apart, shouting into his mobile phone. He returned looking tired.

"That's sorted it out. Turns out that some tourist kids were having a birthday party and they thought how pretty the lanterns would look. Idiots! Idiots! The fire brigade is over there now dealing with them."

"You seem to know a lot of people in authority. What exactly do you do?" asked Antonis.

"As I said, you get to meet a lot of people at the gym," Antonis seemed to buy this for now. Events had shaken everyone but luckily there has been little real damage. The blackened sides of the lane were still smoking, and a few trees were half burnt. Suddenly, from inside the hut, a sleepy figure emerged, rubbing his eyes. The dogs rushed out barking. "What happened?" asked Jacob.

"Your roof caught fire," replied Nikos.

"Yeh, really, is it out? Wow!" he exclaimed and disappeared inside again.

"He's really out of it, today," commented Kitso.

"Who is that boy?" asked Petroula.

"That's my son actually," said Betty who had come to check for any damage. "He lives there at the moment, cleans up the beach and guards the café at night."

"Are those his d-d-dogs?" asked Tom.

"Yes, dear, they are."

"Why does he live there?"

"Because he got sad and doesn't want to be with people anymore."

"I'm s-s-sorry."

"Me too," said Betty, as if she had resigned herself to the situation.

The winter swimmers started to go home, and Betty lit her little lantern in the seaward window. Alexi picked up his skateboard and gave it to Lt Mavromatis. "Show me your stuff, yo!"

"Next week, you big kid. I think we've had enough excitement for one day and they walked off down the lane together. Poppy started to follow them.

"Hey, can I give you a lift to the metro?" asked Kitso."If you don't mind me being covered in soot?"

"Yes, that would be nice," she replied. They drove off on his bike.

In the evening, the TV flickered in the darkness of the empty cafe, showing smouldering woodland all blackened and charred, Marina couldn't bare it, so she switched it off. She helped her grandad up. "Let's go. Every year, it's the same scam. They burn the land, then it's sold, and they build on it. It seems such a waste of time and money getting those little kids to replant trees. Its sheer hypocrisy!" Arm-in-arm, they walked down the lane to look at the damage.

Sunday 5

An Awkward Revelation

It was a real winter day, especially by Greek standards! Clear and cold with clouds racing across the sky and seagulls flying sideways against the wind. It was nearly Christmas and the café had been decorated with fairy lights around the windows. A small artificial tree, dripping with tinsel and other decorations stood in one corner where Louli was enjoying herself lying on her back, pawing at a large, low hanging, crimson baubles. But she was living dangerously, as Marina, armed with a mop, started to shoo her out before the whole tree got pulled over. Red tablecloths had been laid on the tables, on top of which, hand-painted silver pinecones and seed pods had been placed in the centre. The Russian stove had been primed and flickered away.

On the beach, a recent storm had washed up a lot of debris. Jacob, wrapped up in jumpers and scarf with his dogs dancing around, surveyed the mess and meticulously started to pick it up … plastic bottles, rotten food, some life jackets, sheets of thin, silvered paper from insulation blankets, as well as the usual cigarette ends. He lifted up a small pink shoe with flowers on it and for a moment, tried to imagine the little girl who had worn it, thinking she must have been upset when it got lost. When he was finished cleaning up, he put the shoe onto the windowsill of the café and whistling for his dogs, retreated to his sanctuary before the winter swimmers arrived.

Within minutes, Matthew roared up on his motor bike, sand flying in his wake. On entering the café, it was obviously that he was visibly limping and had a black eye.

He greeted Betty, Marina and the three regulars wearily. Lt Mavromatis examined him and to make light of the situation said, "I hope they pay you enough, young man!"

Matthew shrugged. "I've ceased to think about it. It's getting to be a routine. The hours of waiting about for something to happen, then the noise, the demonstrations, the burning cars, the tear gas, the attacks, the Molotov's exploding around you. It all happens so fast. Then, there's the insults, the swearing, the stones flying, the spitting followed by a counter-charge. The street dogs are running in and out barking. Then, just as suddenly it's all over, we dump our gear in the bus and go and have a cup of coffee and joke about. Just another day at the office! Jesus, I ache all over!"

Betty came over, wiping her hands on her apron. "Let me have a look at that eye. How about a pack of frozen peas?"

"Anything is worth a try." He sat nursing his eye. "To be honest, I don't know how long I'll last. I'm getting sick of it all. It's like a giant puppet show and we're all dancing around, and God knows who's pulling the strings."

Alexi pointed up at the TV. "Look." There, was extensive reporting on the death of a teenage boy who had been shot by a policeman. "That's bad," said Alexi simply and he crossed himself.

Matthew added, "and quite unnecessary, that cop was out of control, a real loose cannon. If I'd been in charge, he'd have been taken off duty weeks ago."

Poppy bounced in, looking happy, with books and towel in her hand. She too, was wrapped up in an old ski jacket and furry boots. "Morning everyone. Ah!" she gasped, "Matthew did you have a bike accident? "

"You could say so!" He motioned to the others not to say anything.

"Get well soon. Did you hear about that boy being shot? It's disgraceful!" They all nodded. She continued, her words tumbling out. "I got caught up in the demonstrations on my way to work. In Omonia, the tear gas was so thick, that some people were being sick. Themistokleous Street was blocked by burning dustbins and the restaurant on the corner had been burnt out. It's just gone. I tried to get into the school, but the secretary had locked up and left. I had a look around for any students but Akademias was nearly empty. So, I started to walk home; I saw people breaking shop windows and looting. One man was carrying out a large plant from a florist's shop. Some women were pulling the clothes off a manikin in a clothes shop and collecting boxes of shoes. It was surrealistic." There was silence, as Julia slipped in quietly.

Matthew nodded, "Surrealistic, that's a good word."

"We live in interesting times," Julia added.

Petroula, Nikos, Kitso and Tom arrived together, and their eyes widened when they saw Matthew but said nothing. They just looked at him in dismay. For once, Alexi didn't react to Julia, so she just sat down next to him and he reached for her hand and together they watched the TV replays; the smoke, the hail of stones smashing onto the MAT shields, the flash bombs, the demonstrators shouting in anger at the senseless death of a kid. They were voicing deep frustration with the government and the state of the economy which had turned many peoples' lives upside down. "Were you there?" he asked Julia. She shook her head.

Outside, Antonis could be seen cycling slowly up to the café. He propped his bike against a tree and when opened the café door, everyone turned to look at him. He also looked beaten up and he sat down heavily, as far away from Matthew as possible. "Black coffee and Metaxa, please Betty," Antonis requested, obviously suffering too, as his face was swollen and bruised and a cut on his mouth still had blood oozing from it.

"Have you been to hospital?" inquired Betty, immediately.

"Yes, I had an X-ray. It's only a hairline fracture. I got a nasty crack on the head from some baton-happy fucking MAT. I'll have a headache for a month!" He coughed dreadfully. "The tear gas they used last night was years out of date. We found the canisters, look." He pulled one out of his pocket and threw it on the table.

Kalim and Nadeen arrived arm-in-arm. When they saw the two men, they sensed that something was going on. "I think we'll go for a walk on the beach," said Kalim.

From across the room, Matthew and Antonis glared at each other, "That fucking MAT might well have been me!" Matthew said menacingly.

"So, you're not a gym instructor then, you lying bastard!" Antonis tried to get up but staggered, then raised his fist, "I'll ..."

"Sit down man, this is not the time or place to settle your differences." Lt Mavromatis took control. Antonis, exhausted, muttered "Okay" and slumped down holding his head, blood was beginning to ooze through the bandage. He looked across at Matthew. "You knew what I believe in. We've talked about it a hundred times and you said nothing, why?"

The other winter swimmers started arriving and stayed to listen. "You know I feel we've been so badly let down time and time again. All this corruption, the only way is to take the system down and start again. My mum is a classic case: She worked all those years, for what? They reduced her pension and she's been waiting for it for nearly three years now. She cries a lot. I can't bear it. The system is crap, crap!" He hit the table.

Everyone was listening. "And what about the state of our universities? Lecturers don't turn up, papers don't get marked, exams are cancelled, the place isn't cleaned anymore and there are junkies in the corridors. Going to university is hardly an enlightening experience! It is just breeding a disillusioned generation. Unemployment is running at twenty-five percent or more, damn it! "His voice was rising. He pointed across at Matthew. "And you lot beat us up when we raise our heads and demand change. Too much has gone down. You can't kick some foreigner senseless because they've got no papers to sell a few handbags, you should be after the real criminals ... the politicians who have skimmed off millions of EU money in scams and pay offs, the ones who've built their enormous summer houses on stolen money, the ones who have stashed their wealth abroad." He pointed at his friend, "You know all this, and you, of all people, support the establishment. Why man, why?" He slumped back. Blood began trickling down the side of his face.

Matthew took a deep breath and said quietly, "I didn't tell you about my job because you probably wouldn't have given me the time of day. It's just a job. I needed to work. There was no money for the extra lessons necessary for the university exams in our house." He was now putting Antonis on the spot. "You had the benefit of a middle-class home; books, music, educated parents who were sensible with their money. So, don't talk to me about cuts. My father walked out years ago and my mother went from one low-paid job to another, the places kept on closing. Then she got depressed. The doctor gave her some pills and she's like a zombie most of the time now … and my kid sister, the one who's married, got pregnant." He choked, "We were so happy, and then, they decided to have an abortion because they felt that they couldn't afford to bring a kid up right now. My mum was heartbroken." He beat his fist emphatically on the table. "So, don't talk to me about the problems caused by this economic crisis, you haven't a clue. You anarchist types, some are idealists, but most are spoilt, arrogant, bored kids, who have never had to work a day in their lives and are looking for a cause. When things get rough, they run home to Psychico or wherever and get daddy's lawyer to sort things out."

Everyone was silent, Louli jumped up onto Julia's lap and she stroked her, then she started to cry. "Dear God boys, that it should come to this. It's like the civil war. We're all Greeks and you two are special friends. You get on so well and have fun together, so please, please stop it!" Both Matthew and Antonis turned to look at Julia who was obviously very upset. Suddenly, they saw an older lady whose glamorous facade could not hide her vulnerability.

"Sorry," they both mumbled. Then, Betty saved the day with a practical suggestion.

"Now that you've got all that out boys, why don't you go for a little swim? The water is a bit cold, but I have a feeling it will help you cool off and come to some sort of agreement." They both stiffly got to their feet and she gently pushed them outside. "Anyone for coffee?" she said, trying to restore a semblance of normality.

The TV was still on, showing a long row of school kids dressed in whatever white clothes they could find, sitting in front of Syntagma. It was their way of protesting against the murder of the teenager … and avoiding lessons!

"I have a feeling it's not over yet," said Julia to Alexi as he handed her a none-too-clean handkerchief! "Thanks." She turned to look at Alexi critically and did a check list. Haircut, tick. Nails clean, tick. Shaved, (nearly). Clothes okay. Shoes, Oh dear! Scuffed but newish! "You'll do! Where and when?"

Alexi's eyes opened wide in amazement and horror. "Really?"

"Yes, I hope you aren't backing out now, I've got a new outfit?"

"Okay, okay, I know just the place." Lt Mavromatis raised his eyes to heaven and crossed himself.

"Hallelujah!"

Dimitris held out his hand. "At last, you owe me fifteen Euros, Michael." Everyone laughed as he handed over the cash reluctantly.

Outside, Matthew and Antonis could be seen walking along the shoreline near to Kalim and Nadeen who were sitting on the beach looking at a magazine. Julia had decided to swim and was making progress in a choppy sea with short sharp strokes. Poppy and Kitso were standing with their feet in the sea, watching Nikos trying to get Tom to float properly. Suddenly, Kitso jumped up, grabbed a toy bucket, waded in, and scooped up a jellyfish and dumped it on the sand.

"It's okay," He waved at Petroula who was obviously concerned.

"Are there anymore?" she called over to him.

"I don't think so, but I'll keep my eyes open," he replied. Tom was shivering now, so Nikos brought him out and showed him the jellyfish. Bartholomew, who was still feeling ashamed of himself sat under the umbrella hoping he was invisible! In the distance, Lt Mavromatis could be seen wobbling away on a skateboard.

Kitso had picked a small blue flower from a bush and gave it to Poppy. She smiled at him and he started to twiddle her hair curls with his fingers, but she seemed unaware of this as she was watching Matthew and Antonis. "That was an awful row. Do you think they will ever be friends again?" Kitso glanced up at the men who were now washing their feet together at the makeshift shower.

"Oh, I don't know ... probably." She followed his train of thought, and giggled. Then, he reached forward and kissed her ... for the first time in public! After a while she asked, "Were you in the city centre the other night, Kitso?" "Yes, I was. It's not usually my thing. I'm too sceptical but sometimes, you've got to be there. It wasn't just students or anarchists, there were ordinary folk and all those pensioners, decent peaceful people, they were angry beyond words." He took her hand.

"What is it?" He was being serious now.

"Listen, I'm a bit like Nikos. I'm the youngest and I won't inherit anything, and my land is rented out for wheat. You can't build there anyway, and my boss has just cut my wages by one hundred Euros, so there won't be much in the way of fancy extras if you are with me. Do you understand?"

Poppy didn't flinch. "Yes, I understand. I'm working and I'm used to being independent. We'll manage, somehow." He leant forward and kissed her again. Framed in the window, the three regulars, ever watchful, cheered and gave the thumbs up sign.

As evening was beginning to draw in, Betty began to light her lantern. Louli was weaving in and out between her legs. "Hussy," she said to her and picked her. For a moment, she held the cat close and looked out to sea. Meanwhile, George was busy at a table arranging the wedding invitations.

"Gather around, come on," he called out when everyone had arrived. "Here we are, the arrangements have been made. The church, the taverna, the band, she's even found a dress! Now, one thing is missing, Bartholomew, don't hide at the back there, man, come here." He pulled him forward. "Would you be prepared to sing at Maria's wedding?"

Bartholomew looked flustered, "I'd be honoured to."

"Perfect. Here, there's one each," and he handed out the invitations. When he got to Matthew and Antonis, he stopped and said, "Do you think you two can put your differences aside for the wedding?"

They smiled at each other with embarrassment. "Yeh, why not!"

George then picked up Jacob's invitation. "I'll just be a moment" and he popped outside and knocked on the hut door. Smoke was rising from the chimney and a plastic Santa Claus hung down on a string from the roof. He could hear the dogs jumping around inside, so he knocked again and waited. There was no response. To kill time, George examined an old wellington boot that had probably washed up onto the beach. It was now full of soil and had a geranium growing out of it and stood at one side of the door. Next to it, a small pink shoe with flowers on had been placed. He walked to the back and frowned when he saw the graffiti-covered wall then he stopped for a moment to examine the lovely owl. That's new, he thought. What does 'LOAF' mean? I thought it was bread in English. He returned to the door and tried again.

"Jacob, Jacob, open up boy. It's me, George. Come on, I've got a wedding invitation for you. Maria is getting married to Vangelis soon and we'd like you to come." He knocked again. "I know you can hear me. There will be food, drink, a band, dancing, pretty girls ... Antigoni will be a bridesmaid. Come on, open up. Your mum would be happy if you went ..." The door opened a crack.

"Okay, okay, George I can hear you and so can half the beach. Antigoni is going to be a bridesmaid, you said?" Jacob emerged, looking bleary eyed.

"Yes, she's all grown up and as beautiful as her sister. So, will you come?"

"Maybe yes, maybe no. I don't know ... it must be costing a lot ..." George was visibly startled.

"What do you mean?"

"Just that, weddings cost a lot of money." George wondered how much dope Jacob had smoked today.

"Well, let's say I inherited some money. No, I won it on the lottery and spent it on her wedding. Is that a crime?"

"No, it's not ... I know ..."

"What do you know, tell me?"

"About Kalim, taking that man's body into the sea to get rid of it and about the clothes on the beach. I saw you take the cash ..."

George interrupted him. "Yes, I did. Are you going to report me?"

"No."

"Do you know who that man was?"

"No."

"Ha, I knew him well. He was my ex-boss, the one who never paid me compensation when his faulty old machinery sliced into my arm and then sacked me when I couldn't work. The same man who owed me back pay and never paid me on time. We used to get paid cash in hand years ago, but now the law has changed and we've all got to have bank accounts. This means you have to check up what has actually been put into your account. Instead of two hundred Euros a week, you'll see one hundred and eighty-seven, for example. It's common practice. If you complain or ask the company accountant what's going on, you never get a straight answer ... because they are both in it together."

"I had no idea." This was a lot for Jacob to take in, but George felt he had to justify his actions.

"What do I feed the girls on, cornflakes and lentils? Even my doctor told me he was owed about ten thousand Euros in back pay. He says he'll never see it. Jesus, everyone is screwing each other, from top to bottom. Jacob, I'm so tired of being at the end of the food chain. Yes, I stole the cash from his wallet. Yes, I'm ashamed of it. I know it was wrong but all I wanted was for Maria to have her fairy tale wedding!"

He was now breathing heavily. "The way that man ate, God, it was disgusting! I couldn't bear to watch. He would order far too much food, just for show. I could have fed all my family for two days on the amount. He would lean forward and attack the plates with his fork, stabbing at the food and stuffing himself. The noise was gross! Then, when he was full, he'd gulp down his drink and order another and proceed to tell stupid jokes and be rude about everyone." George was sweating now, and Jacob couldn't cope with the barrage of information, so he went inside and brought out a chair for George to sit in.

"Steady on, George! You're going purple. Calm down please. I won't say anything. I promise. Here, sit down.

"Thanks, it's not just the work situation. Did you see that car, the one Kalim uses?"

"Yes."

"Did you know he has a so-called employment agency? No, well it's a 'ladies of the night' business. That girlfriend of his was probably involved. The boss was always bragging about what he did to the coloured girls. He had no respect for anyone, a nasty bastard … it makes me sick."

"Chill out, man!" Jacob was becoming alarmed.

"Please keep quiet about this. Maria, Antigoni, my wife, they must never know … promise me!" He was gasping for air now.

"I said I promise, and I will." Jacob took the invitation and closed the door on George who took a deep breath and returned to the café where the fairy lights were twinkling, and the Christmas tree had a timeless magic about it.

Betty took Tom by the hand and led him to the tree. "What can you see?" She pointed under the tree to a little square present.

"Is it for m-m-me? Can I open it now?"

"Of course," and he sat under a table with Louli to pull off the paper. In the grown-up world, there was a lot of loud talk about what to wear for the wedding. Julia favoured a cream-coloured suit with black accessories, Poppy preferred a dress with a matching coat and heels, Nadeen intended to wear something traditional in a bright pattern, Betty thought her evening dress in cobalt blue would do, if she added a lace jacket over the top, Marina intended to go with something more punky. Petroula smiled smugly at Julia. "I've got a KK original dress to wear!"

"No!" "You lucky girl," "Wow!" The noise was rising as the women giggled and planned what to wear. "Listen to them, George. It's like a henhouse in here!" Alexi shouted above the noise.

"I rather like it!" Lt Mavromatis shouted back.

"Oh, you big poofta! What are you going to wear then? A pink suit, perhaps or a spotted bow tie, maybe?"

"Nothing wrong with being presentable. Talking of which, where are you taking Julia on you big night out?"

"Top secret, mate!"

"I know, I know," chirped up Dimitris.

"Jesus man, can't you keep a secret?"

As the light faded, everyone started to leave. Antonis and Matthew were now actually talking to each other or rather exchanging jibes. "I once waited three quarters of an hour in the post office and there were only sixteen people in front of me, then less, because some gave up."

"That's reasonable" replied Matthew. "My mum once waited six hours in IKA; there were hundreds in there. The staff cuts have made it a nightmare for everyone. She said that one woman had a breakdown and was really howling, something about her brother who needed psychiatric medicines that couldn't be found now."

"You see, that's the price we're paying. It's wrong, all wrong! All these people suffering; the system needs to be upended. We need to start again from scratch."

But Matthew was not having this. "You're dreaming again. Half of us would starve before anything got organized."

"See you next week?"

"Of course." They stiffly raised their hands for a high-five and parted company reasonably amicably. Kalim and Nadeen, who were relieved to see them friends again, waved, as they drove off. George departed on his groaning Vespa. While Nikos, Kitso, Poppy, Petroula and Tom walked away down the lane trying to ignore the depressing blackened verges and bushes which had been burnt. Bartholomew offered Julia a lift home which she accepted, leaving Alexi kicking the furniture with jealousy!

"Relax man," teased LT Mavromatis. "She's only got eyes for you!" When everyone had gone, he collected his skateboard, which had been hidden away all day, and pushed off. He was getting better! From the window, Betty, Marina and Dimitris watched in case he tumbled, and Betty lifted the lantern, put the candle inside and lit it. Then, she noticed that Jacob was standing outside his hut, smiling happily, and looking at his wedding invitation. He bent down to pat his dogs and waved when he saw her standing at the window. Betty waved back, thinking that this was the best Christmas present she could ever have had!

Sunday 6

A Bittersweet Celebration

It was a miserable day, smelling of damp, as it has been raining for some hours, not the short, sharp rain of summer but long rain, grey and slow, wonderful for the land but dampening for the spirits. The sea looked uninviting, calm, and chilly, which would test the resolve of the hardiest of winter swimmers.

Outside the café under the trees, Dimitris, dressed up in Wellington boots, a large woollen jumper, and cord trousers was carefully sweeping up the fallen leaves. "He's making a good job of it," Betty said to Marina approvingly, as they wiped the tabletops and organised the chairs inside.

"You have to keep an eye on him though. I caught him setting up the ladder the other day, in his underwear! He said he was going to check the roof for loose tiles before winter!" Marina watched him fondly." Now I supervise his wardrobe!"

By early afternoon, everyone, except for George, was in the café gathered around the stove enjoying the heat, showing no interest in the sea at all. "This is lovely," said Bartholomew. "We haven't had petrol in our block for three years, most of the people can't afford it now. So, we use a gas heater with a bottle. It's much cheaper than an electric radiator but it only heats one room."

Sitting apart from the gentle buzz of conversation, Poppy was marking exam papers with her gloves on! Kitso stood by the window smoking and stroking Louli, who was sprawled on the windowsill enjoying the attention. Nikos was showing Tom a picture dictionary while Bartholomew,

Petroula, Kalim and Nadeen had set up a game of Monopoly. Matthew and Antonis were sitting together joking about and comparing each other's injuries. Dimitris was again holding his newspaper upside down, so Marina gently corrected this and kissed him on the cheek.

"Thank you, my dear, I was beginning to wonder why I couldn't make sense of it."

Alexi was deliberately examining the Christmas decorations around the room, much to the annoyance of Lt Mavromatis who was becoming increasingly impatient. He clicked his worry beads around in annoyance. At last, Julia's taxi dropped her off. She waved goodbye to Pavlos as he departed. Today, she was wearing a fur jacket, trousers, and boots and looked very glamorous but still carried her swimming gear with her. "Afternoon all," she said, cheerfully.

Alexi rushed to open the door for her, "Ah, my sunshine on a winter's day!"

"Come on! Tell us the details," Lt Mavromatis burst out.

"All in good time," she said, as Alexi gave his seat to her and helped her remove the fur jacket. Caesar immediately jealous, jumped up and started to snuffle at it. "No, you don't. Get off, Caesar!" There was a brief tug of war and for a moment, Caesar had thought he might win! But the jacket was retrieved, and Caesar banished to a corner. Lt Mavromatis was almost desperate now.

"Well?" Julia joined in the teasing. "What would you like to know?"

"Where did you go? Where did this misfit take you, madam?"

"If you must know, we had dinner in a perfectly respectable tavern with live music and excellent sea food!

Then, we walked through Plaka, the moon was full, there was a busker playing a saxophone and couples were dancing in the streets. It was very pleasant."

"Ah, what a night," added Alexi dreamily. However, Lt Mavromatis was not yet satisfied.

"Then ... after that?"

"We had some ice cream."

"Then?"

"Then, he took me home and I'm saying no more! No more!" She put her finger to her lips and winked, and the conversation was closed, leaving Lt Mavromatis in a sceptical quandary.

Nadeen, who had been admiring Julia's outfit, asked, "Why do you always dress like this, with so much style, like a lady from Vogue?"

"Thank you my dear, it's nice to be appreciated. Since I was young, I've been interested in fashion. My mother had an old sewing machine and she taught me how to sew and make patterns. I never became a designer, but I worked for a fashion magazine for many years as a journalist and now I have my own blog. Actually, I have quite a following. My style isn't original though! I've always been a fan of an American designer called Iris Apfel, who wears the big glasses and beads."

Poppy raised her head and pen. "I've heard that the next fashion market will be for the over sixties,"

"Yes, that's correct because they're probably the only ones with the spending power these days."

"I can't remember the last time I just went out and bought clothes or boots for the fun of it," Marina said wistfully, "I don't like this mass produced stuff anymore and retro is getting so expensive now."

Betty came in from the kitchen carrying a plate of Christmas kourabiedes biscuits drenched in icing sugar. "Help yourselves," she said. "I remember, not so long ago, we always got changed into our best clothes in the evening and put on our gold jewellery ..."

"Then, we went for coffee or just a walk about," added Julia.

Marina looked startled. "I wouldn't dare wear gold now. I heard of a woman, who was walking down the steps of Saint Nicholas church, and had her gold cross and chain pulled from her neck in broad daylight."

Nadeen spoke up, "In our area, the latest trick is for a thief on a motor bike to drive past someone with a bag on their arm and pull it off or push them to the ground. One old lady died because she hit her head when she fell down."

Antonis was incensed. "You see, that's wicked. This damn economic crisis is making some people desperate, but there is no excuse for that! "Matthew nodded in agreement.

Marina continued, "A student friend of mine works in a kiosk for a pittance. One night, he was walking home, and two burly Bulgarian types grabbed him from behind and nearly strangled him. They grabbed his bag full of books and notes. Of course, they stole his wages and cell phone. He yelled at them and surprisingly, he found his bag, books and ID under a bench near the church."

"Maybe there is honour amongst thieves," said Poppy ironically. "Last week, two kids, brothers actually, got stopped outside my school and a man waved a knife at them. He got away with their mobile phone. Thank goodness the boys weren't hurt."

Nadeen continued, "My friend got her flat broken into recently. They pulled everything apart, all for thirty Euros! When you've got nothing, that's a lot to lose."

"Amen," said Julia. "So much has changed. In the early seventies, I did the American thing, dressed like a hippie, went to Woodstock, did Route 66. I was supposed to be studying to be a secretary, but I was rebellious: I tried everything once! But I was drawn back to Greece. In the eighties, we had a good lifestyle and partied a lot. It had its dark side though, when AIDS arrived. People started getting paranoid when good friends started to die. Then, my first husband, who was a TV journalist and drank far too much, was killed in a car crash. Yet, we seemed to have work and money and enjoyed spending it."

"That's right," confirmed Poppy. "When I first came here, I was able to eat properly. Look at me now!" She patted her hips!

"A bag of bones is no use to any man," Kitso said very quietly, and the regulars smiled, knowingly.

Poppy wasn't sure if that was a compliment or not. "Thank you, I think. Nadeen, what about you?"

"When I left my home and my village in West Africa, I had no idea of what a city was or life or different people. It's strange when you think about it. I believe that everyone is the same. You go to school, try to get a job, get married, have a kid, make a nice place to live in. Well, that's how it's supposed to be."

"And survive," said Poppy.

"Yes, that's about it."

Tom was now playing with his Christmas present, "Thank you," said Petroula over the top of his head to Nikos, "That rubric cube really keeps him busy."

"Nothing," he replied. Petroula looked across at Nadeen. "Do you think you'll stay here?"

"I've nowhere else to go. France sounds nice, the welfare system is good, but I wouldn't want to live in one of those higher rise ghettos, all gangs and violence. Anyway, maybe one day Kalim and I ..." She blushed and pointed to her tummy, "I'm pregnant!" she whispered with her finger on her mouth, so only the girls could hear.

"Congratulations!" both Poppy and Petroula replied quietly.

"What about you, Poppy. Will you stay?"

"Probably, I've got a job, a flat, some friends. There's no reason to go home, whatever that means." She turned to Julia, "And you?"

"I've been thinking about it. I'm not getting any younger. I could go to my sister's girl who lives in Denmark but I'm not keen on the idea of living with months of rain and cold! It would probably kill me! On the other hand, I'm not sure I want to end my days watching a cockroach waving at me in a local hospital bed! Please let's change the subject."

Bartholomew pulled his chair round to join them. "You girls put me to shame. I've never been further than Crete and that was on a school trip. I could never imagine living somewhere else, having to speak a different language and eat new food. All this mobility worries me. I think it will cause a lot of problems, eventually. I wonder what terrible circumstances force them to move?"

Nadeen looked at him quizzically, wondering if he was naive or stupid. "That's easy," she said and pointed at the TV, which was showing a montage of refugees in rubber boats landing on Greek islands, being kept in camps, walking along railway lines, men with kids on their shoulders, women struggling with bags, tents in the rain and the mud of some middle European crossing point ... an endless river of hope and despair. After a moment, she said, "Its war, fear of death, knowing that your tribe, colour, religion, is enough to get you killed. Trust me, rape and torture are commonplace in many countries," and she bit her lip.

To divert his attention Poppy said, "I think there are quite a few economic migrants like me who just want a chance to work and make a living."

"Don't I know it!" Petroula turned around to face the regulars. "Gentlemen, you have all been fortunate in some ways. Of course, you've had your share of troubles, but you know who you are and where you are from and you have a sense of identity. We are all mixed up, and we're cosmopolitan. Many go abroad to find a more tolerant place to live, somewhere peaceful." At this, Matthew and Antonis exchanged a knowing look.

"Somewhere you don't have to make your living by crowd control!" Matthew said.

"Or fighting the system every day!" added Antonis.

Suddenly, Kalim asked, "Where is George?"

""He's often the last to arrive. Wasn't the wedding lovely?" Marina asked everyone.

There was a chorus of "Yes," "Yes," "Yes."

"Maria's dress was heavenly," said Julia. The others chimed in with, "the food," "the cake," "the church decorations," "the old car, so romantic," "the music," "the dancing" ... "What an evening," "the singing ..." This put Bartholomew into the spotlight, "Bravo!" and there was a short round of applause.

"Thank you, but things didn't go so smoothly for me," he replied reddening.

"What happened?" asked Betty carrying Louli out of the kitchen, giving the cat to Tom to play with.

"When George introduced his wife Roula to us, she recognized me immediately from the church food bank services. Of course, my wife had a fit. She thought I was having an affair! Dear me! So, I had to tell her there and then about losing my job and pretending to go to work every day and working at the church."

"Jesus man!" said Alexi, "You're lucky to be standing!"

"At first, she was quite understanding and then she stuck her high heel into my toes and kept on smiling … Now, I'm banished to my son's room." They all laughed at this.

"That will teach you. There's no chance of keeping anything secret from your wife for long!" Lt Mavromatis reprimanded him.

"Where is George? He should be here by now." Julia glanced at her watch, which had a huge face studded with strass and a chunky strap. This latest fashion statement was a Christmas present from Alexi, which she thought was fabulous. "The last time I saw him was after the first dance. Then, he dashed out of the tavern for some reason. Did you see him again, Petroula?"

"No, I didn't."

As the sun was trying to break through the clouds, Kitso, Kalim and Nadeen decided to play ball on the beach with Tom. As the girls watched them go, Petroula smiled at Poppy. "He's a good man. I think he will make you happy,"

"I hope so," she blushed and returned to her marking. But she was biting her pen, nervously, "These test results are pretty bad: only six passes out of fourteen." Louli jumped onto the table and settled down to watch her work.

"Betty, did I see Jacob at the wedding?" Julia asked

"Yes, you did. He had his hair tied back and he was wearing a white shirt, and black trousers, I couldn't believe it! He said, "Hi Mum," as if everything was normal again."

"That's wonderful."

"He even asked me for a dance" said Marina, "But he only had eyes for Antigoni!"

"Well, I never! By the way, you looked incredible, so Amy Winehouse. Your hair was superb!"

"Thanks, I'm glad you noticed me, no one else did!"

Poppy was getting crosser whilst marking. The papers were bleeding red ink.

"Steady on, girl!" warned Lt Mavromatis, "You'll blow a fuse."

Poppy was going red with frustration. "These test results are rubbish! The kids aren't stupid or particularly lazy but this year, the teaching hours have been cut, because the school owner wants to make a bit of profit. But they still expect you to cover the same amount of material. It's impossible!"

The game of ball on the beach ended. So far, no-one had swum today; it was just too miserable.

"Are you okay?" Kitso asked Poppy immediately, "You look upset."

"Not really, it's just work ... business and education just don't mix. When you work with people, you can't treat them like a commodity. Then, there's the hassle with the pension stamps never being correctly paid, if at all ... then, the extra hours that they forget to pay you for. It's one big scam, the kids being force-fed education. They do so many extra hours and their parents pay through the nose for it. It's ridiculous!"

Those listening agreed. "Recently, a little girl said to me, 'Miss, if you've been unemployed, what chance do I have?' I had to bite my lip not to cry."

"Aww," said Marina. "That's so sad. Kids these days know everything." Poppy looked at Kitso and Nikos. "Kids these days don't have the freedom like you had. No trees to climb or fall out of! They just sit at home playing video games, eating junk food and getting lost in the world of social networking. Virtual reality doesn't encourage them to think independently or use their imaginations constructively. I've had enough!" She picked up her red pen and continued.

"Feeling any better?" The Lieutenant inquired.

"Not really!" Everyone laughed. "It's not just that. Every night, I have to get the bus home and at that time of night, there are always a few ladies going to work downtown. No offence, Kalim, but some of these girls are so young. It hurts me that it seems to be their only way to get by." He shrugged, "There's one foreign girl, about twenty-two. She passes me at the same time every night. She's usually in white boots, a mini, with braids in her hair. She's really sweet looking. After a few weeks, we started saying 'goodnight', and laughing! It's our joke, she's starting work and I' m finishing it."

Nadeen smiled sadly, "That's nice."

"Then, when I get off in Omonia, I have to walk down the back of Rio Arcade where the junkies are. At that time of night, they are in their first throes of oblivion, it's heart-breaking."

"Try taking the ten-thirty train from Kifissia to Piraeus. The last carriage is full of them. They're zoned out, moving in slow motion, like underwater ballet dancers. Then, at Omonia station, they spring into life," Kitso added. "Why not get off at Victoria and get the train from there?"

"It's not much better. Last time I was there, it was full of young Afghani men sleeping rough in the park. God help them when it rains. I don't suppose they let them sleep in the train station downstairs."

Kitso concluded, "I think it's the same in every city now, refugees sleeping out until they get moved on or they can pay their way out. Someone's making big money out of their misery, that's for sure." The others nodded in agreement.

Betty emerged from the kitchen, a mouth-watering smell following her. "Where is George?" she asked again. "Maybe, he's tired after the wedding."

"He was certainly the life and soul of the party, wasn't he?" Lt Mavromatis commented.

"He certainly was," said Betty.

The café door opened slowly, and everyone turned, expecting to see George, but it was only Jacob who stood there looking very pale. "Come in darling" called Betty, about to return to the kitchen.

"Mum, stop! Wait, I've just had a text from Antigoni." He held up his phone and took a deep breath, "It's George, he has had a heart attack!" Everyone fell silent.

"When?"

"She said that he left the wedding to get some cash from the ATM to pay the band but there was a queue and he was hot from dancing. He must have got stressed because he had to wait and there was a rumour that the money would run out. All he wanted was to get back to the taverna as fast as possible. After the wedding, he collapsed at home and died later in hospital. The funeral is in a few days."

"Dear God." Most of the winter swimmers crossed themselves, lost for words. Betty automatically turned to light the candle in the little lantern. "How many more?" she whispered.

The TV was still on, silently showing refugees clambering out of half-sunken boats watched by a group of holiday makers, some of whom were giving out bottles of water while others just moved their sun loungers, rubbed in more oil and continued sunbathing. It was being reported that many didn't make it. A stricken coastguard stood numbly for the press, holding a tiny drowned girl in his arms whilst behind, her father was being manhandled into a black plastic body bag, to be dragged up the beach. One leg of the toddler was caught on camera dangling down. She was wearing a distinctive pink shoe with flowers on. Jacob gasped when he realised that her other shoe was sitting outside his hut. The young man broke down and the tears which should have been shed months ago now started to pour. Betty took her sons hand and led him away to mourn in privacy.

Alexi, Dimitris, and Lt Mavromatis sat huddled together. "I never thought he'd be the first to go."

"Let's get a taxi to the funeral together."

"After all these years … At least, he saw Maria married."

"Roula must be devastated." At last, Lt Mavromatis stood up wearily, grasping the top of the chair for support

"Marina, Betty, could I trouble you for some glasses and a drop of Metaxa for everyone please?" The glasses were laid out and the brandy poured. When everyone had a glass, he said, "If I may speak for us all. Let's honour our friend and fellow winter swimmer George. Please raise your glasses. To George!" Tom looked confused. "That's right, hold it up son."

Bartholomew took over. "To George, a generous man who gave everything to ensure that his daughter had a glorious wedding and a good friend to me too." Then his voice faltered. When he regained his composure, he said, "If it's okay, I'll organize the wreath?"

"That's very kind of you," said Betty.

The evening was drawing in, a dark leaden sky without stars. Kitso turned to Poppy, "I'll take you home, and if you like we'll light a fire and grill some fish. Then I'll play you a tune on my clarinet."

"If the neighbours don't call the police!" Nikos winked at him.

"I'm not that bad, am I?"

"There's plenty of room in my car," Bartholomew offered, "No Tom you can't bring Louli. She lives here." He took Petroula, Tom and Julia home. Matthew roared off on his motor bike with Antonis clinging on behind followed by Nadeen and Kalim in their own car. Alexi and Lt Mavromatis walked down the lane in measured paces with their heads bent, followed by Caesar, padding behind.

Nikos was left alone with Jacob watching TV.

"Are you okay, Jacob?"

"Not really. I made a big fool of myself crying like that." He went outside and returned with the little pink shoe and laid it on the table." I'm sure this is the other shoe that little girl was wearing, the kid that drowned. I found it a while ago on the beach when I was cleaning up."

"I have an idea. Let's put it in the shrine at the end of the lane, shall we?" said his mother. So, Nikos, mother and son went off together sharing an umbrella.

Marina and Dimitris were also preparing to leave for home. She helped him into his coat. "Grandad, how can we be so happy one moment and so sad the next?"

"I don't know. What is it they say about life? You should light the candle before the night comes."

By now, it was raining quite hard and the remaining leaves were being blown off the trees. Jacob had retreated to his hut while Betty went to the window and traced the rain splattering on the windowpane with her finger. The candle flickered and the glass reflected the beads of light. She looked seaward and picked up Louli and cuddled her for comfort. On the surrounding hills, the village lights were coming on in the dusk, making patterns like distant starry constellations. She gazed at them and murmured, "So many lives each with their own story to tell and soon I'll be saying goodbye to another dear friend."

Sunday 7

Competition Time

On a tree outside the café, a handmade notice announced that the 'Winter Swimmers Annual New Year's Race', was imminent, offering prizes of medals and hot meals to all participants. In the sea, orange buoys had been laid out to mark the distance of approximately one hundred metres there and back. It was a perfect day. The sky was clear and the sun shining but the water was distinctly chilly. However, experienced winter swimmers knew that if you swam hard, you'd start to 'burn'.

The regular swimmers were already lined up on the beach along with an assortment of athletic-looking, newcomers who had turned up for the race. Not surprisingly though, no-one seemed willing to be first to strip off. On the beach, Tom stood between Betty and Nadeen holding their hands, whilst from the warmth of the café, Dimitris, Alexi, and Marina watched from the window. Back at the starting line, Lt Mavromatis who was in charge, had everyone lined up and was checking their goggles.

"Right, everyone ready? There and back." He held up the starting pistol and fired. "GO!" There was a flurry of activity as most participants ran towards the sea and dived in while others waded in, prolonging the agony only to gasp as they started to swim the course. Out of the regular swimmers, Matthew was leading, closely followed by Jacob, Kalim was next, surprisingly, Bartholomew. Julia and Antonis were not far behind. In the middle section, Kitso and Nikos were swimming together, with Petroula trying to keep up but Poppy was swimming slowly at the rear. One by one, they circled the last buoy. Eventually, they all made it back to dry land and wrapped themselves in towels and were presented with medals made of cardboard and glitter glue by Tom! He solemnly shook their hands and put the medal with a ribbon around their necks. The swimmers were all delighted, if cold and shivering.

Back in the café, everyone was drying off and thawing out, but Poppy was suffering from the cold. "I didn't think I'd make it but I'm glad I didn't give up. Oh ... I don't feel too good ..." By now, she was trembling and looked pale and dizzy.

"Quick, get her next to the stove, Kitso. We must start rubbing her back, arms and legs, to get her circulation going and Betty, a hot drink please, with sugar." Antonis had come to the rescue. Within a few moments, Poppy was regaining her colour and could move her feet and hands.

"Sorry about that," she said sleepily. Kitso sat her on his knee and wrapped his arms around her.

"Nothing like a little body warmth. You'll feel better soon."

"I once saw Russian soldiers breaking the ice to get a swim," said Lt Mavromatis.

"Idiots! I bet they froze their balls off," scoffed Alexi.

"Nonsense, it's good for you."

"If you're a penguin!"

Petroula joined in. "My sister Jenny married into a Finnish family and she met her new in-laws by first going naked into a hot sauna with them, then jumping into a freezing cold lake. She thought that she was going to die but actually, it was quite pleasant."

"Sounds masochistic to me," muttered Alexi.

Undeterred, Petroula continued, "She was married in a wooden church, dressed in a white satin gown with white fur around the wrists and hood. There were large white candles and branches of green pine for decoration." She looked wistfully into the distance. Nadeen, who was now obviously pregnant, touched her hand.

"It sounds very romantic."

"It was. They live in Sweden now and they have a little girl."

"Has Kalim said anything yet?" Petroula patted Nadeen's tummy.

"No, not yet. Obviously, I'm not at work. I haven't been for months since ..."

"Since what?" inquired Petroula.

"It's nothing. Something happened at work. A man died, and I couldn't go on, so I refused. Kalim could easily have thrown me out but instead, we began to see each other and now I work for a cleaning agency. We do shops in the morning and offices in the evenings mostly. I hope this is meant to be."

"Nice words, 'meant to be'. I wasn't so lucky. One careless night when I was young, I got Tom. His father, well let's say, he's a waste of space!"

"There seems to be a lot of them around."

"But I loved having a baby and I'm sure you will too, don't worry."

Kalim noticed the women together. "Women laughing, talking; it's not a good omen. They're plotting something. It makes me nervous."

"You're being paranoid man," said Bartholomew, then "By the way, when is Nadeen due?"

"April or early May."

"Good, plenty of time then."

"Time for what?"

"To go to the town hall and get a civil marriage."

"Oh!"

"Don't play dumb! Think about your residency papers, your football dreams. I hope you're still training?"

"Not much, I get bored training on my own."

"No excuses, join a training programme, no more beer or souvlaki. Think success! Don't you want your son to say, my daddy plays for …?"

"It's just a dream."

"Make it happen. Don't give up on life like I nearly did. God, I'm stiff after that swim! I need a hot drink." He ordered a mountain tea with honey from Marina.

"Make it two," said Kalim.

At the other tables, Poppy was paying more attention to Kitso than her marking, Julia was playing tavli with Alexi and Dimitris was listening as Lt Mavromatis read to him from the newspaper. "Over twenty bodies have so far been recovered from the latest tragedy at sea … including that of a three-year-old girl and her father …"

Dimitris shook his head in disbelief. "Why did they come in such a bad boat? Who would do this? How much did they pay? Where are they from? Where will they go? Where will they be buried? What about the kids?" He rubbed his face, tired out with trying to understand the enormity of the situation, so he closed his eyes to take refuge in sleep. Lt Mavromatis folded up the newspaper and lifted Louli off the table.

"I don't know my friend, I don't know," he said quietly.

Petroula, Tom and Nikos were busy looking at an animal picture book with numbers on it. Nikos said, "Tom, if I have two elephants plus three giraffes and one hippo, how many animals have I got in the zoo?"

"Six," yelled Tom, happily. "S-s-six!"

"Bravo!"

At the table in the corner, Nadeen and Kalim were talking seriously. She was showing him something in a mother-and-baby magazine and he was looking at it with interest. The TV was on, silently showing reruns of the war in Syria, including the IS atrocities, and the blowing up of the ancient temple at Palmyra. This caught everyone's attention, as the fate of ancient monuments and antiquities were close to the hearts of most Greeks.

"Didn't the Taliban blow up a huge Buddha some years ago?" Nikos asked.

"Yes, they did," replied Poppy.

A young voice piped up. "Why?" asked Tom. "I d-d-don't understand, it's so old."

"Because these people believe that any culture, other than their own, should not exist," Poppy explained slowly. "So, they destroy statues and buildings so no one can see or remember them."

Tom seemed satisfied. Then asked, "Why are those women w-w-wearing f-f-funny clothes?" His mother came to the rescue.

"Lots of Muslim women cover their heads and faces and wear long dresses because it's a tradition and they believe it's modest. Some do it because they choose to, others are forced into it and get punished if they don't."

"I don't like it; you can't see their f-f-faces, only their eyes. Like a ninja! It's creepy! Can they go swimming, Mummy and w-w-wear a bikini like yours?"

"I don't think so Tom. Let's have a look at your book, shall we?" she suggested, trying to distract him.

Matthew began talking to Kitso, over the top of the boy's head. He said quietly, "I saw some awful video made by the IS on the internet a few days ago. They had cut the throat of a young girl and were draining the blood into a plastic washing-up bowl, like a sheep … she was still a child for God's sake, someone's child. I can't get it out of my mind."

"Yes, I saw that. It was wicked, and the bastards were standing around laughing and cheering. If that's what they get off on, then they are sick."

"We don't know half of what's really going on. What about those men beheaded on the beach? The sea turned red," Antonis added.

"Hey, Kalim, what do you make of this IS?"

"In my opinion, they are not true Muslims. They have taken the Koran and twisted the words for their own agenda. They use medieval torture and murder plus high-tech media to spread fear. I heard that one man was severely beaten just for smoking a cigarette!"

"Shhh! Shhh! That's enough," said Petroula, pointing down at Tom. "Please don't say any more. I don't want him to know all this just yet." The men nodded.

After the lunch, which had been promised by the notice on the tree, Betty was busy cleaning up in the kitchen, Jacob and his dogs were on the beach pulling in the line of marking buoys and Marina was gazing out of the window, absentmindedly stroking Louli.

"Penny for your thoughts," inquired Julia.

"I'm just feeling a bit stuck and that nothing is ever going to happen for me. You've done it all; travel, education, marriage, career."

"Ah, it's taken a long time and I never had the baby I so desperately wanted. You're so young … I know it's difficult to be patient."

"I know I shouldn't complain, I've got this job and Betty always pays me on time and feeds me and also, grandad. It's just that when I graduated, I thought I'd go on and do a masters, or go abroad on an Erasmus programme." Julia nodded sympathetically. "Most of my friends are still living at home and just sleep for most of the day and go out all night. I'm not into that and anyway, I've got to care for grandad. I doubt if he could manage on his own now. He's getting forgetful. The other day, I found him out in the yard watering the plants with his pyjamas on!"

"Never mind, I'm sure no-one noticed."

"Ha, we've got nosey neighbours. They don't miss much! As I was saying, there is so much despondency at university. Many of my teachers haven't been paid for six months and some of them are leaving to work abroad."

"Ah … the brain drain."

"Yes. To be honest, my friends haven't been of much help and I got fed up with my boyfriend. Every time we went out, we talked about the same stuff or analysed other couples' relationships, it was so boring and negative. Many kids don't go to lectures anymore. They say it's all theory and they can get the notes online anyway. It's a form of educational tourism and they still complain."

"It was very different in my day. Lectures were compulsory, all our notes were handwritten, and we had seminars to give and essays to write. It was very time consuming in the pre-computerized age. It sounds as if some of these kids are spoilt brats!"

"Some are. They don't realise I've done a full day's work, plus helping grandad and I have to earn my pocket money. I enjoyed being at university but now I feel insecure. Some people I know cling onto the political groups for a sense of identity. The first few weeks at university, I remember being bullied to join this party or that. The conservatives promised a weekend in Arachova skiing! Who fell for that one, I'll never know! Then, there were the anarchist types pretending to be important, dressed in their compulsory designer black clothes, all to score with the village girls! What a joke." She sighed. "It was all so obvious. I hate politics, it's the same blah, blah every year, recycled and repeated. I got bored with it all. I just want to get on. I'd love to get onto one of those graduate training schemes in England but how can I leave grandad?" She held her head in her hands.

"It's Catch 22, as they say," said Julia. "Just try to stay positive. I'm sure something will turn up."

"Thanks, at least girls here don't have to do army service." She looked at Jacob on the beach. "He was like a vegetable when he came out. He wouldn't speak to any of us. He just wanted to hide away and smoke dope. We were really worried. Betty even wanted him to see a psychologist.

"Did he go?"

"No, he said he doesn't trust them or anyone else for that matter. Half of my friends have been to see a psychologist at one time or another. It's the in thing at the moment."

"I'm sure time will heal. He seemed to enjoy the wedding. I saw him dancing with Antigoni. I think I'll take a short walk on the beach after such a big lunch." She left the café and Marina returned to the washing up.

There was an unexpected crunch of brakes on the gravel, a van pulled up outside the cafe and an old familiar

Vespa bike was pulled out. The driver entered the café and yelled out, "Delivery for Jacob. Is he here?"

"No, he's on the beach. I'm his mother."

"Sign here, please. The bike is for Jacob from Roula," and with that, he left in a cloud of dust, narrowly missing Julia who was walking down the lane.

Betty stared at the Vespa. "Well that should give him an interest, getting that old wreck to work properly again. George wasn't much of a mechanic; he never did take care of it."

Julia stood in the doorway, wrapped up in a tartan scarf on top of ski pants and jumper.

"How's my little darling?" said Alexi, opening the door.

"Quite well, thank you. That van nearly got me though," She pushed Caesar down before he could do much damage. "But I do have one problem."

"Shall I kiss it better?"

"I'd rather you didn't,"

"What's the matter, has someone stolen your Varoufakis poster?"

"No, it's still above my bed, please be serious. It's a matter of finances. I've got rather behind with the rent. What with Christmas presents and the cat needing to go to the vet and this outfit was so nice, I just had to have it!"

"In short woman, you're in trouble."

"Yes, my landlord died last year, and his daughter took over. She has no idea of economic realities. I know I'm careless with money, but I always pay up eventually. Just because you live in a certain area you are now expected to pay a ridiculous amount of rent. Trust me, thirty years ago no one wanted to live where I do, now it's considered to be chic. Now you can't find anything to rent because it's all

Airbnb for tourists who can afford to pay ridiculous rates and the Chinese seem to be buying up anything that's for sale. Local people don't have a chance." Tears of anger stung her eyes.

Alexi waited a moment, then asked, "So what's the solution?"

"Pay up or leave. She knows full well that some aspiring outsider will pay three times what I can afford."

"After thirty years?"

"After thirty years."

"Good God, how mean!"

"She seems to forget that I paid for the earthquake damage, a new toilet, a new hot water tank, a new front door, not to mention painting, over the years."

"Get some legal advice."

"I did. They say that I can hang on for a few months without paying before I have to go," Kalim and Nadeen, who had been listening, came over to offer support.

"Don't worry, most people we know owe rent. Some don't care; others worry so much they get ulcers!"

"It's not funny. I love my home, my little yard, my quince tree ... " She wiped away a tear and looked at Kalim and Nadeen. "Nothing seems to last forever, just hold onto each other. When the baby comes, your life will change completely."

"Yes, we've been talking. I've decided to apply for that football training course at the stadium. If I'm accepted, it could lead to a place on a second division team or coaching or a referee's job, who knows?"

"Good for you," said Bartholomew, who had been listening. "Now you can give up the other business!"

Kalim just gave him a charming smile. "One thing at a time man!" They laughed.

"Ahh!" Nadeen held her tummy. "Ohh. The baby kicked! It's all this talk about football. He must have been listening!"

Outside, Kitso and Poppy were examining the state of the Vespa. Jacob was already prowling around it, "You've got your work cut out. It's caked in salt and dirt," said Kitso.

"You'll see! Now, all I've got to do is find the cash for lessons and get my diploma."

"Good luck with that one, "he said.

Kitso and Poppy were now sitting on the secluded bench at the back of the café.

"I still can't believe that George is gone, I keep expecting to see him at any moment," she said.

"Me too. He was such a character."

"To die in hospital, it seems so impersonal. My mum died at home, years ago. We sat up with her all night and she just drifted into unconsciousness and died. Later, some men from the mortuary came and put her in a black plastic bag and pulled her down the stairs and into a van. My dad had vanished with a bottle of whiskey by this time. I couldn't even cry. It was the fifth of November, Bonfire Night, when we have fireworks. I went out alone to watch them. I didn't feel the cold. I was numb, like I'd died too. To be honest, I was glad. The pain she went through at the end was too much as the morphine wasn't helping."

Kitso pulled her close and gave her a kiss, "We've all been there," he assured her.

"My dad died when I was eight or so. He was working away from home at the time in a factory in the city. The rest of us were in the village; mum, kids, horse, goats, cats ... He used to come home on Friday night and leave on Sunday. On Friday night, we were waiting for dad and there was a knock on the door and my sister opened it expecting dad, but it was a local policeman. Everyone rushed to the door to see what was happening and all eyes were on him. My mother was waiting. He couldn't tell her the truth, he said something about the bus breaking down and dad being late. In reality, dad had fallen asleep on the bus after work and had woken up suddenly at a coffee stop. Being half asleep, he hadn't looked properly before crossing the road. He'd been knocked down and killed instantly."

"Ahh."

"I was the youngest, so I never got to know him properly. Come on, let's see what the others are doing."

As they walked to the edge of the sea, a group of kayaks were passing by. Tom was excitedly pulling his mother to the shoreline.

"W-w-what are those?"

"They are canoes," she said patiently.

"Can I have a c-c-canoe? I want a canoe, a c-c-canoe!" They all watched as the three kayaks paddled rhythmically away. On their return to the café, the three regulars were playing cards, Marina was on her computer and Matthew and Antonis were trying to find something worth watching on TV. At the moment, it was between an old black and white Greek film and a documentary on Salvador Dali.

"All exciting stuff," said Alexi, who had just lost at cards. The boys grunted and kept on flicking. There was an old clip showing horses at work during the war years. Kitso glanced at the TV. "My dad had a horse called Canella. I've still got the stirrups at home."

"I never learnt to ride; it's a very expensive hobby."

"Most village families had a horse, up to forty years ago. I think we've lost a lot not by having donkeys and horses around," he said.

Alexi joined in, "It's all very romantic but I have to take in the poor brutes that have been abandoned and neglected. At the animal shelter where I work, last year, two ponies turned up. They were starving. One had to be put down, the other one was so sad, she just stood for days with her head down, then we put her in with an old donkey for company and she's okay now."

"I suppose you get a lot of unwanted pets at this time of year?" asked Poppy.

"Not only now. Because of the economic crisis, people can't afford to keep a pet. Louli here, was found in a city dust bin. The driver, who's a friend of mine, put her in the cab until he'd finished work and brought her to me, and I brought her here."

"I wondered where she'd come from," said Betty, popping her head out of the kitchen. Alexi grinned guiltily.

"Kittens, puppies, we've got them all. It breaks my heart."

"You old softy," said Julia, putting her arms around his neck and he blushed.

"They were going to put this one down." He bent to pat Caesar, "but I couldn't bear it, so I took him home."

Tom looked at Petroula, "Mummy, can we have a d-d-dog?"

"No, no dogs! I've got no time to walk one, no space or extra money for food or the vet." She replied sharply.

"A cat then?"

"Maybe."

"Come here Tom, you can play with Caesar any time you like," Tom hugged Caesar and the dog thumped his tail on the floor. Outside, the kayaks could be seen returning. The boy rushed to the window.

"Mummy, Mummy look! I want a c-c-canoe-a canoe!" he yelled.

"Hush Tom, that's loud enough."

"Canoe, I w-w-want a canoe!"

"Shut up!" snapped Betty.

Petroula gasped and Tom started to cry. "I'm sorry. He can get over excited sometimes.

But Betty was not listening. "No canoes, never. Promise me, Petroula!"

"Yes, okay," she replied, getting a little frightened by this outburst. Tom was still snivelling.

"Forgive me child."

Matthew and Antonis turned to see what was going on. Betty was obviously becoming distressed. She twisted her apron around her hands. "My boy, Yannis, Jacob's twin brother, had a canoe. One day, he just paddled away saying he said he would be back in half an hour. It was a lovely day, but he never came back, and his body was never found. Eventually, the canoe turned up on an island, miles away. It had been smashed up down one side. That's why Jacob and I keep the café on ... just in case he comes back ... every night, I light this little lantern ... just in case ... I'm sorry ..." and tears of pain and loss streamed down her face. Those present were stunned, as Betty crumpled.

Julia helped her into a chair and gave her a glass of water, "So the boy in the photo in the shrine at the end of the lane is yours?"

"Yes, that's Yannis. He was only fourteen years old." The three regulars, who all knew this, crossed themselves. Then she then picked up Louli and held her close.

Matthew and Antonis had now found something of interest on TV, a travel show about Amsterdam. The city seemed to be a beautiful place with canals, quaintly shaped buildings and people riding bikes. They were watching it closely.

"That's the place to be, look, bike lanes, flat roads, free thinking, dope on demand and decent architecture."

"You mean law, order and tolerance!" added Matthew and they smiled into each other's eyes, "I think we could be happy there."

Alexi glanced out of the window and gasped, "Oh my God! I don't believe it!" which drew a crowd to witness Lt Mavromatis on his skateboard gliding about the park, looping and flicking and turning direction like a pro. "The rotten dog! He's been practising on the sly! I'll show him." and with that, he picked up his skateboard from behind the door, walked smartly out and skated off down the lane shouting, "You old bugger, Mavro! I'll get you." Lt Marvomatis had, of course, seen him coming and just skated gracefully away giving him the finger!

"Come and get me … if you can," he yelled back at his old friend. The spectacle of these two big kids showing off to each other did wonders for Betty's spirits. But as dusk crept across the sky, alone in the café, she lit the candle in the lantern and placed it on the windowsill, facing the sea … just in case.

Sunday 8

Time for Changes

Springtime in Greece was often over in the blink of an eye. Traditionally, it was marked by the arrival of one or two swallows flitting about, then before you knew it, there were dozens swooping and twittering everywhere, rebuilding last year's nests. Also, before the temperature soared, many city-bound housewives did the annual heavy jobs and the thud of carpets being beaten echoed off the walls, after which they were scrubbed, hosed down, and left to drip over their balconies. Or, if you had money for such things, the local dry cleaner would collect, clean, and store them until wintertime.

At the coast today, though the bright sunshine was mercifully tempered by a north wind, the sea sparkled invitingly but it was still quite chilly, keeping the beach relatively empty. Near the café, the blackened verges of the lane and skate park had sprouted green and the spindly trees had recovered enough to produce clouds of purple blossom.

Inside, the cafe was still bedecked with paper streamers hanging from the rafters and curtain rails and littered with other remnants of a carnival party. On a tabletop, there was a wicker basket full of red eggs and the menu board had been extended to include sweet Tsoureki bread, Taramasalata and halva in preparation for those who wished to eat Lenten fare before Paska. The exact date of this celebration was decided by the guardians of Gregorian calendar and it was, so to speak, a moveable feast!

On this particular Sunday, Dimitris was sitting with the red eggs in front of him and he was showing Tom how to polish them with olive oil and a cloth.

"You know, Paska used to be my favourite holiday," said Dimitris staring at the eggs, ignoring the fact that Tom had already cracked one and was busy peeling it. As he nibbled, Dimitris began to reminisce, his early memories now more real and vivid than those of a few weeks ago.

"Before Paska, we were always given a new outfit and shoes to wear, courtesy of a Godparent, and those 'best' shoes had to last until school started in September. Do you have a godmother, Tom?" The little boy just shrugged. "Oh, well, never mind." He slowly polished some eggs and continued. "Then, on 'Big Saturday night', we would all get dressed up and gather outside the church before midnight, with friends and families standing in groups, talking quietly. There was the sense of expectancy. The bell would toll and, in the darkness, candles started to be lit. Then, the sound of the priest singing 'Christos Anesti' was followed by the explosion of fireworks and bells which drowned out the priest, whose litany was not yet over. Then, people kissed each other, trying not to burn each other's clothes or hair! Next, we'd walk home carrying the candles carefully so they wouldn't go out ... I remember being lifted up to make a black cross with the candle flame above the front door ... We would have margarita soup before bed."

Dimitris smiled, then handed Tom a paper napkin and he wiped the red colouring from his fingers and mouth." Don't get it on your clothes," he warned." Do you want to know what else happened?"

The little boy seemed quite happy to listen, so he carried on. "But Sunday was best." He went on to tell him all about how his father carefully washed the lengths of lambs' intestines and made Kokoretsi from liver and other bits and how to wrap it on a skewer and about the smell of roasting lamb that made your mouth water. "Us kids would steal little bits of burnt skin to eat and take turns revolving the lamb on the spit." By now, the boy was getting restless and banged his heels against the wooden bars of the chair.

Dimitris touched the child's hand, but his memories were compelling. "As the day progressed, small glasses of raki or wine were drunk, accompanied by endless plates of feta, bread, olives and tomatoes. Our neighbours came and went, then, when an assortment of chairs had been gathered and arranged around a large table, the lamb would be cut up and served. Then, we'd listen to the talk of family histories and long dead relatives, of scandals and politics. Then, the music would blare and we'd all dance in any space available, amidst the crashing of plates. Ahh Paska!" Tom's seat had been empty, for some time. He was now lying on the floor playing with Louli.

From outside, the sound of a clarinet being played drew both of them to the window and sitting alone on some rocks, they could see Kitso practising, his music held down by a large stone so the wind wouldn't blow it away. High above him, a goat and a young, brown and white kid descended daintily down the cliff to drink at the freshwater spring that trickled from the rocks and to investigate the new noise!

Tom, whose patience had run out, tugged at Dimitris hand, "Come on, let's go ... p-p-please." So together, they walked slowly towards the sea, the boy trailing a piece of seaweed and clutching his plastic dinosaur and Dimitris taking short stiff steps. Behind them, Jacob carried a plastic chair and a rug for Dimitris, with a towel around his neck as he wanted a quick swim. Tom looked up at the old man who still seemed to be in a world of his own, asked "Are you feeling any b-b-better?"

"Yes, I am, but let's take it steady," said Dimitris, as Jacob helped him into the chair and put the rug around him.

"Okay?"

"Fine, don't fuss. Take off this damn rug. Just go for your swim," and he waved him away.

Tom persisted, "W-w-what happened?"

"I don't know really. I felt a bit tired then one leg wouldn't work properly,"

"W-w-what did you do?"

"Marina called for a taxi and we went to the hospital."

"I've n-n-never been there. Is it big?"

"Yes, it's all corridors and rooms with numbers on them and people rushing about."

"Did you see a d-d-doctor?"

"Eventually, a foreigner, I think. She was a nice lady, very polite. She said I'd had a little stroke and my heart had a murmur."

"If you're okay, can we swim t-t-today?"

"I'm fine and no, we can't swim today. It's too cold."

"Can we p-p-play sandcastles?"

"Why not, let's make a central fort with a moat around it," he suggested, so Tom began to construct his castle enthusiastically. But Dimitris was drifting. "Oh, to be young again," he said, watching the child playing. "What I'd give to bend and stretch and run and dive down to the yellow coral by the rocks over there and to dance again." Tom wasn't really listening.

"When I was your age I used to walk with my father and the men after the sheep. Every year, they drove them from Sklesko to Kalambaka to graze them and sell them at market. We often slept rough around a campfire on thick sheep skin rugs, listening to the sheep bells clanging, and if the weather was bad, we'd sleep in a hani for the night. We had an enormous white sheep dog called ... strange, I can't remember his name, that guarded the flocks."

"Like C-C-Caesar?"

"Even bigger than Caesar and he wasn't a pet, he was a working animal and when it rained, most of the men put on heavy cloaks of sheep skin to keep dry. I learnt a lot about life on those journeys. The men would smoke at night and tell dirty jokes or talk politics."

"Did you become a s-s-sheepman ... s-s-shepherd?"

"No, my father had other ideas for me. He made me stay on at school, but I still helped with the animals. He wasn't good with letters or numbers, so I started doing the paperwork. When I left school, I went to Ioannina and began working as a junior in an accounting firm. I worked my way up slowly, took some exams and became a partner."

"What's a p-p-partner?"

"Someone who is in charge of a business with other people, you share the work. Then I married Martha. She was a beauty and a good girl. She was very clever with her hands. Our house was always immaculate. She couldn't go to school much. The war years stopped many young people getting an education. She had to look after her younger brothers, gather firewood, keep the house, cook, and survive. They were difficult times."

"I hate s-s-school! Some of the kids are m-m-mean. They spit at me and call me nasty names."

"It's always been like that, I'm afraid. Some kids think they're richer or stronger or more popular and like making the others' lives miserable."

"I know!"

"I heard Antonis and Matthew talking the other day. Did you know that they were both bullied at school?"

"No." The little boy found this difficult to believe.

"Look at them now, both good looking, strong young men. I have an idea: whenever someone makes you afraid, imagine them in an old-fashioned pair of stripy pyjamas or a horrid, pink, frilly nighty." Tom laughed at the thought.

"T-t--tell me, what happened n-n-next?" he said, continuing to work on the sandcastle.

"And then, our son Petros, that's Marina's dad, came along a bit late in life. I've been a lucky man, compared to many."

"I don't have a d-d-daddy!" Tom said suddenly. "All the other kids have a d-d-daddy. Mummy said that he was a waste of space. W-w-what's a waste of space?"

Dimitris sighed. "It's your mummy's way of saying that some men don't deserve their children. Don't let it worry you."

"D-d-do you have any grandchildren?"

"Yes, Marina is my granddaughter. Her parents went to live in Canada about five years ago." Then, out of the blue, Tom asked, "Will you be my Pappous?"

Dimitris opened his arms, "Come here child," he lifted him up onto his knees and brushed off the sand. "Of course, child, that's the best medicine I could ever have. Come on, let's finish this sandcastle."

In the café, Lt Mavromatis and Alexi were playing tavli, Betty was cooking and half watching TV. Outside, Jacob was tinkering with George's Vespa, wielding a selection of spanners and an oily rag. The machine was now in a pristine condition. Bartholomew arrived dressed up in a smart leather jacket and stopped to admire the bike. "You've made a good job of that, Jacob," he said.

"Now let's see if Antigoni will come for a drive with me!"

"I'm sure she will. Did you get your diploma, then?"

"Ha! Don't start me with that one!" snarled Jacob.

"What's wrong? I can't believe you failed,"

"I did all the lessons and theoretical stuff. Then, on the day of the test, the two kids in front of me failed immediately on small details."

"No!"

"When my turn came, I thought I'd done okay, then I turned too sharply in front of a parked car and the examiner failed me. Then, he asked me for two-hundred Euros to pass!"

"What a nerve!"

"Of course, I didn't have that kind of money. Then, the instructor arrived. He was very angry and told us to repeat the test rather than pay a bribe to the examiner."

"What did you do?"

"Just that. A few days later, we retook the test with another examiner and we all passed."

"Bravo!"

"Those creeps make me sick. I bet they are making over one-thousand Euros in bribe money alone!"

Bartholomew shook his head, "It's unbelievable. Why can't someone stop this kind of blatant corruption?"

"I don't know. Are you going to swim today?"

"No chance!" he replied, and they went into the warmth of the café where Jacob started to wipe the oil off his hands.

"Mum, can I have a hot chocolate, please?" He pulled out the spoon he had found from his pocket and was about to take some sugar when his mother spotted it.

"Hey, where did you get that?"

"I found it a few months ago on the beach with the metal detector." Betty picked it up and started to polish it.

"I haven't seen this in a long time. It was your grandfather's. He made it himself during the civil war. Your dad always kept it in his jacket."

"I can hardly remember dad now."

"It's been fifteen years now. For me, it's like yesterday … it was hard to see him waste away. He refused to have any treatment for the cancer, so the doctor sent him home. Ah, he was such a big, healthy man, a man of few words. At the end, all he wanted to do was sit on the beach and look at the sea. He said it was timeless and peaceful …"

"That I can understand."

The game of tavli ended rowdily. Alexi was now holding his mobile phone at arm's length, much to the amusement of Louli who was sitting on the table next to the tavli board.

"What are you looking at, cat?" he said crossly.

"Put your glasses on, man," advised his friend.

So, Alexi dutifully put on his glasses. "I still don't understand, press this, then that, wait, what code? Enter where? How? SIM cards, recorded messages, texting, selfies, photo box, strawberry crush, apps … all I want to do is make a simple call!" He began to shake the phone with frustration!

"Careful Alexi! Get Jacob to help you." He banged the phone down and Louli jumped off the table in fright.

Jacob came over and held out his hand, "Give it to me please, before it gets broken!" Alexi handed it straight over for him to fix.

"I was given a tablet for Christmas", announced Lt Mavromatis proudly. "It's a wonderful gadget. Instant information but this internet, I feel it's a mixed blessing. Kids today know everything it took us years to work out!" They all laughed.

"It's not funny," said Betty emerging from the kitchen holding a large wooden spoon. "Last year, my sister took some photos of her grandkids in the bath. When she went to collect them, the manager told her that they were not supposed to print photos like these. She had no idea what he meant, at first. Then she was horrified! So much has changed. There's no innocence anymore," and she tapped the spoon on the table for emphasis.

"No sweet years of dreaming! Ah, Margarita in the fourth class." Alexi clutched his hands under his chin and gave a silly smile.

"I thought you'd got over her, Alexi, it's a lifetime ago!"

"I'm all for the slow approach."

"So slow that you nearly let Julia slip away. Get a grip man, for the love of God!"

"Hey, wait a minute, you can talk. What about that girl you once saw at the bus stop?" Lt Mavromatis smiled wistfully, remembering a moment trapped in time when a gaunt tongue-tied teenage schoolboy was lost for the words to say to the beauty standing so close to him. The summer wind had blown her dark hair back off her face and her cotton dress had billowed out and flapped against her legs. Then, without so much as a glance in his direction, she had climbed aboard the bus, the gears crashed, and dust and diesel fumes enveloped him, and she was gone.

Betty sat down with them," I think it's sick, those little girls caked in makeup, dressed up like adults for beauty pageants or those sexy music videos on TV. No wonder kids are precocious. If you believe what the news says, you can't trust anyone. What about those Catholic priests messing with boys or that teacher who put a camera in the boys changing rooms at a school or that lawyer who was selling child porn?"

"God help us all," said Lt Mavromatis, who crossed himself, then drew his hand across his throat. "I know what they deserve."

"For once, we agree" Alexi said and shook his hand which his friend cleaned discreetly with a napkin afterwards!

Kitso entered the café carrying his clarinet. "Sorry about the noise. I've got to practice somewhere!"

"Well, Louli liked it, mate!" teased Alexi. Kitso picked up the cat and held her face to his.

"Really?" She purred at the attention. "You little hussy!" He put her down gently. "It's a bit empty in here these days. Where is everyone?" Betty held up a postcard.

"This is from the boys: Matthew has given up his job and they have gone to try out life in Amsterdam."

"Where?" asked Dimitris, holding his hand to his ear.

"Holland!"

"Oh, all tulips, windmills and canals, far too flat. What does it say?"

"It says that they have found accommodation on a canal boat and met some interesting people. Matthew has got a job as a security officer for a politician and Antonis is working in a shop that sells special cigarettes!"

"Nice one!" muttered Jacob, which his mother ignored.

"… and they are going to the opening of a performing arts festival tomorrow. They sound happy."

"At least they are out of the Exarchia scene. Any news of Kalim and Nadeen?"

"Not recently, the baby must be due soon."

"What about that redhead of yours, Kitso, where is she today?" asked Alexi.

"She phoned to say that she wasn't feeling well. There is some bug going around the school."

"Oh dear."

"Nikos should be here soon. He'll have some news, I'm sure."

Lt Mavromatis turned his attention to Bartholomew who was doing a killer Sudoku. "You look smart today, isn't it a bit much for the beach?"

"Yes, actually I've come from the church. I've been appointed as one of the Psalters in the Cathedral. At last, I can say I have a paid job."

"Bravo!" There was a short burst of applause.

"And I don't have to sleep in my son's room anymore!"

Nikos arrived carrying a large bag of artichokes for Betty and watched Tom playing with Louli, rolling pinecones along the floor for her to chase. He bent to pat the boy's head.

"Hey, what's going on?" Alexi asked.

"Well," he looked embarrassed, "Don't laugh, but I've gone back to third school!"

"Good for you man," he replied, "Wish I had."

"I'm not doing so well at the maths to be honest, but my teacher is so polite and patient. I never thought they could be like that!" He handed the bag to Betty who disappeared into the kitchen.

"I'll tell Poppy, she'll be so proud of you," she said.

"Where is Petroula? I haven't seen her in a while," Nikos ventured.

Betty emerged from the kitchen, carrying a large bowl and a knife to prepare the vegetables. "Well, she has really landed on her feet! "You remember that she worked as housekeeper for that rich lawyer? The one she hardly ever saw?"

"Yes."

"Well, he died suddenly and left her everything, the house and the money!"

"Wow! I had no idea. What will she do?"

"She's planning to open a bridal and wedding services shop in Kolonaki. It's going to be very posh. Julia pulled a few strings with her fashion connections that arranged for the promotion and with the help of some frilly type of designer from Mykonos, so it's all go."

"Lucky for her. I'm glad she got a break in life but ..." he looked down at Tom, "What about the boy?"

"Don't worry, Bartholomew brings him here after church and takes him back home in the evening. We can all keep an eye on him during the day."

Bartholomew looked about. "I haven't seen Marina for a while either."

Dimitris replied, "Didn't you hear? She has got a six-month Erasmus placement at Manchester University in social psychology."

"What a wonderful opportunity." Bartholomew was impressed.

Betty stood behind Dimitri's chair and patted his shoulders, "so I decided to take him in until she gets back.

He's got Yannis' old room. I'm very fond of them both. Marina's like the daughter I never had."

"You're a gem, Betty," said Nikos and gave her a kiss. She pushed him away and blushed.

"Get away with you!"

Alexi was now hovering by the door keeping watch for Julia's taxi. "Where is my girl? That's what I want to know?"

"She probably got fed up with waiting around for you ... you old jail bird!" teased Lt Mavromatis.

"Come on, three days in the local cells was nothing. The food was okay, and I wasn't even drunk!"

"At your age, what were you thinking?"

"Aww, it was nothing, just doing a favour for Sergeant Dimotrakis, his father was in my class at school."

"What exactly happened?" asked Bartholomew stiffly.

"Relax man. It's nothing serious! Dimo arrived with this G3 and says he can't make it work. As you may know, I do have some skills ..."

"Get on with it and stop bragging man," snapped Lt Mavromatis.

"Anyway, I stripped it down, cleaned it properly and thought I'd just try it out."

"Snipers' tricks, I suppose?"

"Well, yes but my eyes are a bit out of focus these days."

"My God man, you could have killed someone." Bartholomew was really startled.

"I lined up the sights and shot, tap, tap, tap ... perfect. Until I realized I'd shot up the storks' nest on top of the telephone pole opposite Saint Augustine's church. The young priest came running out in hysterics."

"You idiot, Alexi!" But Lt Mavromatis had his hand over his mouth trying not to laugh out loud.

"Aww, it was sad. There were bits of nest flying everywhere. Then, there was a blue flash and the power went out. Of course, some nosey neighbours phoned the police and two teenage cops appeared in a patrol car with their sirens blaring ... All for show, the police station is less than one-hundred metres away! They arrested me and put on handcuffs. Caesar was barking madly, and the priest looked as if he'd pass out!"

"What happened next?"

"When he'd calmed down, the priest offered to look after Caesar, but the telephone company and the electricity board had to be informed. There was only a little bit of damage to the pole ... but it took hours to reconnect the power."

"You're lucky not to be to going to court."

"Sergeant Dimo got me off. As I said, I was doing him a favour and he shouldn't have had a gun like that in the first place. Where is my girl?"

"She's out of your league mate, give it up."

"No, we had a moment; there may be more." Alexi insisted. Bartholomew shook his head in dismay.

"What about you, Lt Mavromatis?" he asked, "anything new?"

"Thank you for asking, I've taken up the tango! Once a week, free lessons if you buy a drink. I've found a charming teacher. In fact, I'm thinking of inviting her one Sunday. If you promise to behave yourself." He poked a finger at Alexi.

"You old fox! "Alexi clapped him on the back, "I'm impressed. Does Mrs. Tango have a name?"

"Valerie, if you must know, with the French pronunciation!"

The TV was on showing the sports news and results. The announcer, who for some reason had no front teeth and was wearing a stripped tee shirt, lisped that El Paso had just signed up a new player, a rising African star and there on the screen was Kalim, grinning broadly!

"He's made it," shouted Betty! "He's made the team!" then added, gesturing towards the TV, "I wish that man would get his teeth fixed."

"W-w-will he still come swimming on Sunday?" asked Tom.

"We'll have to wait and see. He'll have a lot of training to do now"

Alexi was again hovering about waiting for Julia's taxi to appear.

"By the way," she began cautiously, "Alexi, did Julia tell you that she has lost her house and that she has had to move out into a much smaller cheaper place which she hates!"

"No, she didn't tell me. I wonder why not?" He was taken aback at this.

"She must have had her reasons, best not to say anything, wait until she tells you then, okay? What is new with you then?" Betty asked Alexi, trying to distract him.

"Someone dropped off a tiny puppy at the shelter yesterday, I've called her Ruby. I was hoping Petroula might let Tom keep her, a pet would do him good."

"I should warn you she's not keen on dogs and she is very busy now."

Lt Mavromatis was studying his friend critically! "You look different. Have you had a shower?"

"No." He gave a wide smile which showed off sparkling white teeth!

"Wow, they are bright! Do they glow in the dark?"

"And," he put his feet up onto a chair, "I've got new trainers and I've cut my toenails."

"Spare me the gruesome details, mate."

"Ha, ha, I've bought a new skateboard and I can really ride it, better than you," he taunted.

"We'll see about that," The two men picked up their boards, jostled each other at the door, then rushed outside to the concrete park, yelling at each other.

Back in the café, Tom asked, "W-w-what's for lunch, Betty?"

"Stuffed vegetables, but first let me hear you read that story about Peter and that nasty Wolf!" They sat together to read the book. Julia's taxi drew up. She got out wearing jeans and a big jumper together with the usual accessories of beads and sunglasses, just in time to see Alexi and Lt Mavromatis crash into one another and fall down in a heap of laughter and swearing! Pavlos just shook his head in disbelief and drove off.

Back inside the café, they all sat round the stove. "You could both have hurt yourselves badly," she reprimanded them.

"Just a bit of fun, that's all, don't worry," said Alexi. The regulars all sat in companionable silence for a while. Then Julia said suddenly, "There's so much I want to do before, you know … George."

"We could make a bucket list," suggested Lt Mavromatis.

"What's that?" asked Dimitris, holding his hand to his ear. "Buckets? We've got three, one for the mop, one for the garden one for the …"

Julia cut in, "No, you make a list of what you'd like to do before you die."

Quick as a flash, Dimitris said, "Oh! That's easy. I want to live long enough to see Marina happily married and with a baby."

"Nice one," said Lt Mavromatis. "I'll go with something more cultural. I'd love to visit Russia; Moscow, St Petersburg, see the Winter Palace, travel on the Trans-Siberian train all the way to Vladivostok."

"I'd like to dress up in sequins and feathers and dance in a carnival in Barbados! What about you Alexi?"

He looked puzzled, "Never thought about it before. I'd like to find a good home for Ruby or take my special girl for a walk in the moonlight again."

"That sounds lovely." She peered at him, "You look different." Alexi gave her a pearly white smile. "Wow, your teeth are super!" and she kissed him then she gazed at the sea. "Pity it's a bit too cold today, I could do with a swim. I'm getting soft in my old age!"

"Let's take a walk then," suggested Lt Mavromatis. The four of them sauntered as far as the swings, where they stopped and got on. They swung up and down as the chains creaked back and forth. By now, the sun was going down and in the window of the café, a tiny light could be seen flickering, the lantern had been lit, just in case …

To be continued …

148

Season 2

New Opportunites

New Characters

Father Efthemias - Quick-witted local priest from St. Augustine's, in his mid-thirties.

Sophia - Also known as Foffie. Glamorous nurse to Dimitri. In her mid-twenties.

Amber and Joshua - Kalim and Nadeen's baby twins.

Thanisis Katssargyris – Online 'Catfish' in his late fifties. Top civil servant and pretend butcher.

Kosti - Flamboyant businessman from Santorini and 'frilly character'. An eternal thirty!

Manos - Shy TV cameraman and friend of Kosti. In his late twenties.

Valerie - Smart woman in her early sixties. An estate agent. Becomes the Tango partner of Lt. Mavomatis.

Antigoni – Pretty, nineteen-year-old daughter of George and girlfriend of Jacob.

Panos - In his mid-forties. Opportunistic petty criminal and Petroula's ex and father of Tom.

Andy - Young Scottish doctor and boyfriend of Marina. In his mid-twenties.

Cameron – Andy's younger brother in his early twenties. An archaeologist.

Stewart and Margaret MacAlister - From the Isle of Skye. Retired parents of Andy and Cameron.

Manolis - Elderly farmer.

Gypsy family - Three men, five women, four babies, three toddlers, three primary school-age children and seven teenagers.

Roberto Castillini, his wife, and son - Italian tourists.

Calypso - Alexis' horse. Rescued from near starvation.

Spinach - Tom's kitten.

Sunday 1

Busy-Bodies

Summer had blasted its way through Athens again, exhausting and draining its citizens of enthusiasm, confidence, and financial resources. By September, it was time for a change and for many this could not come too soon. Surprisingly, it had rained, just enough to clean the streets and cars and drench the trees, all thanks to some far-off invisible jet stream that had changed course. Sadly, the same deluge was more extreme in other parts of the country resulting in flooding and mudslides which tore through basements, street level shops and living quarters, leaving the occupants dazed at the enormity of the clean-up operation ahead of them.

On one such rainy Sunday, Julia was standing under a large umbrella waiting for a bus to take her to the coast. Behind her, stood the lovely church with its Moorish influenced design work and square and her beloved ground floor flat where she had lived for over thirty years. She stood with her back to all this deliberately in order to avoid the inevitable wave of sadness that comes with looking at something you desperately want but know is out of reach. She tried to focus on the passing traffic and then from a short distance away, two black-clad figures descended the church steps and began to cross the marble square with measured pace and click of block heels. Shrill accusative voices, the kind that can break glass, reached her. But Julia did not flinch, as she knew all too well that Lydia and Litsa had spotted her and were moving in for the kill. Their moth-ball smell was now intense, and Julia put her finger under her nose instinctively. They were now standing behind her, so she turned and smiled politely.

Litsa opened with, "Ah, Julia, so sorry to see you've lost your little flat. You must be so upset." They oozed hypocrisy.

"And after thirty years." Lydia rubbed salt into the wound. "What's life like down in Petralona then, more affordable, I suppose?"

Julia remained impassive, so Litsa continued, "You should see what they've done to the place, complete modernization, new windows ..."

"And the yard, you would hardly recognize it without that old tree!" gloated Lydia. Julia bit her lip involuntarily, as she hadn't been prepared for this one. She remembered a similar rainy day many years ago when her husband had planted the quince tree as a birthday present for her.

"Are you going swimming today or have you got a date with your friend from the animal shelter?" they giggled. As Julia didn't answer, Litsa continued, "Well, despite the hard times, you look very chic, I must say. We must keep up appearances, mustn't we?" She looked Julia up and down disdainfully. In fact, Julia was perfectly dressed in Wellington boots, which were in fashion again and a Burberry-style trench coat, both courtesy of a second-hand market. Her usual accessories of beads and large sunglasses pulled the outfit together.

Julia, in turn, took off her sunglasses and surveyed them and was just about to say something she might later regret, when the priest scurried by holding up his jacket collar. "Ladies," he said in acknowledgement and kept on going to avoid confrontation. Julia smiled at him, either a coward or experienced, he widened his eyes knowingly at her. Julia leant out into the road. Please let this goddamn bus come!

However, Lydia and Litsa were becoming bored with their game. "Let's go for coffee, shall we?" Lydia obligingly and imperiously, waved her arm at an approaching taxi.

The taxi drew up and the driver wound the window down and said to Julia, "Sorry I'm a little late, madam."

Without hesitation Julia got in and glanced at the astonished faces of the two black-hearted women. "Thank you for rescuing me, Pavlos. Those weasels were about to go for my jugular! If those women were to bite their tongues, they'd poison themselves!"

He grinned at her in the mirror and threw his cigarette end out of the window. "I could see that. Those lovely ladies were Litsa and Lydia, I presume?"

"Indeed."

"Why didn't you call me? I was just cruising about."

"I was waiting for a bus, Pavlos. I don't really have the money to pay you for these Sunday trips anymore."

"Don't worry, after all these years, I enjoy the drive out to the beach. If I stay in the house all Sunday, my wife starts nagging me to do housework. Who knows, maybe I'll swim this winter!" They drove through a once-vibrant commercial neighbourhood where sadly, whole blocks now stood empty and boarded up with 'For Rent' or 'For Sale' signs on them. The abandoned properties were already being dismembered by thieves and vandals who, like hyenas, had attacked, ripped out and carried off what they could. Julia gazed out of the window and commented on the obvious.

"Look, so many shops have closed down. Even the Chinese clothes shops are disappearing. The only places that seem to be doing well are fast food and coffee shops."

"Or those Euro shops," added Pavlos. "So many small businesses have gone bust."

"I did hear that if you work for a multinational company, your job will be secure, and the wages won't get cut."

"Lucky bastards!" Pavlos spat contemptuously out of the window and drew on his cigarette. "Try working for yourself. It's hardly worth it under the new tax system." They fell silent for the rest of the journey. As they cruised by the Aqua Palace, Julia noticed that it had been repainted and the rusted balcony rails replaced. Then, she saw a new sign with 'Sunny Smile Travel Services welcomes visitors from Yellow Rose Tourist Corp. Shanghai'. There was even a stone lion creature crouched at one side of the entrance. Little did she know that the Aqua Palace had now begun to refurbish one of its restaurants to create a suitable ambiance, complete with large red and gold lanterns, tassels and all, circular tables with revolving centres, menus in Mandarin and Cantonese and a plethora of kitsch, predominantly those sitting cats whose arms waved up and down. Below stairs, private enterprise was also blossoming. A certain insider on the kitchen staff, in cahoots with one of the receptionists, was making a decent living by organising company for unattached men using the City Escort Agency run by Bozzman from Mombassa, as well as selling certain pharmaceutical products which were said to prolong sexual performance.

The rain had begun to ease up and by the time they reached the beach, it had stopped. Within half an hour, it was warm again and everything bone-dry. As they drove slowly down the lane, Julia noticed that the swings had been painted yellow and along the verge that got burnt in last year's fire, a series of small fir trees had been planted.

On arriving in the car park, Pavlos ground to a sudden halt when he saw a horse tied to one of the trees outside the café. "What the …?"

"That's new!" said Julia. "I suspect I know who it belongs to though." He drove off with a gesture that signified that the situation was a little crazy. To one side of the café, Julia examined an old cart which was being restored to its former glory. The large wood-framed wheels had new metal surrounds, the shafts had been replaced with new wood and they had been varnished.

Inside the café, Julia found a few more changes: the walls had been painted in an off-white colour; the tables and chairs in pale complementary colours; and there were blinds at the windows in peppermint green. The old settee had been covered and several patchwork cushions placed there.

"What do you think?" said Betty emerging from the kitchen. They exchanged kisses on each cheek. "Kalo himona."

"Great! It looks very fresh. How are you keeping? You look …" she had, in fact, lost about twenty kilos and was wearing a stylish striped dress and sandals, "… wonderful!"

"Thank you," she said blushing. "It's about time I started looking after myself. I started doing a local Zumba class and found a diet that suited me. I have to be very careful when working in the kitchen. It's very easy to nibble all day!" The three regulars gave the thumbs up sign to show their approval. Alexi and Nikos looked up from the newspaper they were sharing, then Alexi jumped up with his arms open wide and Caesar bounded forward, tail wagging furiously.

"At last, my winter princess has returned!" Alexi for once, looked quite smart, suspiciously so.

"Lovely to see you boys, and kalo himona," she said, kissing them both. "How's the farm going, Nikos?"

"Okay, nothing too dramatic has happened. My tractor has broken down and I've decided not to keep geese this winter as they make far too much noise. I might give turkeys a try. There is always a local market for them."

"Good idea. Keep a small one for me." She eyed up Alexi. "I suppose the horse outside is yours?"

"Of course, isn't she a beauty? A year ago, she was skin and bones, remember the pony we rescued and put in with the donkey? That's her, she's called Calypso, clip-clop Calypso!" He was just about bursting with pride.

"Why is she here? Are you going to ride her?"

"Not exactly … She's in training."

"For a race?"

"No, to pull the cart I'm fixing up."

"For Nikos' farm?"

"No offence, but I can't tell you yet, its top secret!"

"Men!" Julia shook her head. "I'm off for a swim then, bye!"

Lt Mavromatis, dapper as ever, was pouring over his tablet, nervously clicking his worry beads around and around.

"What's the matter man? You've done nothing but fiddle with that all morning." Alexi demanded.

"If you must know, I'm studying the opposition."

"What?"

"Valerie and I have entered a tango competition and I'm checking out the other dancers. Most of them are extremely good and much younger."

"Well, if you will play such dangerous sports," chortled Alexi, imitating a tango movement.

"Don't mock me, man. Tango is an exact science, never mind an art form. You have to get it perfect, its passion and performance!"

"When will we get to meet your lady fair Twinkle-toes?"

"All in good time. What are you dressed up for anyway?"

"As I said to Julia, top secret!"

Meanwhile, at another table Dimitris had been sitting alone quietly, hardly reacting to the banter around him. Louli was snoozing on his knees. Betty came over with a drink for him, sat down and took his hands.

"Cheer up, Marina will be back soon. Her university placement has finished, she's done her dissertation and she's gone to Scotland with her boyfriend, Andy something. Come on, she'll be home soon." She spoke quite slowly so the elderly man could follow her.

Dimitris roused himself. "I know, I know ... It's just that I miss her so much. It's been such a long time since she left. Maybe, she'll find a job over there and never return?"

"Don't get sentimental now. Of course, she's coming home. She's gone to Scotland to see the sights for a few weeks. Come on, let's put on the TV." She helped him lift the drink and flicked the control to find something to distract him.

Outside, a small expensive car crunched to a halt. Nadeen got out and waved to the regulars who were, of course, looking out of the window to see who had arrived. She went to the back of the car and lifted a double buggy out of the boot. She then unstrapped her babies and put them into the buggy. Lt Mavromatis opened the café door wide for her. "Welcome and congratulations!" She pushed the babies into the café, and everyone gathered round. "What beautiful babies, how old are they now?"

"Nearly six months old, this is Joshua, and this is Amber."

"Double the fun!"

"Double the trouble!"

"How are you keeping?" asked Betty." It must have been a surprise to have twins."

"It was and I'm quite well, thank you. As you can see, I've learnt to drive, I have had to become much more independent, what with the babies and Kalim being away training most of the time. Also, we moved into a bigger apartment up in Kifissia. It's very nice but I don't know anyone in the area, and I get a bit lonely."

"At least you can get here for an outing on Sunday."

"Now the weather is a bit cooler I think I'll take the twins out for a walk to get some fresh air." Nadeen manoeuvred the buggy out and headed for the park.

"Is Kalim still playing for El Paso?" asked Alexi.

"Yes, and he scored a goal last week. I always follow what he's doing," replied Nikos.

"Well, good luck to him."

There was another arrival. A pristine Vespa pulled up smartly driven by Jacob. He too, had made some changes. Gone were the hippie ponytail and baggy clothes. He was now a hipster with slick hair style, patterned shirt, and bright coloured trousers. With him, was a tall, slim girl of about nineteen with long blonde hair that tumbled out of her motor bike helmet. She smiled shyly at everyone.

"How is your mum?" inquired Betty immediately.

"She's doing okay. Some days, she doesn't speak much. She misses dad so much."

"I know darling. It took me a long time to get over the death of my husband. You just take it one day at a time." She cuddled her. "We all miss your dad, Antigoni. George used to come here nearly every Sunday in wintertime for a few hours."

"I know," she turned her face away.

"That's enough, Mum," Jacob admonished her. "Come on Antigoni, what would you like to do, swim or take the dogs for a walk?"

"Walk the dogs."

As they left, Jacob turned to his mum. "For God's sake go easy, she gets upset too."

Betty, stung from being reprimanded, retreated into the kitchen.

The next arrival was the familiar sight of Bartholomew's car. Inside, was Tom, Petroula's young son. After singing in the Cathedral in the morning, Bartholomew collected him and together they would go to the beach for a few hours as Petroula had a lot of work to do keeping her bridal business running smoothly. Julia offered advice from time to time, but now the business was expanding beyond just dresses. Bartholomew undid Tom's seat belt and the boy ran into the café towards Nikos, who stroked him on the head, then to Dimitri who automatically lifted him onto his knees, pushing a startled Louli onto the floor.

"Ah! You're getting a big boy! Tell me about your week."

"We went to the s-s-shop and mummy put a new dress in the window. A lady came to t-t-try on a dress but her top bits," he pointed to his chest and giggled, "didn't f-f-fit inside! Mummy brought out m-m-more dresses. In the end, Joanna had to t-t-tie her into a glittery top, then she went a f-f-funny colour because she couldn't b-b-breathe!"

"Did the lady buy a dress?"

"No, she said she'd have to go on a c-c-crash diet but Kosti said that was dangerous and that she should get a b-b-bigger size. Then Kosti let me watch *Shrek* on his computer because they were talking about f-f-foreign people who come to San ...tor ...ini to get married and need wedding d-d-dresses."

"Who is this Kosti?" asked Nikos, suspiciously.

"I don't know. He's a funny man. He has orange skin and a big t-t-tattoo down his arm and a big earring, and he waves his arms ab-b-bout when he talks. The lady with the big, you-know, really liked him, she kept g-g-giggling when he said something about t-t-tweaking ... or was it t-t-twerking? He calls mummy, P-P-Petty."

"I'm sure I don't know," said Dimitris signalling to Nikos for some help.

"No need to worry about that one, Nikos," scoffed Alexi. "A real frilly character!"

"When does school start?" asked Nikos changing the subject.

"On M-M-Monday. I don't want to go!"

"Remember I'm going to school too, so in a way, we both start on Monday, okay?"

"Okay." He slid off Dimitris' knees and went to cuddle Caesar, who rolled over obligingly and thumped his tail against the floor.

"I'll be interested to meet this Kosti person," said Nikos.

"Well, here's your chance." Betty pointed to a new car that had pulled up. Petroula got out and waved. She was accompanied by the 'funny man'. Tom's description had been quite accurate, and the regulars examined the new arrival. He had a mop of carefully arranged, lacquered hair, a fake suntan which had gone a bit orange, rather tight trousers, and a printed shirt. It was all a bit too obvious. Lt Mavromatis just rolled his eyes and clicked his beads around. Bartholomew, sensing the tension, rescued the situation by offering to take Tom for a swim, while Dimitris leant forward to get a better look!

"Interesting indeed, I wonder what his story is?" he said.

Julia returned from her swim, looking refreshed and more relaxed. The hurt caused by the nasty comments of Litsa and Lydia had been washed away in the rhythm of swimming in sun speckled sea and she went to sit with Petroula and Kosti. Petroula was looking business-like in a grey suit and heels. Julia kissed her fondly and complimented her, "You look very corporate, my dear."

"Lovely to see you. Where's Tom?"

"Gone for a swim with Bartholomew," Nikos said abruptly, Petroula looked a bit surprised.

"Okay, this is Kosti everyone. He's in town this weekend to help set up some business between his shop on Santorini and mine."

Kosti waved his hands at the regulars, who nodded out of habit! Betty came forward to greet him, "Welcome, I'm Betty."

"Charmed madam, you have a delightful establishment here." He gazed at her and with a flourish, kissed her hand.

"Oh, thank you. Lunch will be ready at two o'clock." Betty flustered! For once, the regulars were lost for words. They looked at him as if he was from another planet! Nikos took advantage of the silence and asked bluntly, "Will you be staying here long?"

"Ah! Darling, as long as it takes! It could be an eternity! There's so much to do; what with the dress alterations, the Japanese and Korean ladies needing such small sizes, the men's suits and black ties to be ordered and not to mention the black patent shoes, which are a must, this season. Then, there are the candles, the flowers, the bonbons, the rice, the carpeting and finally, we need a cameraman for the sunset photo shots. It never ends! He gesticulated wildly for emphasis. The regulars were mesmerized like rabbits before a weasel!

"Thank God for political weddings ... quick and quiet!" said Alexi, under his breath.

"I heard that!" said Julia. "Have some imagination. These people travel halfway around the world to get married in one of the most beautiful places on earth, and they pay for perfection."

"It must cost them a fortune; I'm glad someone's got money to burn," said Nikos, uncharacteristically sarcastic. Petroula looked hurt now. Oblivious, Kosti continued.

"Oh darling, if only you knew what they are prepared to pay; the business opportunities are endless."

"Indeed."

"What's wrong Nikos? Don't you want me to try something new and maybe do well?" Petroula was now annoyed at his rudeness.

He reddened, painfully aware that he was out of his depth. "Whatever. I'm going home. I've got a tractor to fix." He muttered and with that, he stalked out.

"Was that your country-cousin Petty?"

"Yes, that was Nikos. He's not usually like that. I don't know what's got into him."

"You'd have to be blind not to see why, my dear," Betty said quietly.

"Are you going for a swim today?" Julia inquired politely.

"Me? Swim! Darling, in the sea? I think not." He was horrified at the idea. "I'm strictly a hot tub and Jacuzzi man, I need warmth and bubbles." The idea of this left the regulars completely dumbfounded.

Nadeen returned with the twins who were now sleeping. She sat down next to Petroula and Kosti and confidently introduced herself. Kosti, of course, recognized her!

"Aren't you Kalim's wife? The footballer?" She nodded. Kosti put his hand to his mouth when he saw the beautiful babies, "They're so perfect," he exclaimed, instinctively touching their cheeks and little hands. "Oh! You lucky lady! And what a gorgeous man your husband is, and so talented. He's really pulled that team up."

Rather surprised at being so recognizable to a stranger, she mumbled, "Thank you." So, this is what fame is like, she thought, a mixture of loneliness and being public property. Before Kosti could continue, she rose and said, "I think I'll take the twins home before they need feeding again. Bye everyone." As she reached the end of the lane, she noticed a red sports car parked a little way down the road. For a moment, she wondered if the paparazzi were following her. Instinctively, she put on her sunglasses and drove carefully past.

Back in the café, Kosti was certainly acting like a cuckoo! A big, pushy, fluffy, flamboyant bird in a new nest. Jacob and Antigoni engaged him in conversation while Petroula went to collect Tom from the beach, much to the relief of Bartholomew, who was getting tired.

"Where's Poppy and Kitso?" inquired Bartholomew on his return.

"No idea. School term starts soon, so she should be here today," said Betty. "Nikos told me that Kitso had started to play his clarinet in a band on Saturday night in an old-fashioned place in Gallipoli. So maybe they are too tired to come swimming on Sunday now, what a pity, I'll miss seeing them."

The TV was on, the same monotonous drone about closures and cutbacks and those in the red with their bank loans and about those who would be forced to sell off their second or third or more, houses. Lt Mavromatis was watching with interest, slowly clicking the beads around and around. "Planning your next property acquisition, man? Alexi teased.

"More like saving up to pay the rent!" Lt Mavromatis replied. "I never did buy a place and judging by how much tax you have to pay, I'm glad I didn't."

"It seems ridiculous to charge some old granny, living in the middle of nowhere a fortune for some half-broken-down old farm buildings that no one wants to rent or live in. It's not fair."

"Did you know that Valerie works as an estate agent? If you thought that there would be no business, well you'd be wrong. Apparently, the number of foreigners, especially the Chinese, buying up Greek properties, is amazing. Then, there are many Greek buyers investing in property abroad as a way of protecting their wealth, I suppose. Take Petroula and Kosti over there, trying to do business and looking for new ways to make it work, and then, there are traditional businesses, which you would think of as secure, that are now floundering."

"It's all a question of supply and demand and creating that demand in the first place," chimed up Kosti. "It's basic first year economics. Take our dear Turkish and Bulgarian people-smugglers. They provide a service and sell life jackets and rubber boats. I hear they can make up to five million Euros a month."

"That's not what I call work," he said, glaring at Kosti, "More like exploitation! They've got blood on their hands. I don't know how they can sleep at night."

"You don't have to like it, it's just business. Sadly, when people drown, the business gets a bad name." Alexi had had enough. "I'm off to feed Calypso." He stamped out followed by Caesar. Julia watched him go. He put a feeding bag over the horse's neck and stroked her, all the time talking quietly. Then, he untied her and led her around to the cart, then backed her into the shafts and secured her in position. She was now ready to pull the cart. When the cart was balanced, he clicked his tongue and pulled the horse around and slowly they began to walk down the lane. In the park area near to the swings, they stopped, and he turned her around and returned. "That's enough for one day, girl," he said patting her neck.

"What on earth is he up to?" she wondered. She was even more curious when Kosti, who also had been watching, tore a picture from a magazine he was reading and went outside to show it to Alexi. She watched as they examined it together and Kosti waved his arms about over the horse and cart like a magician! Slowly, Alexi smiled and then slapped Kosti on the back in a friendly manner, which nearly knocked him over! He then folded up the paper and put it in his top pocket, then they shook hands. When Alexi wasn't looking Kosti quickly found a paper hankie to clean his hand with. "Only God knows what those two can possibly be up to," Julia said to Betty, who just shook her head in disbelief.

By late afternoon, the sky was looking overcast again, but the air was sweet and clean. The lunches had been served and eaten. Betty had washed up and sat down with Dimitris to watch TV for a while. When most of the winter swimmers had left, Alexi led his horse down the lane accompanied by Lt Mavromatis. For now, they seemed to have forgotten their skate-boarding craze, which was probably a good thing, as it was only a matter of time before one or both got hurt. At the end of the lane, Lt Mavromatis stopped to light the oil light in the little shrine for Betty, the light shone on the photo of Yannis standing proudly next to his canoe and the tiny pink shoe belonging to the drowned refugee toddler, both items serving as a reminder of the cruel indifference of the sea and to those who sought to make a profit from those who needed a safe passage. Inside the café, Betty lit the lantern and put it on the windowsill, then she helped Dimitris into his jacket, and with a last look around she prepared to leave.

Sunday 2

A Matter of Seconds

It was one of the last days of real summer. A beautiful hot day but not so hot as to start fires. There was a gentle wind running through the reeds and trees, the sand shimmered, and the sea sparkled. It was perfect for swimming. Already, there were a few groups of picnickers on the beach whose children ran in and out of the sea endlessly. Nikos and Jacob were already swimming quite far out, and Betty kept checking up on them nervously, using the binoculars which were kept next to the lantern on the windowsill. Antigoni was sitting quietly in a corner, her long hair pushed back by a band and surrounded with paints. She was engrossed in an icon which she was copying from a book. Lt Mavromatis and Dimitris watched her progress with interest.

Outside, Alexi was manoeuvring Calypso up and down, pulling on the shafts of the cart. The horse happily snuffled in her feeding bag and didn't seem to mind the weight of the cart which trundled behind her. Caesar obediently padded along behind. Alexi watched Julia's taxi approaching slowly. She got out and Pavlos reversed back down the lane so as not to spook the horse that had now stopped abruptly and was stamping her forelegs in distress. Alexi whispered to her and patted her neck as Julia approached. "She's not so good with cars yet, is she?" Julia commented, "Does she need to be?"

"Don't be tricky, lady," he laughed and tapped the side of his nose. "I'm not telling you."

"Well, there are only so many jobs a horse and cart can do these days."

"Oh, you would be surprised!" They walked on either side of the horse with Caesar behind, tail wagging. Today, Julia was wearing a well-cut summer dress with matching material around a large hat and heels. They escorted Calypso back to her tree and unhitched the cart to let the little horse have a rest.

"That's enough for now. I don't want to over-tire her in this heat," Alexi said, as he filled up a large plastic basin with water for her. He pinched Julia's cheek and smiled wickedly. "You look lovely. Are we going to the races later?"

"I thought you'd never notice," she replied and playfully flicked some water at him.

A moment later, Poppy and Kitso arrived on his bike. She shook out her hair as she squeezed out of her crash helmet." I really dislike these things. They are so hot!" she complained.

"Nothing to do with ruining your hair style then?" he teased. Betty greeted everyone. She seemed to be very chirpy and Poppy complimented her on her weight loss.

"You look great. I wish I could lose a bit."

"You're fine as you are," Kitso said, quickly.

"We expected to see you last week," said Betty who was now cleaning the tabletops in preparation for lunch.

"I was playing my clarinet in that club in Gallipoli on Saturday night and I was really tired out the next day," explained Kitso.

"It wasn't just that. I wasn't feeling very sociable," added Poppy.

"Why is that?" Betty leant on a table and looked at Poppy, a little alarmed.

"It's unbelievable. My school has closed down, just like that, with no warning. If they had told us before summer, then we could have looked for jobs but now, it's too late. There's not much left. I went for one interview last week and was offered a pittance. I'd be better off cleaning, no offence, but you'd think experience and qualifications would count for something?" the regulars all nodded sadly.

"Aren't there any schools near you?" asked Lt Mavromatis, habitually clicking his beads around.

"Not many now. A lot have closed down and those that are open already have staff."

"Have you got any private lessons?" inquired Julia.

"A few, but I hardly live in an area where parents can afford private education. I feel like I'm passed my sell-by date!" Julia bristled indignantly.

"That's harsh, my dear. No woman is ever passed her sell-by date. It sounds like something a male marketing manager would say on a vicious tweet to an unfortunate middle-aged co-worker. You must adapt and move on somehow; maybe, try something completely new."

"Remember," added Betty trying to sound positive, "As one door closes, another one opens."

Poppy looked at her sceptically. "Really, we'll see. First, I've got to get used to the idea of being unemployed. I feel so lazy and I resent it when I hear the other teachers bitching about how busy they are!"

Kitso came to the rescue, "Come on, it's a beautiful day. Let's go for a swim!" So, Julia and Poppy accompanied him.

"That's rotten luck," said Antigoni when they had left the café. The regulars indicated agreement. There was nothing much more to be said when you lived in the throes of an economic depression, where closures and unemployment were an everyday occurrence.

Bartholomew's car approached, and this time, only Petroula and Tom were inside. There was no sign of Kosti. Tom ran straight inside the café and climbed onto Dimitris' knee, knocking off Louli who landed on the floor with a thud, then just stretched and sauntered off to find another warm refuge.

"Steady on child!" said Dimitris, gathering his senses.

"L-l-look, look!" demanded Tom, clutching his school backpack.

"Yes child. What is it?"

Tom proudly pulled out a blue textbook and showed him his homework. nine out of ten for spelling. "I got one wrong."

"Never mind. Well done, my boy," said Dimitris, stroking his head.

"Bravo!" added Lt Mavromatis. Tom caught sight of Antigoni painting carefully.

"W-w-what are you d-d-doing?"

"I'm painting an icon. Come and look." Tom approached cautiously and looked at it seriously.

"W-w-why does he look so cross and s-s-strict? He's like the men on the c-c-church walls. Why don't they s-s-smile?"

"I don't know. Maybe, he was thinking about all the troubles in the world ..."

"Oh."

Petroula caught up with them. "Sorry, I hope he didn't annoy you," she apologised,

"Come on Tom, let's go for a swim."

"It doesn't matter; I've got some spare paper. Would you like to come and paint with me after your swim?" Tom's eyes lit up.

"M-m-mummy, please?"

"Okay." She smiled at Antigoni. "Thanks a lot. The kids never get taught drawing or painting at his school and I know it's good for their development. I've got no talent, so when we paint at home, everything looks like a Kandinsky!"

Bartholomew, Tom and Petroula arrived at the beach just as Jacob and Nikos were finishing their swim. They'd been out with spear guns and had caught several palaminda. Both men look fit and tanned. Nikos just nodded, said good morning, and walked by, picked up his towel and left.

"What's wrong with him?" she asked Jacob.

"I don't know. Ask him. Maybe, he didn't like your new friend."

"He's not a friend exactly. We work together. He can be a bit ... you know ... over the top, but he's good at what he does, and he's helped me a lot with the business."

"Don't worry, he'll come around," and with that, Jacob also picked up his towel and left. Petroula and Tom remained in the shallows where she tried to coax Tom along, but he could only manage a few strokes, so she gave up and went to lie on the beach whilst Tom played with Jacob's dogs nearby. She applied some oil briskly and lay back again to let the sun work some magic on her rather pale skin. When a shadow blocked out her sunlight, she presumed that some clouds had passed over but when she opened her eyes, she saw Nikos standing there.

"Hi, would you like to hire a tuxedo?"

"Very funny, what would I do with one of those? Muck out the chickens or plant some cabbages?"

She ignored his sarcasm. "You'd look very suave, I'm sure."

"Really?"

"What is the matter? I hope you're not jealous of Kosti? He's only helping me at work: he is full of new ideas."

"Well, I hope he hasn't any ideas about you!"

"Don't be silly. He's so camp and I know for a fact he's interested in a cameraman who works for TV channel 4!"

Nikos started to go red. "Oh! I didn't realize. It's just I wanted to tell you ... but ... things got in the way ... and I was hoping that one day you and I and Tom ... but now you've got the new business .... and ..." He gave up and sat down beside her on the sand with his head in his hands. "I made a mess of that, didn't I?"

She leant up on an elbow and looked at his eyes and laughed. "Yes, you did a bit, but you could ask me again ... soon!"

"I think I'll take Tom and the dogs for a little walk before I make a bigger fool of myself."

"Men!" she said and lay back on the hot sand to soak up the sunshine.

Back in the café, the TV was on as usual, providing an endless background drone of party politics and election forecasts, to which Bartholomew was listening intently. One new candidate looked familiar. "I thought he was an actor," said Lt Mavromatis, glancing up from his game of cards with the other regulars.

"He was," replied Bartholomew." If he can do it, so can I. Maybe, I'll give politics a try ... at a local level of course..."

"It's a dirty business, mate! Half of them would sell their grandmothers or cut your throat to get the better of you. Are you sure about this? Alexi inquired.

"Maybe, I could make a difference. I'm an honest man!"

"Ha!" scoffed Lt Mavromatis. "As I remember, not long ago, you kept your wife in the dark regarding your unemployment for some months, I'd say you've plenty of experience at being devious. You might do well."

"Thanks for the vote of confidence!"

"Be realistic," said Betty picking Louli off a table, where she has been basking in the sunshine. "Getting elected costs money and you need connections and promotion and God knows what else."

"Okay, I'm not running for president! I just thought I'd try to get on the local council to get the streets and parks cleaned up a bit ..."

"Good luck with that one man," warned Alexi shaking his head.

The cafe door opened and a lady in a pale blue summer suit and strappy sandals, carrying a large bag full of swimming gear stood there looking around. Lt Mavromatis glanced up from his cards, for a moment he was stunned! Then he remembered himself. "Hello, welcome, my dear! Come in, make way, men." He took her by the hand and swept her into the room. "This is my tango partner, Valerie," he announced, and she did a twirl.

"Good afternoon," she said politely and then turned to Betty. "Could I have one of your famous ice cream sundaes, please. I've been told they're excellent."

"At last, someone with taste!" I won't be a moment," and she retreated into the kitchen.

"Welcome," said Dimitris, half rising, "to the Winter Swimmers' Club."

"So, this is where it all happens. What a lovely place. I never knew it existed." She turned to Alexi. "Is that your horse outside?"

"Yes, why?"

"I used to ride my father's horse in the village when I was young. I adored her, you're so lucky to have one."

Alexi was now bursting with pride and smiled broadly when Julia returned from her swim. She was now wearing a bright-coloured kaftan and her wet hair was pushed up under a straw hat. "Hello, you must be Valerie. I'm Julia."

"So, you're the face behind the fashion blog! It's a small world."

"What do you do?"

"I'm an estate agent actually ..." Before Julia could interrogate her any further, Betty bustled in carrying the sundae, which really was a work of art. A large glass filled with different layers of ice cream and jelly, topped with cream and chocolate bits. "Thank you. This is glorious!" Then, she picked up a long-handled spoon and settled down to enjoy it.

"By the way," said Betty," I forgot to tell you that Matthew and Antonis are back in town. Jacob got a text the other day, so they should probably arrive soon." She turned to Valerie, "They were winter swimmers from last year who decided that Amsterdam was a better place to live than Athens."

"It's a lovely place but I wouldn't be happy living there permanently ... When I was young, I went on holiday to Turkey and fell in love with Konstantinopolis, Kadikoy to be exact. It used to be the old Greek area of Chalkidonia. I dreamt of doing up one of those old abandoned houses and spending my old age watching the ferries going up and down the Bosporus and feeding the seagulls. Ahh … now there are so many people there … I've heard that Izmir, old Smyrna, is the place to be. It's cheaper, more liberal and it's still got a mixture of cultures. I'd love to go back one day …" She fell silent.

"Who knows, one day, we might make a trip?" said Lt Mavromatis. Valerie just smiled, still caught up in her fantasy. The others arrived and were introduced to Valerie who was still in the middle of her sundae. Tom's eyes lit up when he saw it. "Mummy, c-c-can I have one of those?"

"After lunch, perhaps," replied Petroula.

Betty was now distracted by the computer that Marina had left behind. She read a message, then all smiles, sat down to reply to it, all thoughts of cooking forgotten … but her smile faded when she smelt burning from the kitchen. "Oh my God! That will teach me!" and she ran into the kitchen to rescue the food.

"What is she up to?" said Jacob quietly, opening the computer.

"You can't snoop like that, it's wrong," said Antigoni. As he had an audience watching him, he muttered, "Okay" and closed it, making a mental note to check it out later.

The familiar noise of a large bike roaring up announced the arrival of Matthew and Antonis. Within minutes, they were in the café, surrounded by everyone asking questions, and Caesar bounding about barking with excitement. Matthew looked about the same, although he now had blond highlights in his hair. He was still good looking and charming as ever. Antonis also had a new hair style, shaved at the sides and long on top but he looked a bit fatter and more chilled out. Betty embraced them both. "Sit down boys, lunch is on the house. Come on then, tell us all about it. "Everyone settled down to listen.

Matthew began, "Well, as you know, I got a job as a security man for a diplomat. I work twelve hours on and off with another guard. I have to go everywhere with him, even wait outside the bathroom if we are out of the house!"

"Is he so famous?"

"No, not really, but an extreme Islamist group are after his blood because he made some comments a few years ago. The pay is good, and I've been to some incredible places, posh hotels, conferences and restaurants … but I'm on duty, so I can hardly enjoy it."

"Do you h-h-have a bullet-proof v-v-vest?" asked Tom.

"How do you know about them?" Petroula said sharply.

"Saw it on Ninja Turtles," Tom replied. She shook her head in disbelief.

"Yes Tom, I do have one but most of the time, I'm the man in the background with dark glasses on and a communication device, scanning the crowd for anyone or something unusual. When he or his family go anywhere, the area has to be searched in case a bomb has been left."

"Makes life as a MAT seem safe to me," said Alexi.

"All security jobs are mostly routine. The chances are nothing will happen, but you just can't become complacent."

"What about you, Antonis?" asked Betty.

"I've been working in a shop, one that sells … a variety of cigarettes," he said diplomatically.

"Any free samples?" asked Jacob. Betty glared at him and Antonis just laughed.

"Not today! Do you know how many times I've heard that one! It may sound strange but once legalized, it didn't mean that everyone was stoned all day. In fact, many of the customers are older men, some of whom are poorly and use it to take the edge of their pain or help them relax. Our stuff is all natural. It's these new packs of legal highs with crazy names that worry me. They target a young market and they are full of chemicals, so many kids have ended up in hospital out of their heads because of them. Dope is safer than those or alcohol, in my opinion."

"Do you enjoy life there?" asked Julia.

"On the whole, yes. It's been great. Of course, everything is new and interesting. We have work and the pay is reasonable and things seem to run smoothly. I don't feel as stressed as I did. I had forgotten how frustrating life here can be. I went to get an EU medical card only to be told to come back next week as there was no staff available. It seems like things have got worse since we've been away."

Antonis went on, "The food is okay, and the choice of beers is amazing, and you can bike around the city safely. Also, we've met some interesting people and some of our friends live on a floating house!"

"Really, it floats? Like a houseboat?" asked Lt Mavromatis.

"Yes, they float but you're not aware of movement and they are linked to water and electricity. The idea is that you can be towed to another place if you want to."

"Building on the waterways is the latest ecological idea to save the land for farming."

"Then, there is the Arty scene and the night life; there is always something going on."

"Where do you want to live then?" asked Alexi bluntly. There was silence and they looked at each other pensively.

"We don't know yet. This is home. We speak the language, know the humour ... like the food! Give me tomatoes from my uncle's garden any day some of the fruit and veg up north seems tasteless."

"The mentality is different too … sticklers for punctuality … rather inflexible … a mind-set that things must be done in a certain way, on time, in time, yes. It is efficient, but I find it stifling."

"Here you are boys, red stew and rice." Betty announced, putting a generous plateful down for each of them.

"Looks great, thanks," said Matthew and they tucked in. "Another thing," he said, fork halfway to his mouth, "I can never get used to an inside culture: so many houses and no people on the streets in the evening."

"Then, there is the weather." Everyone laughed. "But more rain means endless greenery, gardens, trees, flowers all year round and wonderful dairy products."

"It's a big decision," said Nikos, simply. They nodded in agreement and looked around.

"Jacob keeps us up to date with what is going on, but we miss being here and our family and friends. We heard some Greeks saying that Greece was only nice for holidays now but that makes you a tourist in your own country doesn't it?" Antonis pointed out.

"Then, others call us traitors for sneaking off to find a better way of life whilst they struggle on and suffer, so to speak. There is no happy medium, is there?"

"As they say, it's every man for himself. You must do what is best for you and don't listen to ignorance and bigotry," said Nikos wisely. Petroula looked impressed. "Anyway, shall we swim later?"

"Probably but we'll need a snooze under an umbrella for a while after all this food. Thanks Betty, you're the best and by the way, you look like a doll!" She blushed and pushed them out towards the beach and café life resumed its leisurely Sunday afternoon pace; coffees were served, and naps were taken behind newspapers. Tom and Nikos shared one of Betty's special ice-cream sundaes, the regulars' started a game of tavli, Antigoni continued with her painting, Jacob went out to attend to the Vespa and Bartholomew decided to sleep on the bench under the platanos tree which had concealed George a year ago. Eventually, Matthew and Antonis swam with Nikos, then returned to the café to say goodbye as they had people to go and see.

"Hope to see you next Sunday," Betty called after them. They put on their leather jackets and crash helmets. Matthew revved up and waved as they cruised down the lane. At the end, he paused and checked for traffic, pulled out and accelerated down the empty road. Suddenly, as if from nowhere, an old tractor emerged from a gateway to a field, driven by an elderly farmer. Matthew swerved to avoid it but clipped a pothole, lost control, and rammed into a telegraph pole.

It all took a matter of seconds. There was a moment's silence that seemed like an hour. Antonis was thrown off the back and he rolled to the side of the road. The farmer stopped his tractor and limped across the road. Antonis gasped for breath as the fall had winded him but he crawled across to Matthew who was lying very still. One leg was twisted, and a broken bone was protruding through his jeans, bleeding profusely. The farmer crossed himself three times, then took off his leather belt and wrapped it around Matthew's leg to stop the bleeding. Antonis searched for a cell phone but found it has been smashed. He pointed at the phone and yelled at the farmer, "Have you got one?" The old man shook his head. "Go to the café on the beach and tell Betty to get an ambulance!" The farmer drove off to the beach leaving Antonis alone. Instinctively, he reached for the cross around his neck, squeezed it and whispered to himself, "Dear God, come on man ..." He gently removed Matthew's helmet and saw that there was swelling on the side of his head and that he was still unconscious. He stripped off his tee-shirt and used it to press down to stop the blood flow. "Don't leave me so soon," he pleaded.

After what seemed like an eternity, he heard the tractor, then bikes and a car approaching; the others stood around feeling helpless but offering advice.

"Don't move him!" instructed Lt Mavromatis. "He may have internal injuries." Meanwhile, Kitso and Nikos directed the passing traffic around the accident scene.

Betty had brought some clean towels to wrap around the leg wound. "A little blood goes a long way," she muttered, trying to sound convincing. The farmer leant against his tractor trying to smoke a cigarette with shaking hands.

At last, the siren of an approaching ambulance offered hope and within ten minutes, the ambulance had administered first aid to Matthew and whisked him and Antonis off to hospital. Kitso had been given the bike keys so he drove it back to the café for safe keeping. Suddenly, it was all over. The police arrived to question the farmer who was now visibly shaking and pale with shock, after examining the skid marks and the pothole they told the farmer to go home. "It was an accident," he mumbled, "an accident."

In all the panic, no one had noticed that a red sports car which had been parked off the road was now moving away slowly, nor the person driving it, who had made no attempt to help in any way.

By now, all the regulars were back in the café standing around in stunned silence. The beauty of the evening passed by unnoticed, even the spectacular sunset. The sky went from pink to pale blue and the first stars began to twinkle. "I'll phone the hospital later tonight," said Betty, as everyone was preparing to leave, "and let you know how he is doing."

"Mummy, will Matthew d-d-die?" asked Tom bluntly, speaking for all.

"I hope not darling. He's a strong man and the doctors will do their best, I'm sure. Let's go home now, shall we?" Left alone, Betty, Jacob and Antigoni stood close together by the window, watching the night fall over the sea, each lost in their own thoughts. Betty automatically lit the lantern, a little flicker of hope in the darkness when events in life seemed inexplicable.

Sunday 3

Avoiding Catfish

The season was turning and high in the sky, above the city, black clouds of starlings dived and whirled like shoals of fish on their ancient migration route, followed by skeins of geese whose plaintive cries could barely be heard against the din of the traffic. Whilst along the back streets of the inner city, where older cafenions and coffee shops still used small square tables and wooden chairs with raffia bases, groups of swarthy gypsies stopped to ask if there were any chairs to be mended.

They usually stayed for a few days. The weavers, sitting outside the shop surrounded by sheaves of raffia, were accompanied by their wives carrying babies on their hips and numerous children who played about, oblivious to city life. The women wore traditional head scarves, and long, full skirts with pantaloons underneath in various shades of red and scarlet, usually bedecked with spangles which glinted and glittered in the sunshine. They spent their time cutting the raffia and laughing uproariously at private jokes or alternatively, scolding one of the children. Their men folk seemed quiet and dowdy by comparison. They were a people who distained the constraints of modern society and deliberately remained on the margins so they could live life in their own way, at their own pace, with the minimum of official interference. Then, when the work was over and they were fed and paid, they would move on and disappear for another year. Where they went or how they lived was largely unknown, a people who refused to be curtailed by convention or borders and communicated in a language which few outsiders knew.

Their sense of freedom was enviable. These anarchic nomads seemed content to go their own way, disdainful of what modern life could offer.

Recently, the weather had been perfect. Warm days and cool nights, allowed people to sleep properly without roaming around at all hours, searching for somewhere to sleep which often meant a tiled floor or next to an open balcony door, where the mosquitoes would get you. However, none of this was of concern to those assembled in the café that Sunday; no one even noticed the sea sparkling invitingly.

Betty announced, "Jacob has heard from Antonis. Matthew was unconscious for three hours and has had surgery on his leg. The bones in his lower leg are broken through and they're now held together with a plate and pins."

"Thank God he didn't lose his leg!" said Lt Mavromatis crossing himself.

"Amen," added Alexi.

Betty continued, "His head is another story though. He had a scan and it showed some swelling. He's got concussion and his speech is slurred and his vision blurred."

"That's not so good," said Lt Mavromatis. Nikos, Petroula, Tom and Bartholomew were all listening attentively.

"We visited the hospital yesterday," said Nikos. "He knew who we were, but he was very tired."

"We all gave blood," added Petroula. "It's the least we could do."

"I gave him my p-p-panda to keep him company," chimed in Tom, "but it made him c-c-cry. Mummy, didn't he like P-p-panda?"

"Yes, dear. He liked Panda very much. Remember he's had a bad accident and he is tired out."

"He still looked pale despite all the blood he's been given," said Bartholomew.

"Was Antonis there?"

"Yes, along with his mother and sister. It's been a close thing. The old farmer turned up as well, but he got terribly upset when he saw Matthew, so the nurses gave him something to calm him down." They all fell silent. "I know it sounds terrible, but I want to blame the old man, even though I know it was an accident."

"Actually, the old farmer is called Manolis and he's a neighbour of mine," Nikos interrupted. "He must be in his eighties now. He is a good man. I used to play on his land when I was young. Then, I would follow him around watching how he did things. He never told me to leave. He has two sons, but they are working abroad, so he is trying to keep the farm going on his own. I doubt he can afford to pay a farmhand. I suspect he's blaming himself. I think I'll call around later to see if he is alright. He was pretty shaken up by the accident too."

"That's a good idea. I'll come with you if you like," said Petroula.

"Okay," Nikos said, although he seemed distracted. Alexi went to attend to Calypso who had been waiting outside patiently and Nikos took Caesar and Tom to the beach. They walked along with Tom holding on to one of his hands whilst Caesar snuffled about in the shoreline behind them. He let Tom talk without interrupting. Occasionally, they stopped, and Nikos pointed something out like a shell or a worm cast. From the window, Petroula was watching them, and for the first time, she realized that she felt secure and happy. Time to make the next move girl, she thought to herself smiling.

Outside the café, Kalim and Nadeen had arrived and were trying to put two recalcitrant babies into the buggy. They also had with them a large bunch of flowers. On entering the café, Nadeen immediately asked if Matthew had made it.

"Yes, he's going to make a recovery and they saved his leg, "Betty told them.

"Thank God!" said Kalim. "Here you are. Would you give these to him?"

"Of course. I'll just put these into some water to keep fresh."

Jacob, sitting with Antigoni who was still working on the icon, looked up." Hi Kalim, how's life? I watched the match on TV. Pity about that missed goal."

"Ha, I could have easily got it if … let's put it this way … We sometimes get told how to play before the match … do you understand me?"

"You mean match fixing?"

"Quietly man, you can call it what you like. But I'm not saying that. There is a lot of investment as they say, in certain matches. So, you do as you're told if you want to be chosen for the team."

"What about the others?"

"It's something we don't talk about. The guys are fine, a mixed bunch. We train, we play, we go home. It's just a job," he said, sounding disillusioned.

"Come on! The pay's okay!"

"I never thought I'd say this but … money isn't everything man! Hang on, the kids are getting cranky." His attention was drawn to the babies who were complaining about being inside and Nadeen started to push them out. "We've brought a big rug so the kids can play on the sand." Dimitris looked up. "Kalim, would you help me down to the sea for a short swim. It will probably be my last one this year."

"No problem. Hey Jacob, will you help me here?" Together, they escorted him slowly down to sea. It was obvious that he was not as strong as he was last winter and needed some support but once in the sea, he swam easily.

"Thank you. This is marvellous, I feel ten years younger!" He laughed joyfully, as the sea sparkled around him and for a while, he was young again and swimming out to the island with Martha beside him. It's strange, he thought, my memories are scattered across the years, like falling snow, yet they are all interwoven in some way, I just can't seem to connect them now. He let the water carry him gently and he started to hum a half remembered song, "How did it go? "Don't go down to the sea, because it is rough and will carry you away. Don't write me letters because I can't read them and it makes me cry." For a moment, he could hear his wife singing with him, then it faded. Why can I remember the sound of my father's whistle when he came home or the embroidered pattern on my mother's apron but I can't remember what I had for dinner yesterday or the name of the man who just helped me into the sea? Oh yes, he's a footballer called 'K' something … No, it's gone. So, Dimitris just swam on peacefully and let his mind drift with the sea.

Kalim sat down with Nadeen on the rug and watched the twins playing with some plastic beach toys. Then, their attention was drawn to some noise and activity at the far end of the beach where three, dusty and battered, open pick-up trucks had pulled up. They were full of an assortment of gypsies. The women wore red-sequined skirts and held onto their babies whilst several children sat among long bundles of raffia. Within minutes, the young boys had run down to the sea, leaving behind them a trail of discarded clothes and trainers. Shouting and showing off, they dived in, and started to play boisterously in the sea. The girls followed more cautiously and paddled, holding up their skirts whilst the adults sat in the shade of the trucks smoking, eating, and talking amongst themselves.

Back in the café, Betty noticed their arrival. "Oh! They're back again. Same time, each year. Here today, gone tomorrow. I'll see if there is anything that needs mending." Sitting alone at a table, Lt Mavromatis was studying a video playing on his tablet in preparation for the upcoming tango competition.

"These couples are good," he said to himself, unaware that Valerie had quietly arrived and was looking over his shoulder.

"Boo! We can do it you know!"

"Hello, I'm getting nervous … at my age … It's a big deal!"

"Rubbish, you're being grumpy now!" She pulled him to his feet, held up an arm and did a twirl. Antigoni was painting quietly, Nikos had taken Tom for a swim and Petroula and Bartholomew were watching TV. "Come on, the cafe is almost empty. Let's put on our music and practice our routine."

"Here?"

"I'll push some of the tables and chairs out of the way," says Bartholomew. "I'm sure Betty won't mind."

"Mind what, exactly?" she said appearing from the kitchen.

"If we do a little dance practice ..."

"Wonderful, come on, let's make some space." Lt Mavromatis and Valerie stood up and waited for the music to start and then, they danced concentrating on each other's movements, Valerie following his lead, strutting, and stamping and moving her feet in a series of complicated steps. When the music ended, everyone applauded.

"That was incredible!" said Antigoni.

"But not perfect. We were rather stiff," said Valerie critically. "The judges are ruthless."

Julia arrived, wearing jeans and a smart checked shirt, Pavlos could be seen driving off in the distance, swerving around the three trucks which were parked halfway across the road. "Have I missed a preview? Would you mind doing it again. I'd love to see you dance." The music started again and this time, they give a star performance, responding to each other's steps with passion. Outside the café window, a group of gypsies clapped politely. One man who was mending a table shouted, "Bravo!"

"That was a bit better," said Lt Mavromatis as he caught his breath and began to replace the tables and chairs. "I wasn't aware we had an audience!"

"You'll get used to it," said Valerie, making a curtsy.

"We had a lucky escape on the way here. Pavlos nearly hit a red sports car that was turning around at the end of the lane, I suppose he'd got lost," Julia mentioned casually. On hearing this, Petroula froze as she knew exactly who it was, but no one noticed her reaction. Julia then turned to Valerie, "Have you thought about a costume yet?"

"That's a problem actually. Most couples have some kind of theme, but I think its bit kitsch."

"Well, what about a twenties look, in silver and white?"

"Umm, sounds nice, it's probably a bit out of my price range."

"I've got some friends in costume design, I'll see what they have in stock if you like and you can always hire it for the day."

"Oh, thank you. I know Michael has a tuxedo, so he's ready!" Outside, Alexi was manoeuvring Calypso and the cart up and down, followed by a group of gypsy children who wanted to climb on board for a ride and pat the horse.

"I'd better check in with Alexi. He'll think I'm ignoring him!" The two women smiled at each other knowingly.

Jacob and Kalim returned to the café, guiding Dimitris, who settled down for his lunch and a snooze. Louli immediately jumped up onto his knees and started pawing him for attention. "You little hussy!" he said, scratching her ears whereupon she started to purr and then rolled over. Kalim returned to the beach to tend to the babies who seemed to think that sand was to be consumed and Antigoni seemed to be engrossed in her painting, so Jacob with a furtive look around thought he'd take the opportunity to check out his mother's activities on the computer.

"Naughty, naughty!" she said not even looking up.

"I know, I know," he replied sheepishly. "But she is up to something. I just hope she hasn't done anything silly." He clicked it on and up came, 'Over Forties Daring Dating Service'. "Wow. Mum has joined a dating service!"

"It's not a crime you know. She's at work all day then after the shopping and her Zumba class, it's time for housework. What chance has she got to meet people, let alone a decent man? She just wants a bit of fun probably. I know my mum misses dad, but she wants to get out too. It's not easy to make new friends when you get older."

"I'm not against it. I'm just worried some creep will tell her lies or worse, hurt her or take advantage of her."

"Come on, she's not a kid and she's not stupid. I don't think she'd tolerate any inappropriate behaviour." Nevertheless, Jacob kept on searching.

"Here's her profile: 'Cute, 40+ widow lady, with one grown-up son. Runs a small beachside café. Enjoys the quiet life but is now ready to stretch her wings and fly to new experiences'. Dear God, Mum! What have you got yourself into? Hasn't she ever heard of catfish? Well, she's had quite a few replies. I bet half of them are fraudulent. Listen to this Antigoni. 'Climb upon my back, I'll be your eagle and we'll fly away together, Eager Eagle'."

"That's pretty awful."

"How about this one? 'Widow lady, your days of black are over. I can guarantee the long winter nights won't be cold with me to keep you warm!'"

"That's a bit obvious!"

"This one sounds a bit better … To lively lady. Hard-working village butcher, longing to meet someone to spend quality time with.'"

"That's more subtle, at least!"

"As long as he leaves his meat cleaver behind in the shop." He tapped again. "Look, they've been talking!"

"Come on. You can't read that, it's private!"

"Nothing on the internet is private. Half the CIA or whoever, knows what you're up to! It says, 'Greetings, I'm Thanasis. My wife died eight years ago, and I brought up our daughter alone. She is now studying in Germany. I run my own shop, so I don't have a lot of time to socialize. I'm not a high-flyer ... but with you, I could try!' They've been chatting for a while."

"Are they planning to meet up?"

"He's asked her out, but she hasn't replied yet." Unknown to Jacob and Antigoni, Betty was now standing behind them! She took hold of Jacob's ear and squeezed it.

"Are you checking up on me?"

"Yes actually, I am, Mum."

"Why?"

"Let go, you're hurting me!" She let go and he rubbed his ear pouting.

"As I said before, why?"

"Because what you are doing isn't safe ... for anyone of any age. There are some nasty people out there just waiting to take advantage of you ... or worse ... Haven't you heard of catfish?"

"Err, I can probably cook it if you bring me one."

"Jesus Mum! It's the name given to someone who pretends to be someone else online. They stick up a false picture and profile and con you."

"Oh." She just looks sadly into space. "Why?"

"I don't really know. Meanness or a twisted sense of humour or more likely, it gives them a feeling of power. They get off on manipulating people's feelings, often when they are at their most vulnerable. That's why so many kids go to meet someone they met online, only to find they are nothing like their picture or worse, it's some creep who should be behind bars!"

"Oh dear!" Betty sat down. "I was looking forward to meeting Thanasis. He seemed so normal, so nice. What a fool I've been!"

"Mum, if you really want a date with him, go ahead and make the arrangements but I'll drive you there and meet him, just in case he is a fraud. Okay?" Betty looked a bit shaken and absentmindedly picked up Louli to cuddle for comfort.

"I'll think about it," she said and returned to the kitchen with her head down.

"Was I too hard on her?" he asked Antigoni.

"No, I think you did the right thing," she replied.

The atmosphere was broken with the arrival of Poppy and Kitso who both looked tired and pale with dark rings under their eyes. Julia followed them inside, wrapped in a towelling robe and rubbing her wet hair. "You look like you've been up all night!" They glared at her.

"We have!" replied Kitso. "I was playing my clarinet in the club until four o'clock in the morning."

"And I have started working behind the bar. It was fun at first but as the night wore on, I got so tired. The smoke, the noise, the boring chat, and my feet hurt terribly. The boss insists that the girls wear high heels. I'd like to see him run around all night wearing them! I feel so guilty complaining because at least I have some work but it's not what I'm used to. Maybe next week, it'll be better. What's more, the bar staff are expected to clean up and you have to wait until all the customers have left which means that we eventually left about six-thirty in the morning, so we're both exhausted and I've got my regular job tomorrow."

"How about a quick swim?" suggested Julia? "The water is perfect. Just watch out for those kids playing ball." They picked up their things and headed for the beach.

By late afternoon, Nadeen and Kalim had gathered up their babies, who had fallen asleep at last, put them into the buggy, collected all the bags full of essential baby stuff and driven off home looking exhausted. Bartholomew was about to suggest that Petroula and Tom get ready to leave when suddenly, Petroula said, "I've got some business to attend to, would you take Tom home? Joanna is living with me now and she's expecting him, if that's okay?"

"Fine," he replied unsuspiciously. Poppy and Kitso had returned from their short swim and decided to call it a day as they were very tired. The other regulars were all leaving and waved goodbye. Betty put the leftovers into take away cartons and headed for the gypsy trucks for a chat. Petroula walked quietly down the lane unnoticed and sat on one of the swings to wait patiently. She began to swing up and down gently. For a moment, she forgot everything. She swung higher, her blonde hair streaming out behind her ... she was back home in her mother's garden, a child again, without a care in the world! So, she was unaware that Alexi, leading Calypso and Nikos holding onto Caesar were watching her.

"Hello!" she said feeling slightly embarrassed. "I didn't see you there."

"That looked like fun," said Alexi patting the horse.

"It was. For a moment, I was flying like a bird." Nikos was looking a little confused.

"Why didn't you leave with Bartholomew and where's Tom?"

"Don't worry, Bartholomew has taken Tom home, Joanna is waiting for him."

"Oh, why?"

"Err ... I have some business to attend to."

"Well, I won't keep you, my dear," said Alexi, who winked knowingly at her, then clicked at the horse and followed by Caesar started off down the lane.

"What business is that?" asked Nikos suspiciously.

"I was wondering ... if you're not busy ... you could show me around your farm then we could visit Manolis to see how he is."

"Now?"

"Why not ... I've got all night!" She casually touched his arm.

Suddenly he got the message. "Oh, I'm hardly prepared for guests!"

"I'm sure you'll manage." In one gentle move, he lifted her off the swing and pulled her close. She put her arms round his neck. He could feel her hair and smell her perfume as he tentatively started to kiss her. The first touch, that's what you always remember, he thought. How long had he been dreaming of this? Of all the women he'd known, maybe she was 'the one'. They embraced for a while, then walked down the lane, across the road, passed some houses and cut across a ditch and field and took a path that led to his land, occasionally touching, like new lovers do.

"This is my place," he announced proudly, waving an arm at a neat patchwork of small fields growing a variety of crops, "and it's mostly organic." At the end, there was a chicken coop full of odd-looking birds.

"What are those strange chickens?"

"They're guinea fowl ... getting nice and fat for Christmas!" They walked towards the house. At one side, there was a small overgrown sunken garden with a sundial lying on the ground and a rusting barbeque next to an enormous lemon tree. His house, which he had eventually inherited from his aunty, had been in the family for years and every so often, a new room had been added on. A central yard led into the main room that served as both kitchen and living room. The table was covered currently with bits of machinery belonging to the broken tractor. There was a fireplace at one side with a bed along the opposite wall. The other rooms were kept for special occasions.

He took her into the room that had once belonged to his parents and his grandfather and mother before that. Petroula admired the white lace curtains, the stained and polished wooded floor, the thick stone walls, a marble topped table with a blue and white china bowl and jug for washing, a large gilt-framed mirror and a brass bed, the whole room smelt of lavender. Once again, he lifted her and placed her gently on to the thick duvet. "I'll just lock up."

Petroula lay back and stared around. As he was closing the outside door a flash of red caught his attention. A car was parked across the field. 'That's strange,' he thought but as he had other things on his mind, he did not pay much attention to it!

He returned to find Petroula wearing only pale pink underwear, she smiled up at him, "This is a lovely room." He knelt beside her and ran his hands the length of her pale body, feeling every curve, enjoying the smell of her perfume. He rolled her over and caressed her back from shoulders to thighs but stopped as he saw a tiny tattoo on her left hip, one which had always been covered by her swimsuit. He looked closely. It was a tiny green dragon fly.

"What's this? He asked, touching it gently.

She sighed, "I think you know that I once worked as a pole dancer. Well, let's say it was a company logo."

Nikos drew a circle around the tattoo with his finger." Ahh well, I think it's very pretty."

"Thanks." She turned to face him. As he began to unbutton his shirt, she reached up, "Let me." Her fingers were cool against his chest. Then, she slowly undid his belt and unzipped his jeans. Nikos ran his fingers though her hair and bent to kiss her ... and time slipped away.

Later that evening, they walked across the fields to Manos' farm and found the old man and his dogs in the kitchen alone and despondent. After a few glasses of raki and a supper of bread and eggs, courtesy of Petroula, Manos began to brighten. "I'm so glad you came over. I keep replaying that accident in my mind, I can't sleep very well. The doctor said something about delayed shock or trauma. I don't know. I just hope that Matthew recovers ... if only I hadn't pulled out at that moment."

On returning home, Petroula said, "Poor man, he could really do with some company." Company, Nikos thought, when you've got it, you take it for granted. When you're alone, it's all you dream about. He lit the candle which stood on the dressing table in the bedroom. The light flickered and was reflected by the big gilt mirror sending shadows dancing across the ceiling. Petroula was now wearing one of Nikos' thick checked work shirts and little else. "You look lovely," he said simply as she lay in his arms. Then, he listened, as her breathing slowed, and he felt her body relax into his.

Back in the café, Betty had washed up and watched the departure of the gypsies. Lt Mavromatis and Valerie had gone to practice their competition routine and Dimitris was sitting alone with Louli on his knee staring vacantly at the TV in the dim evening light. The café door opened slowly and there stood Marina, complete with rucksack and suitcase and tartan scarf around her neck. He gazed at her unbelievingly. "Welcome, welcome my child!" He stood up and tried to walk forward to embrace her but stumbled and nearly fell forward. Marina dashed to catch him.

"Grandad, don't get up. Yes, I'm here." She kissed him and put him back into his chair.

"I thought I'd seen a ghost for a moment. Let me have a look at you!" He gazed at her. "Ahh, my pretty girl, you look well. Have you gained a bit of weight?"

"Oh, Grandad!" and she buried her head in his chest.

"Now, now, don't cry or I'll start," She sat down next to him and opened her ruck sack.

"I've got presents from Scotland for everyone." She gave him a tartan tie and a box of fudge.

"What was it like?"

"Green, very green, fields full of sheep and cows, mountains, castles, lochs ..."

"What?"

"Lakes."

"Did you see the Loch Ness Monster?"

"No, it's just a tourist thing!"

Betty bustled in. "Lovely to see you my dear, have you had a good time?"

"Yes, it's been a wonderful experience, I've brought you something ... it's a haggis!"

She examined it carefully, "Thank you. What is this? Do I eat it or plant it in the garden?"

"You boil it slowly for two hours and eat it hot with mashed potatoes." Betty gave a rather forced smile, picked it up and sniffed it. Then carried it out at arm's length!

Left alone, Marina focused on her grandad, "I've something to tell you."

"Yes"?

She took a deep breath. "I'm pregnant." Dimitris slumped a little, and then closed his eyes, "Grandad, say something." There was a long pause.

"Who is the father?"

"While I was at Manchester University, I met a young Scottish doctor called Andy MacAlister. We started dating and he took me round Scotland. I met his relatives who live on Skye."

"And does this Andreas know about your condition?"

"Err ... not yet ... he has plans to work with Doctors Without Borders in a refugee camp."

"And what about your plans now"?

"Stop it. I can't think straight yet." She started to cry again. "I really love him. He's a good man. I thought about having an abortion, but I just couldn't do it."

"Well, we'd better phone your mum and dad to tell them everything. I wonder what time it is in Canada?"

"It's too late now. Let's do it tomorrow."

"Come here, my girl." She put her arms around him, and he patted her back gently and Louli jumped up for a cuddle too. Betty looked in but did not interfere. She crossed the room briefly to light the candle in the lantern and admired the finished icon painted by Antigoni which was now propped up behind the binoculars. She touched it and silently asked the Saint for protection. Outside, the evening stars were beginning to show in the sky and the waves pounded on the beach.

Sunday 4

An Important Rescue

It was another Sunday morning. The distant clanging of a church bell called the faithful to early morning prayer but for most, it was a day of rest, a time for reflection and relaxation. For many others, it was an opportunity to work on the black to supplement ones income, or forage on the street market for decent second-hand clothes or retro junk which can be sold later on eBay. In short, business as usual.

Down at the coast, the weather was pleasant, crisp, and cool. The sun was shining, and the smell of percolating coffee and toast wafted around Nikos' kitchen. He walked from room to room noticing the little changes that had been made. Nothing too intrusive, just the impacts of a female presence. In the bedroom, the sun shone through the freshly laundered white lace curtains making patters across the wall. The big, brass bed now had a flowery cover on the duvet with matching pillowcases and there were fairy lights around the mirror. The old settee had an assortment of bright cushions on it and the kitchen dresser had the plates and bowls neatly displayed rather than just slacked up. In the middle of the table, there was a large bowl of chrysanthemums, all the bits of tractor machinery had been placed in the workshop. He noticed that his shoes were in a neat row against a wall and an ironed shirt was hanging from a door handle. He smiled and sighed contentedly and headed off towards the café.

As he was approaching the small park, Bartholomew drove past. Petroula and Tom waved. As yet, no-one was aware of their relationship, or if they were, nothing had been said. Julia's taxi was not far behind them. Alexi was already putting Calypso into the shafts of the cart in preparation for her morning training.

"Ah! My morning sunshine! He greeted Julia who was sporting a dark purple velvet track suit and bright pink trainers. "Are you in a rush this evening?" He asked innocently.

"No, why?"

"Well, I'd like to ... err ... share a moment or two with you and a secret perhaps?"

"Fine, where and when?" She was intrigued.

"Oh, nothing fancy, just here, actually. When the rest of the hoi polloi have gone home."

"I've nothing to change into."

"Give up, woman! You're fine as you are. Remember, you can only wear one pair of shoes at a time!"

"Yes, I do, but it's nice to have a choice!" she fired back. He smiled at her indulgently, as he well knew her weakness for clothes. They began to laugh at each other, and Caesar snuffled in to be involved.

Inside the café, Marina and Betty were fussing around Dimitris who was having difficulty taking off his coat. "Grandad, I think I'm going to need some advice about you. It took you ages this morning to get up, wash, dress and eat breakfast. I can't ask Betty to help. She's done so much for us already. So, I phoned an agency earlier on and they are going to send out a nurse to ask you some questions and assess the situation, okay?" Dimitris hardly responded. "Okay?"

"Don't fuss me. I'm fine!" he replied, quite sharply. "I'm just tired." Outside, a small Smart car could be seen approaching.

"This must be the nurse now." True enough, out stepped a young woman dressed as a nurse in uniform, but one you might see at carnival time with short white dress and cap. She was a very pretty girl with large brown eyes and thick dark hair and a curvy figure. Marina's eyes widened in horror. "Dear God, did I phone the right agency?" By now, Alexi was standing with his mouth open in amazement. Julia elbowed him in the ribs! The other men just stared. Marina welcomed her and just checked that she really was from the agency.

"Yes, I'm Sophie, but call me Foffie, everyone does. So, where is my patient?"

"This is my Grandad, Dimitris. He had a few little strokes a while back, then a few weeks ago, he had a similar incident and now he's gone a bit quiet and he seems to find walking and dressing a bit more difficult but he's still able to go to the bathroom and eat on his own."

"Right." She turned to the old man and smiled disarmingly. "Shall we find somewhere more private and we'll have a chat and I'll examine your mobility?"

"Of course," he melted.

"If that's a nurse? I don't believe it!" Bartholomew whispered to Nikos.

"Seeing is believing!"

"Lucky bugger!" Alexi sighed, "I wish I was ill ..." Julia poked him in the ribs again.

"Shh ... Be careful what you wish for!" The nurse helped Dimitris to his feet.

"Do I know you my dear?" he asked, politely.

"I'm Foffie, I'm a geriatric nurse and I'm going to help you today."

"How kind!" Marina and Foffie led him over to a quiet corner to talk.

Meanwhile, an odd smell was wafting out of the kitchen … Tom wrinkled his nose. "W-w-what's that awful smell, Mum?" Petroula just shook her head and shrugged. Nikos held his nose and Bartholomew opened the windows, then Betty entered the café holding a bowl with a steaming haggis sitting in the middle.

"Gather round everyone and taste this, all the way from Scotland. Marina says it's very popular."

"What on earth is it?" asked Alexi, who had left Julia outside holding Calypso,"It smells wonderful!"

"It's haggis," Marina called over.

"What's inside?"

"Mutton, sheep's insides, liver and oats, I think. All steamed up in an artificial, plastic sheep's stomach."

"Well, open it up, Betty!" Caesar now had his nose on the table and was making big eyes at her. "Wait your turn dog, I'm first!" Alexi pushed the dog away. Betty cut it open and put a spoonful onto some small plates.

"Who's first? Marina?" She took a mouthful, and then spat it out into a paper napkin.

"Sorry, I can't stand the smell of it!"

Petroula tried some next. "It's not as bad as it looks."

Then Nikos had a go, "It's okay, actually."

Betty tried some and smacked her lips professionally. "I think a little soya sauce would help!"

"Or some whiskey," suggested Bartholomew. Everyone else refused to try it. Alexi was losing his patience, "If no one is going to eat this, I will!" and he picked up the bowl and disappeared outside, followed by Caesar, who was wagging his tail furiously. Julia watched him go, wide-eyed in amazement. Within minutes, the bowl was empty, and both man and dog were licking their lips!

Meanwhile, Kalim and Nadeen had arrived with the twins, closely followed by Antonis on his mountain bike.

"How's Matthew doing"? Nadeen asked as Antonis propped his bike against the tree. He looked tired and sad.

"He's going home soon but he can't stand up on his own or walk yet ... He's in a wheelchair for now."

"I'm so sorry, man," said Kalim sincerely; the thought of disability appalled him. "It must be terrifying for him."

"Yes, he's finding it very difficult. Some days, he's very angry, the next weepy."

"It just takes time to recover," said Betty wisely. Julia had now handed over the horse to Alexi and come in to see what was going on.

"How's life at the top then, Kalim? We watched your last match on TV. Well done, you scored two scorching goals. The crowd was going mad!"

"Thanks," he said flatly. "But I got in a hell of a lot of trouble afterwards ... you see ... I wasn't supposed to score any goals at all. The coach and the manager were howling at me, using all kinds of racial stuff, because I'd lost them a lot of cash ... I reckon I'm out."

"Good Lord! Isn't that match-fixing? I thought they'd put a stop to it."

"No, it seems like it affects every sport now, horse racing, boxing, even tennis. Ha, but I may have got the last laugh. As I was leaving the club, a Frenchman from Marseilles approached me and gave me his card. It turns out that he is a talent scout for one of the French teams, and they want to see me next week for trials and an interview."

"Wow, good luck with that one," said Antonis.

"Thanks, by the way, does anyone know who owns a red sports car that is parked up on the road near to the entrance to this lane? Nadeen says she saw it a few weeks ago too."

"That's strange," said Nikos. "I remember seeing a red car across the fields from my house a while ago." Petroula had gone visibly pale and sat down. "Anyway, I'm off for a swim. Anyone going to join me?" Antonis, Bartholomew, Kalim and Julia all decided to accompany him.

"We must keep in shape for the New Year's Race!" announced Julia as she collected her cap and goggles and wrapped herself up in a thick towelling gown before leaving. Nadeen decided to take the twins, who today, were behaving like angels, down to the swings in their buggy to the little park and Tom went with them. The water and wind were quite fresh, so the swimmers paced themselves and after twenty minutes, they were glad to return to the café and dry off and warm up. Betty had lit the Russian stove and made winter soup for dinner. Poppy and Kitso arrived looking exhausted and bleary eyed. They could hardly be bothered to speak to each other or anyone else.

"Soup or coffee?" asked Betty.

"Two coffees, please." Kitso slumped onto the settee and yawned as Betty served them.

"For goodness' sake, look at you both, you're exhausted! Is this club work worth it? You both look so miserable."

"I know, but the money is good, so we've decided to stick it out a bit longer." Poppy had already put her head on her arms and her eyes were closing as Betty tut-tutted her disapprovingly.

Lt Mavromatis and Valerie appeared at the door and held up their bronze medals for all to see and cheering erupted! "Thank you. Now quickly, let's put on the TV. I think they are showing highlights of the competition on a sports channel." Everyone settled down to watch. Tom had returned and was helping Foffie with Dimitris' exercises. He was learning how to stand up and sit down using different muscles. "Who's the new girlfriend?" Lt Mavromatis called across the room.

"This young lady has both beauty and brains and she's my nurse!"

"Lucky man!" He gave the thumbs up sign. The competition was beginning on TV. The camera zoomed in on the venue, showing a posh hotel foyer with glittering chandeliers. There was a huge polished floor with judges positioned around the sides. On the floor, the couples were warming up to the music.

"Where are you?" asked Betty. Valerie pointed at the screen.

"Wait ... here we are, behind those two in the awful orange and green costumes!" The couples were swirling and strutting and stamping, all trying to outdo their rivals' routines.

"Look! That woman kicked you!" Julia pointed out.

"I know," says Lt Mavromatis. "I've got the bruise to prove it! Let's call it an accident."

"Your dress is incredible," said Marina.

"I can thank Julia for that. Here we are. This was the final elimination. The camera span around showing the couples looking suitably haughty or passionate, most of the women had fixed lipstick smiles upon their faces.

"Looks more like a rugby scrum in posh clothes to me," chuckled Alexi.

"Hush up!" warned Julia. Tom stood up and pointed at the TV.

"L-l-look! The l-l-lady in the blue dress, she put her high h-h-heel on Valerie's dress!"

"So, she did! I wondered when that happened. I nearly tripped up."

"It's pretty cut-throat, isn't it?" Petroula commented. Nikos and Kitso were just dumbfounded, as this was a first for them. Poppy, however, had slept soundly throughout!

"Do you think it's fair?" asked Bartholomew. "Or were some of those judges persuaded to vote in a certain way?"

"I don't think so but who knows, these days?" said Lt Mavromatis. "Anyway, the couple in the blue didn't make it." The TV showed elimination and the final dance off. Then the award ceremony came on. The gold went to a young couple dressed in red and black, the silver to the orange and green couple and bronze to Lt Mavromatis and Valerie. The camera zoomed in as they held up their medals, then a full-length shot showing that Valerie's beautiful dress was torn and a train of sequins dangling down at the back.

"Oh dear, what a pity. I hope I can get it mended." The TV programme turned abruptly to football news … and there was Kalim expertly shooting in the goal from the previous match. "Sadly, our rising star may well be moving to France. It has been rumoured that he's been made an offer he can't refuse. However, there has been no comment from him at this time, so speculation is rife …"

"Unbelievable," he said.

"Seems like sport is all about business these days," said Bartholomew quietly, stating the obvious.

Outside, Jacob was busy fiddling about with the Vespa while Antigoni was playing with his dogs on the beach, throwing sticks into the sea. They rushed into the waves to retrieve them and then paddled back to her. Out across the bay, three kayaks appeared, paddling steadily, one behind the other. Tom rushed to the window but said nothing, as Betty was standing behind him. However, once outside the protection of the bay area, the wind was much stronger and the waves choppier. Automatically, Jacob stood up to watch, and as he did so, the last kayak was broadsided and capsized. For some reason, the other kayaks continued to paddle away, unaware that their third party had gone over.

There was a short scream from within the café, as Betty who had been watching events with the binoculars, realized that the kayaker had not yet surfaced. Without a second thought, Jacob dashed down the beach, kicked off his trainers and jeans and started to swim towards the kayak followed by Nikos, not far behind him. Everyone was now standing in silence watching events unfold. Surprisingly, it was Foffie, who the regulars regarded as a bit of a dumb blonde, who sprang into action. She got rid of her high heels and picked up Dimitris' rug and ran down the beach.

By now, the other kayakers had turned around and were approaching the upturned canoe, which was bobbing up and down in the choppy sea, calling out and looking into the sea. When Jacob arrived at the boat, he dived underneath to see if someone was trapped inside. He surfaced and gave the thumbs up sign to Nikos and together, they dived back down to release the person from the seat and harness and then begin to tow her to the shore. Eventually, they dragged the body of a woman out of the sea and onto the rug, where Foffie started to give CPR and mouth-to-mouth resuscitation. The other kayakers paddled in and pulled their canoes out of the sea. A middle-aged man and young son, stood shivering, and holding onto each other helplessly. The man was weeping, repeating his wife's name repeatedly but Foffie calmly continued, then she turned the woman onto her side, and she started to cough and regain consciousness. "Quickly, carry her in the rug up to the café to get warm. She'll be okay now."

"Grazie, grazie, grazie" was all the man could manage to say.

After the kayaks had been dragged up beside the hut to be collected later, it turned out that they were Italian tourists staying at the infamous Aqua Palace. With professional efficiency, Foffie arranged for a taxi to take them back to their hotel, where the local doctor would examine the unfortunate woman. As they drove off, Betty's nerves began to break. She sat swaying in a chair, twisting her apron, trying not to cry.

"Come on Mum, no one got hurt. Cheer up!" Jacob tried to calm her.

"You had to go and be a hero, didn't you?" she snapped at him.

Foffie interrupted to stop the argument." Both Jacob and Nikos did a very brave thing" she said quietly. "If they hadn't brought her to shore so quickly, she might have died …"

Betty bit her lip. "I know and you were marvellous, my dear."

It was now late afternoon and most people had had enough excitement for one day. Betty gathered herself together. "Right everyone, I'd like to clear up a bit early today," which meant please go home! So, most of the regulars took the hint started to leave. As Valerie was going, she handed Julia a note and put her finger to her mouth. "Shh. Read it later."

When the place was empty, Betty could now be heard singing and doing things in the kitchen. Alexi was outside fiddling with Calypso and the cart which now had a carriage lantern attached and rugs inside, so Julia could read the note undisturbed. It said, "Rejoice! I may have found you a decent place to live … phone me. P.S. Tell A. I'll take Ruby." She folded it up and smiled happily. Alexi shouted at her through the open door, "Are you ready?"

"Ready, for what?"

"Just get dressed up warmly. "So, she donned a jacket and scarf. "Well madam, what do you think?" She looked at the horse and cart now transformed into a carriage. "Get in then." He took her hand and helped her in and put a rug around her knees, then climbed up beside her, and flicked the reins. "Move on girl" he said and obediently, the little horse turned the carriage and they progressed slowly up the lane and along the coastal road.

"This is marvellous!" said Julia, "I've never done this before." The breeze was quite cool now, so they cuddled under a blanket together.

"Do you want to know my secret?" She nodded. "I've got an idea to start charging for rides around the coast or some villages for the tourists next summer. What do you think?"

"Brilliant! But won't you need a license?"

"Yes, that will be another story, no doubt." He turned the horse around in the entrance to Manos' farm where a small pomegranate tree grew curved by wind and age, still hanging with glistening ruby fruit and began to return to the café down the main road. As if from nowhere, a car was heard roaring at speed from behind. "Whoa! Girl, stop now," he reigned in the horse. There was a flash of red as a sports car drove by, far too close to Calypso who stamped her hooves and started to shake.

"You bugger!" Alexi yelled at the car as it vanished. "Okay girl, it's okay. We'll have to practice a lot more in traffic, I suppose."

"And I've some news for you." Julia said, as they were trundling back.

"What?"

"Oh, don't be grumpy, we had a lovely ride. That driver was probably a city type who thinks the country roads are always empty for them to play in. Anyway, listen, Valerie says she'll take Ruby." He nodded and helped her down.

"That's only the beginning." He winked.

"You really are full of surprises today." They unhitched the horse and tethered her near to a bale of straw and a bucket of water.

The evening air was damp, and the light was fading. The evening stars were beginning to show and in the scrubland behind the café, a nightingale was belting out a one-man jazz concert which would go on for most of the night. On a patch of hard flat sand, Julia saw that a brazier had been lit and next to it was one of the tables and chairs from the café. On the table, there was a white cloth and a large candle in a glass vase to protect the flame from the breeze. She was spellbound! "What's all this?" He took her arm.

"Top secret, surprise! Cooking by Betty and conversation by yours truly!"

"Look at me! I'm in an old track suit and jacket, I bet my hair is in a mess and I smell of horse."

"Be quiet woman! You never looked better. Come on, let's sit down." Betty appeared carrying a tray with glasses and a bottle of champagne.

"Here you are," and without too much fuss, Alexi popped the cork and filled the glasses.

"What's the occasion?" Julia asked, curious.

"This was on my bucket list, don't you remember? A moonlight walk, with my special girl … so I thought I'd do things in style." Betty carefully carried a loaded tray up to the table. "There is a special seafood starter, then steak with mushroom sauce and potato croquettes."

"This looks delicious."

"Enjoy!" said Betty and returned to the café. Caesar was now standing with his nose at the edge of the table, with his big eyes looking at them adoringly, knowing full well that Alexi would keep on slipping him bits and pieces.

Eventually, Alexi asked casually. "How's the new flat coming along?"

Julia pulled a face. "It's vile! It smells of old vegetables in the hall downstairs and someone drops coffee on the stairs every morning and never cleans it up. I can hear every step the people upstairs take, and the couple downstairs argue most days, then there is a dog that's left alone all day and he barks a lot, poor thing. All he needs is a good walk and some attention." She took a swig of champagne for fortification and continued.

"Then, there's the young men living in the basement. They are into heavy metal and alternative politics, although at least they are polite and one of them, with long curly hair, always carries my shopping up the stairs if he sees me. Then, there is the flat opposite mine across the road. I can see everything they do! Best of all, they've got a large disco ball on their balcony that spins around sprinkling my bedroom with coloured lights! Actually, I quite like that but the music that goes with it, not so much!"

"It sounds 'interesting,' I wish you had told me about losing your house last year. I was wondering if you'd like to …" He faltered.

"To what?"

"Change places …" Alexis' confidence stalled, and he coughed.

"It's funny you should say that as Valerie said in her note that she may have found me a new place," she replied unwittingly.

"Oh great," he said sarcastically. All ideas of asking her to move in with him had now evaporated.

"Pardon?"

"Nothing, shall we share a special ice cream sundae?"

"Good idea." She wondered what she had said to cause his change of mood. When the meal ended, they walked along the beach in the moonlight enjoying the silver light caste on the waves and he seemed to brighten up. Betty watched then from the window enviously.

"I wish that was me," she said to herself, then examined herself in the mirror. "God! I'm a mess! What can I do?"

Julia and Alexi returned carrying the plates, glasses, tablecloth, candle, and empty bottle. "That was wonderful. Thank you both," said Julia gratefully.

Alexi left to take Calypso back to her stable and Betty confided in Julia, "You're so lucky. Alexi adores you. I'm going on a date soon but I've no idea where to start, it's been so long. My clothes are, let's say practical! My make-up minimal and my hair is … no comment."

"What you need is a real make-over to give you a new look."

"I don't know if I dare. Is it expensive?"

"No, I'll do it, if you like?"

"Really?"

"First of all, we both need some beauty sleep. We've had an eventful day." They giggled like teenagers and left arm-in-arm, planning the makeover. The candle flickered in the lantern and the kayak lay forgotten behind the hut. For once, Betty felt happier than she had done in a long, long time.

Sunday 5

It's All Go

Christmas was approaching fast and Marina, now obviously pregnant, had been decorating the café. Ribbons hung from the ceiling, each ending in a series of stars, all carefully cut out and glued together by Tom. The tree, dripping with baubles, was standing in a corner and each table has a red cloth on. The windowsills were full of pinecones sprayed silver and the old gilt mirror had been transformed by fairy lights. Louli was curled up on a chair near to the Russian stove and across the door, a handmade banner said, 'Welcome Matthew'.

Betty and Marina were busy arranging the glasses and biscuits on a table in preparation for his arrival. In the middle, there was a large glass punch bowl full of Sangria with slices of apple and orange floating on it. Lt Mavromatis was reading to Dimitris from the newspaper while Alexi was outside, attaching another carriage light to the cart. Bartholomew, Petroula and Tom all arrived in time, closely followed by Nikos and Kalim. "Quickly … everyone act natural!" ordered Betty, "They should be here soon." True enough, within minutes, Pavlos pulled up with Julia, Antonis and Matthew. The men helped Matthew out of the taxi and into a wheelchair.

"I'll be back later on," said Pavlos, as he drove off. At the end of the lane, he had to swerve, narrowly missing a red sports car that was cruising by.

"Welcome!" Everyone stood up as Matthew was pushed into the café.

"I'm glad to be back … but I won't be swimming today!" The drinks were handed around.

"Not for you, young man!" said Petroula, as she took a glass out of Tom's hands.

"I'll give it a miss too," said Marina. By now, everyone was aware of her condition.

"A toast to Matthew. Raise your glasses," announced Lt Mavromatis.

"D-d-do you like my b-b-banner?" asked Tom, now holding an orange juice, "I made it myself."

"Yes, I do. I'm going to put it on my bedroom wall at home and by the way, do you remember this little fellow?" and he produced the panda that Tom had brought to him in hospital, "He's ready to go home too."

"Thank you." Tom reached out and clutched his panda.

"No, thank you," relied Matthew, patting the boy's head.

Kalim came over. "Hey man, glad you're back. Have you tried to walk yet?" Silence fell, and everyone looked a bit embarrassed.

Matthew shook his head, sadly. "Not yet, I've been told to get used to being in this damned wheelchair. The physiotherapist told me to be patient … It's driving me mad."

"Come on, don't get upset, it's just going to take time," said Antonis.

"What's going on with you?" Matthew asked Kalim. "I heard something about an offer from a French team. Will you take it?"

"I don't know yet. I'm finding that the beautiful game can be pretty dirty. If you can score when they want you to, they love you and the fans cheer but if you miss or fall foul of the management's schemes then its racist taunts and swearing and the fans spit and throw coins at you. I've even had my car scratched. Recently, it's become nasty, some right-wing types started doing monkey chants and saying vile things about Nadeen and the babies."

"I hope you got rid of the other business," said Bartholomew.

"Of course, I did. There's a big guy from Mombasa in charge now."

"What are you going to do?"

"Keep on playing and doing my best. We've had a triple-bolt security lock put on the front door of the apartment but Nadeen is beginning to be afraid to go out. This is no way to live, is it?"

"No, it isn't."

"Anyway, the twins aren't very well today, so they aren't coming to the beach."

In one corner, Julia and Betty were huddled over the computer. Beside them was a large bag of clothes, shoes, make up and a hair dryer. "Here we are," she said, pointing at the screen. "You put your photo here, that's it, then try on all these different hairstyles so you can choose the style and colour you want, print it up and take it to the hairdresser."

"What about this one?

"No, black is too hard and blonde too sassy." Eventually, they made a choice. "Now for the outfit. Where do you think you'll be going?"

"I'm not sure, Thanasis is a butcher. He sounds like a regular type, so I suppose we'll end up at a local restaurant or tavern?"

"How about a matching skirt and winter coat with heels and a soft glittery top, for a bit of Christmas spirit."

"Okay, I'm not sure about the glittery stuff though!"

"Come on, live dangerously! A bit of glam never hurt anyone!"

"What about make-up?"

"Let's go to the bathroom and experiment." Giggling, they collected the bag and went off to experiment.

Antonis, Bartholomew, Nikos and Kalim all decided to have a swim, so they left Matthew outside in the wheelchair, near to Alexi, who was fussing over Calypso, "I'll keep an eye on him!" he said. But when he saw Jacob fiddling with the Vespa, he wheeled himself over. "I'd give anything to get on my bike and go for a ride."

"God willing, you will," replied Jacob. Matthew tried to move his leg and a spasm of pain hit him. "Are you okay? Do you want me to get you a painkiller?"

"Ahh! No, I'm only allowed a few a day because you can get used to them. Err ... I wouldn't normally ask you this, but have you got anything, a small joint even, anything to take the edge off this fucking pain?"

Jacob looked alarmed. "Are you sure?"

"Yes," he groaned.

"Okay, we'll just go over to my hut," he said, wheeling Matthew in that direction. Alexi looked up and said, "Not a good idea, boys."

Meanwhile, a small red sports car had parked up but no-one had noticed. Inside, Lt Mavromatis and Alexi were now watching TV, Marina was helping her father with his exercises, Julia was colouring Betty's hair in the bathroom and the others were swimming or otherwise busy. Petroula and Tom were playing beach tennis. A rather stocky man in his mid-forties walked confidently into the café. He was wearing a black suit and white shirt which was stretched tight across a beer gut. His hair was slicked back, and he sported a lot of gold jewellery. Betty emerged with a plastic bag on her head! The stranger smiled charmingly. "Hi, gorgeous!" Betty was quite flustered; the regulars looked up, nonplussed.

"Can I help you" she asked, composing herself.

"No, I've just come to see an old friend," he replied and with that, he walked away down the beach.

"Who on earth was that cool customer?" asked Lt Mavromatis.

"No idea, but he gave me the creeps" said Julia. Then she noticed the red sports car. "Oh God! It's him, he's come here to see Petroula. It's Tom's father." They watched from the window as Panos stalked up on them from behind. Julia tapped on the glass to try and draw her attention, but they were too far away. Tom had missed a ball and was trying to hit it back to his mum.

"Try again, watch the ball!" she encouraged him. This time, he hit it, but a man suddenly reached out his arm and caught the ball in mid-air. Instinctively, Petroula jumped back and then went pale and squealed, rather than screamed, when she saw him. "What are you doing here? I thought you'd been snooping around when my friends told me they'd seen a red sports car."

"Don't be like that ... long time no see ... So, this is Tom ... all grown up ... Can you speak properly yet?" He tried to touch Petroula, but she drew back.

"What do you want, Panos?" Tom had now come around to his mum's side and was staring up at the man.

"I just thought I'd stop by to say hello and congratulate you on your new shop. Nice little business, bridal wear, and wedding plans. That friend of yours Kosti, he's got brains, hasn't he? What's his cut I wonder? You've really landed on your feet haven't you, ever since that lawyer died … I hope you made him a happy man. I'm sure you did. I taught you well enough!"

"You creep! There was nothing between us, not that it's any business of yours. I was just his housekeeper."

"Whatever."

"As I said, what do you want?"

"How about we start again, you know family … business?"

"You've got to be joking!"

Panos now moved towards Tom who tried to run away but Panos grabbed him clumsily and picked him up. "Aren't you going to give your father a cuddle?"

"I don't have a f-f-father. Mummy said he was just a waste of s-s-space … Get off me!" and with that, he stuck a finger in Panos' eye!

He dropped the boy onto the beach and yelled, "You little brat!"

By now, Matthew and Jacob were watching from the hut. Of course, they could not hear what was being said, but they knew that something was wrong. At the side of the hut door, there hung an old cow bell which Betty used to call the boys at mealtimes when they were young. Jacob now rang this vigorously and out at sea, Nikos heard it, looked towards the beach, and began to swim back followed by the others.

"You owe me, Petroula. I brought you to Greece." He lunged forward and grasped her wrists.

"Get off M-m-mummy!" Tom shouted and started to pummel Panos on the back.

"Then you dumped me. I owe you nothing. I want nothing to do with you. Go back to your wife!" she shouted at him.

"She went back to Russia and took the kids with her."

"Good for her!"

Nikos was now swimming strongly towards the beach. "Hey, you, let go of her!" he shouted.

"Or what? So, this is your farmer boy is it?" He was still holding Petroula's wrists tightly.

Suddenly, Nikos was there, "This," and with one short punch, Panos was flat on his back on the sand, stunned. The other swimmers gathered around to pin him down. Nikos took Tom by the hand whilst Petroula collected the bats and balls and together, they returned to the café.

Bartholomew and Kalim escorted Panos to his car where Lt Mavromatis was waiting for him. He took him by his suit collar and quietly said, "Never, ever interfere in Petroula's business again or try to contact Tom! Do you understand me?" He stared at Panos menacingly. Panos realized that this man meant what he said. "Now, go away and do not return, understand?" Panos eased himself into the sports car, revved it up and drove off in the dust. Petroula was now holding Tom close and together they watched him depart. Back in the café, the swimmers had dried off and Jacob had wheeled Matthew back inside ... all ideas about having a joint had long been forgotten.

"Who was that man, Petroula?" Matthew asked.

"Panos, Tom's father. He thought he could try and muscle in on the bridal and wedding business."

"What a nerve!" said Julia.

"He always was an opportunist," she replied, flatly.

"Are you okay, Tom?" asked Nikos stroking the boy's head.

"Yes," he replied looking down.

"Mummy? Did he say he had kids? That m-m-means I've got brothers and sisters."

"Yes, dear."

"Will I ever m-m-meet them?"

"Maybe, one day, who knows?" She noticed that her hands were shaking.

"I don't think he'll bother you again," Lt Mavromatis reassured her.

"If I were you, I'd get a restriction order on him," advised Bartholomew.

"Err ... I've got some friends who could teach him a real lesson!" added Kalim.

"That's not necessary," Petroula said, becoming a bit overwhelmed and tearful, but then Betty, still with the plastic bag on her head, appeared with a hot drink and made her sit down quietly for a while.

Poppy and Kitso arrived looking tired. "We nearly got hit by a red sports car on our way here," said Poppy and everyone laughed! "Hey, what's going on?"

"Later, it's a long story," said Betty.

"How is your club work going?" asked Julia.

"I'm exhausted, but business is good at Christmas time which means a lot of tips! You'd never think there's an economic crisis the way some people spend money." They sat down together and started a game of *Scrabble* with Tom. The TV news was on and the announcer indicated that the Greek economy had shrunk by half a percent this quarter ... Bartholomew looked around and stated the obvious, "I see the economy has gone down again."

"What did you expect?" said Antonis with his old fire.

"I thought things were supposed to be getting better."

"You're joking man! We're like beggars ... Worse, we are like junkies waiting for our next fix just to keep us going."

"That's hard," said Lt Mavromatis. "What's the solution then?"

"I don't know. Cut us free from Europe, bring back the drachma, write off our debts, anything but this economic dependence upon those faceless, soulless suits from Belgium or Germany." Antonis had not lost his passion.

Bartholomew tried again, "Well I think they will have problems when all these refugees arrive from Syria, Iran, Afghanistan and Africa. Where on earth will they live or work? It will cost a fortune to set up housing, medical facilities and provide food for them all and there will always be a few criminal types who'll get in and make trouble. Did you hear that they'd been chopping down olive tree for firewood? And desecrating the churches, slashing the icons and pissing against the walls. It's sacrilege."

"I bet Germany will turn the situation to their advantage. They'll select the wealthy and well-educated and set them to work and those farther down the ladder will be a cheap source of labour ... These new slaves are a Godsend for them!" Everyone was listening now.

Julia held up her hand to speak.

"Let me play devil's advocate a moment, I don't want to seem alarmist, but if all these millions of refugees settle across northern Europe, they will probably have larger families than us, so in thirty years or less, there will be a considerable shift in the demographics between Christians and Muslims ... What do you say to this?"

"Sadly, I agree," said Matthew. "It's called Islamification. It's quite a talking point in Holland,"

"What's all this?" asked Bartholomew.

"It's the idea that the Muslims are deliberately moving north to spread their religion by immigration and then the settlers are encouraged to have lots of kids. They run their own businesses, shops, schools, then take over existing communities and councils and create Muslim enclaves."

"I may sound naïve, but this sounds very extreme to me," Bartholomew observed with some scepticism.

Poppy put up her hand now, "As you know, most schools in England are multi-ethnic and they work quite well on the whole. But it's the independent Muslim schools, where they follow their own curriculum and preach Sharia law and enforce strict segregation and dress code, it's these places which divide communities and create mistrust."

"I bet the Brits don't like that!" said Matthew.

"They don't. Government Inspectors were sent in to close them down but when the school has the backing and funding from the local council that's predominantly Muslim then it's not easy. They passed a law banning female circumcision, but it still goes on."

"That's a disgrace!" said Julia, horrified.

"Of course, but they argue that it's their cultural right and we should respect it."

"What ever happened to, 'when in Rome, do as the Romans'?"

"What's it really like in England?" asked Antonis.

"On the surface, the government says everything is progressing and doing well, if you live in the southeast! They're good at demonizing any critics and passing on the costs to those who are least able to afford them or defend themselves. If you have a job and a reasonable wage and are content to go with the materialistic flow and talk about houses and cars and where to go on holiday, then you'll be fine. However, I also know that the UK has one of the worst child poverty levels in Europe, so everything is not right. There are so many homeless and unemployed, the majority just scrape by. Then you have these ethnic areas, societies within societies, full of youngsters who feel that they don't belong anywhere and get disillusioned and are easily radicalized. And now, they have voted to leave the EU, I think there will be big problems!"

The sombre mood was broken by the entrance of Betty. At first, no one took much notice. Then, "Mum! What have you done?" Everyone turned to look. Betty looked incredible! She was dressed in a Chanel type suit and heels, her hair has been cut and coloured and flicked out in a modern style, her eyebrows attended to and nails polished. "Wow!"! All the regulars gave the thumbs up. Suddenly, everyone was talking at once, "You look lovely," "So stylish," "A vision my dear," "So cute," "What's the occasion?"

Betty cleared her throat, "As you all know, I've been communicating with a gentleman I met through a dating site on the internet. He is a butcher called Thanasis and tonight, I've got a real date with him … so I just wanted to look my best."

"I'm going along as well to see if this butcher really is who he says he is and not some freak," said Jacob.

"Well don't be rude to him. I'm nervous enough as it is," Betty confirmed.

"I won't be, think of me as your bodyguard!"

She slapped him playfully. "Stop it! I'll have to leave early tonight. Would you mind closing up for me, Marina?"

"No problem, enjoy yourself and If you can't be good, be careful!" she whispered.

"You can talk! That's enough teasing, I'm not fifteen anymore!"

Outside, Pavlos drew up in the taxi to collect Matthew and Antonis. The evening was turning dark early. The trees and surrounding rocks and farmland were for some time silhouetted against the pale evening light, then the street and house lights started coming on. The Winter swimmers were about to leave when a courier bike turned outside the café. The rider crunched on the stones and popped his head into the café. "Anyone here called Jacob, Nikos or Foffie?" he asked. Nikos and Jacob raised their hands.

"Yes, but Foffie isn't here today." They were handed an envelope which Nikos signed for.

"And this is for Dimitris." The courier gave him a parcel, which he handed to Marina to open.

"Thank you. Who is it from?" The courier shrugged and left. She opened it to find the rug that was used by Foffie to wrap the Italian tourist lady in.

"Come on, open it then," said Kitso.

Jacob gasped, "It's a letter and some cheques! Oh, It's in Italian, I can't read it."

"I'll do it." Kitso took the letter and silently read it for a moment before saying out loud, "It says, 'Thank you for saving the life of my lovely wife. My son and I are grateful beyond words. Please accept this as a Christmas gift. Yours, Roberto Castillini, Milan'." and Jacob held up three cheques for three thousand Euros each!

"This is unbelievable, three thousand each!" There was a chorus of congratulations from the others. Nikos looked stunned. "I can get the little tractor fixed now," he said quietly.

"Foffie only sees dad once a week now, I'll contact her and tell her the good news" said Marina. "What will you do with all that cash, Jacob?"

"No idea," he replied simply. Then he added, "I'd better get ready to act as chauffeur for mum."

Betty appeared looking lovely if a little apprehensive. Alexi pulled her ear playfully like a big brother, "Go for it, girl!"

The others started to leave. Kalim was first, followed by Bartholomew who offered to take Tom home to Joanna. Nikos and Petroula walked away down the lane with Lt Mavromatis, Julia, and Alexi leading Calypso behind them followed by Caesar wagging his tail. Behind them, the lantern flickered in the window and the lane fell silent for a moment before a blackbird began his evening recital.

Inside the café, Marina and her grandad were sitting together watching the TV with Louli snoozing on his lap. The door opened slowly and there stood a young man with a rucksack on his back. He was tall and wiry with very short red hair and eyes the colour of a pale winter sky. He was wearing jeans and a bright red Christmas jumper with a smiling reindeer on the front. He didn't speak, he just looked around calmly and took everything in. He then swung his rucksack to the floor and propped it against the old chest with the crystal knobs. Marina just turned around and smiled, then she ran across the room into his open arms. Dimitris turned round to see what was happening.

"Grandad, this is Andy." The young man extended his hand and shook hands firmly.

"I'm Andy MacAlister. I love Marina and we'll be wed soon. Do we have your blessing?"

"I'd better translate for you," Marina said, so she did.

"Slow down young man, we've just met!" Andy turned his attention to Marina, "You should have told me," he said gently rubbing her tummy.

"How did you find out?"

"Your flat-mate told her boyfriend who happens to have gone to school with my brother; it's a small world."

"I didn't tell you because I didn't want to spoil your plans of working for Doctors Without Borders in Syria."

"Bah! Plans can be changed, or they can wait. Life isn't much fun without you around." He held her at arms' length and looked at her intently, "So what do you say, yes or no?"

"Since you're asking, yes, of course."

"Good." He patted his pockets. "I hope you like this." Then he placed an old gold ring with an amethyst set in circle of tiny diamonds on her finger. "It belonged to my great Aunt Fiona. Apparently, she had an affair with an airman during the war."

"What happened to him?"

"I'm not sure, missing in combat, I suppose."

"And Fiona?"

"She moved to London and did something a bit hush-hush at MI6."

"It all sounds very romantic." They were in each other's arms again when Jacob arrived back after leaving his mum for her date. He popped his head around the door.

"Hello, who's this?"

"This is Andy, my boyfriend from Scotland and it looks like we've just got engaged!" She held up her hand for him to see.

"Bravo, congratulations, it's all go tonight."

"Did Betty meet her date?"

"Yes, he looked a bit posh for a butcher to me. He had a grey XJS and a very expensive suit on. He seemed quite impressed that I'd turned up to check up on him. He even told me where they were going and when they'd be back ... so I hope he is genuine."

"Sounds too good to be true," said Andy deadpan, "Sounds like a catfish to me."

"At last! Someone who agrees with me."

"Well, we'll just have to wait and see when she gets back," said Marina. "Now, we'd better go home, we've got lots to talk about, haven't we?"

This time, it was Jacob who was left alone in the cafe." So, this is how it feels when the kids go out at night!" He laughed to himself and looked out to sea, then into the darkness and the distant sparkling lights of the villages. He automatically checked the candle in the lantern and picked up Louli, who started to purr in his arms.

Sunday 6

Santa on the Loose

It was the Sunday before Christmas. As the darkness lifted in the silent city, a lone blackbird, high up on a TV aerial, sang his heart out in the pale light of early morning. Today, rose shafts of sunlight streamed down. At street level, the orange trees were laden with fruit like baubles on a Christmas tree. Such peace was illusionary though, as it was a time for last minute shopping for presents, making arrangements, buying of food, baking of biscuits, decanting of wine, and making one's living space suitably festive in case of visitors. The sending and receiving of cards seemed to be in decline, probably due to the expense involved and the increased use of e-mail; for those left behind in the wake of computerization Christmas was becoming a time of isolation rather than inclusion and only trendy, arty types or the desperate, make their own cards these days. By mid-day, the city streets were packed and the traffic heavy, to escape from all this. The winter swimmers headed for the coast.

The café was surprisingly full, considering that most people should have been busy, as Christmas was only a few days away. Poppy, who was neither trendy nor desperate, had decided to make her own cards this year and had enrolled Tom and Antigoni to help. They were engrossed in cutting up old cards and showing Tom how to arrange them and glue them onto new card paper. Then, inside, in best capitals, he wrote, 'Happy Christmas' which was all giving him a great sense of achievement. Jacob was helping Alexi outside decorate the cart in red tinsel and to brush

Calypso, as she had an important event coming up later in the day.

Andy was, of course, very much the centre of attention, although there were problems with his English, which was Scottish! Marina had to keep translating for the regulars who didn't speak a lot of English. They were very much taken with the young man who had made his intentions very clear regarding Marina and their baby, although Lt Mavromatis still had a few questions. With a steely gaze and clicking his beads around he leant forward.

"Andreas, have you done your military service yet?"

"No, we don't have military service in Scotland, but I've got my gold Duke of Edinburgh's Award. Does that count?" After a translation, Lt Mavromatis seemed satisfied that a three-day expedition in the wilds in bad weather carrying all your equipment and using navigation skills and living off the land was good enough!

"Ah, but did you also carry a gun?" he asked.

"No, no guns! We've got a hunting rifle at home, so I know how to use it, if necessary." Lt Mavromatis seemed satisfied. In his mind, Andy had passed the test!

Kitso was fascinated by a tattoo that he had on his arm. "What does it mean?" Andy held his arm up for all to see.

"It's an ancient Celtic circle, where the pattern never ends. You can see the same design carved into rocks all over Scotland."

"Do you have a kilt?"

"I do. It's made of our tartan for our clan. I only wear it on special occasions, don't worry." He winked at Marina!

"Can I ask you something?" Antigoni came over to sit with him. "Last week, we were talking about the ethnic tensions in England and it sounded awful, so much distrust and division. Here, we take it for granted that nearly everyone is orthodox with the same beliefs and culture, so life seems much easier. What's it like in Scotland?"

Andy looked thoughtful. "When I was a kid, we only had a few foreigners in our village. There was a Greek man who ran the Spar Supermarket. He married a local girl. Then, there was a small Pakistani family who had a clothes shop and finally, a handful of retired English and ex-pat types. But we had other deep divisions to deal with like class and religion, the Protestant-Catholic identity is even reflected in which football team you support! It seems ridiculous, but it's true.

"I've heard about that. Isn't it Rangers for the Protestants and Celtic for the Catholics?"

"Aye," it is.

Since I worked in Manchester, I think that society can benefit from being ethnically diverse. In the NHS, we have to work together for the greater good. I doubt the NHS could operate without a large foreign medical community … In short, we all need each other in this world. He spoke slowly and clearly, measuring his words. Marina smiled proudly at her sweet man of reason.

Poppy looked up from making the Christmas cards. "Look, it's not so bad. For example, at normal state schools, kids mix quite well on the whole, but the problems start when they go home.

"Why?" Antigoni asked, naively.

"Because, they have to live by the rules of the ethnic group they belong to. Teachers must be very careful what they say in order not to offend any student. However, this unofficial censorship or political correctness, doesn't stop people being racist. What's your experience, Andy?"

He just nodded, "Sadly, you're right about that." After a fair bit of translation, the regulars also agreed.

The cafe door opened and Antonis and Matthew arrived unexpectedly. Matthew slowly manoeuvred the wheelchair inside and up to the stove to get warm. Although it was a lovely day with clear blue sky, the wind was chilly and the sea cold.

"Who's swimming today then?" asked Antonis. Jacob, Nikos, Andy, Bartholomew even Julia indicated that they were going to have a go.

"I want to make sure I can still do the New Year's race," said Julia. "I'm a bit out of practice."

"Race?" asked Andy. "That sounds like fun."

"It's the annual Winter Swimmers' Club race, held sometime in January. Anyone can enter. Jacob puts up buoys and lines across the bay here and we have to swim there and back. It's about one hundred metres."

"Okay," he said, nonplussed. "Count me in."

"I suppose you're used to a cold sea?" asked Kitso.

"Aye. When we were kids, we didn't know any better, so we'd put on wet suits and play in the sea for hours when the tide was in."

"Tide?"

"Yes, where we live, the tide goes out as far as a mile sometimes."

"Really! That must be a strange sight. I had no idea it went out so far."

"Well, I think we shouldn't swim just yet. Let's wait for a while until the sun is high. That wind is quite cold." There was general agreement.

Matthew turned his chair around to Andy now. "Marina tells me you are a doctor."

"Well, I've just qualified. Now, I've got to specialise."

"Do you think you could look at my leg? I had a nasty motor bike accident a few months ago."

Andy rolled up his trouser legs to compare them. "Were you a sportsman?" he asked, immediately.

"Yes, I was."

"Well, your bad leg has lost quite a bit of muscle tone, but the wounds have healed nicely. I suppose you've got plates in?"

"Yes."

"I think you are ready to stand and walk again. Antonis, could you give me a hand?"

"Wait, the physio in the hospital told me to start moving but I think I've lost my nerve."

"Okay, don't worry. Let's use this chair. I want you to lean forward a bit and put your hand on your good knee, then hold onto the chair with the other. That's it, now raise your bottom and push up like you are learning to dive. Okay, we've got you, now straighten up, slowly, slowly … do you feel dizzy?"

"No, it feels great!"

"Now hold onto the chair and push it in front of you, like a walking frame. Balance … Stand on your good leg … Swing the other forward a bit … Stop … Again … This time … Down with the heel and toe … It takes time."

Everyone was cheering but after three steps, Tom rushed up with the wheelchair behind him.

"Well done, now sit down and tomorrow, you'll go a bit further."

"I have an idea!" said Tom and he went across to Poppy and whispered in her ear. Petroula was doing some business, surrounded by papers, bridal magazines, and a mobile phone at the ready. She was now watching Betty arranging a tray of sandwiches on the kitchen countertop.

She gently lifted Louli off and onto the floor and the cat immediately jumped up onto Dimitris' knees for sanctuary.

"I'm dying to ask you; how did your date go?" Immediately, all conversations ceased."

"It seems I have your attention!" She laughed. "As you all know, I met a man called Thanasis through a dating site on the internet, who said he was a widower of eight years with two daughters and was a butcher in a small town. We had been talking about this and that, nothing important, for a few weeks. Then, he asked if we could meet up and go out for dinner."

"In case you're worried, I acted as a chauffeur and bodyguard," Jacob interrupted.

"Thank you, dear. As I said, I'm not a teenager."

"You never know, Mum. People in chat rooms and dating sites are often not what they seem to be or even look like their photo."

"Let me go on. Thanks to Julia, I got myself looking presentable."

"You looked marvellous," said Julia. "Simple and sophisticated, with a flash of seasonal bling."

"Those heels were killers by the way. I'm not used to them." The women laughed. "At about eight o'clock, Jacob dropped me off outside a snazzy Italian restaurant called *Giovanni's* and he waited in the car. I felt very excited, standing there looking so glam. Then, an expensive, pale blue XJS purred to a halt and a man of about sixty got out, wearing a well-cut suit, shirt and tie, grey hair … in short, immaculately groomed! Not quite the butcher I'd been expecting in checked shirt and jeans. He was very polite, introduced himself and suggested we went inside. Jacob seems satisfied that he wasn't waving a meat cleaver at me, so in we went."

"And what happened next?" Lt Mavromatis asked.

"We made small talk about the weather and families, then I asked him about his business … and after a few moments, I realized that he knew nothing about being a butcher or meat, so I stopped being polite and just looked at him and Thanasis went quiet too. Who exactly are you?'" I asked. He looked quite embarrassed and said that he hadn't been entirely honest. So, I said he had to come clean or I was going to leave before dinner."

"Never waste the chance of a good meal," muttered Alexi and Julia elbowed him in the ribs to be quiet.

"Never fear, I sat still and waited. Eventually, he took out his identity card and gave it to me. Sure enough, he is called Thanasis, but it is his brother who is the butcher and whose wife is very much alive and they have two daughters. This Thanasis is none other than Thanasis Christopoulos, a top consultant to our Minister of Foreign Affairs!"

"No! Never! That explains the car … and the clothes …" chimed a chorus of listeners."

"I told you it would be a catfish!" said Jacob smugly.

"Yes, you did, but it was in reverse. I was expecting a normal chap, middle-aged, probably a bit chubby and boring, a man who lived a quiet life. This Thanasis is a high-powered politician, used to travelling around Europe regularly and knows all the top people. He's a real power player. I listened for a while, and then we ate the main course of lobster thermidor and mushroom risotto. I found myself getting cross! I felt cheated! So, I told him that I didn't like being deceived by anyone and that he should take me home!"

"Oh dear, Mum. I hope you didn't make a scene?"

"No, I didn't. When we left, the waiters were a bit upset. They thought we didn't like the food, but the tip Thanasis left was outrageous!"

"Wow! We are talking money!"

"No, Jacob, we are talking ostentation. He's out of touch with real people and economic realities."

"Did you tell him that?" asked Nikos.

There was no stopping Betty now. "As a matter of fact, I made my feeling quite clear in the car on the way home. I told him that most politicians and decision makers lived in ivory towers, so far up in the clouds, that they had no idea of what life was like at ground level! I told him about the way some bosses treat their workers, remember George and also, Bartholomew. The poor man lost a good job and pretended to be employed so his wife wouldn't feel his disgrace. Then, there is Marina and her friends from university, who haven't a chance of finding a decent job and the rest of us struggling, living from hand to mouth, trying to hold onto our dignity or searching for alternative work. I told him that all normal women, like me, wanted was a decent life without the stress of economic insecurity."

"You really gave it to him. What happened next?"

"He just listened to me. He had little choice, after all. Then, he said he was sorry that he hadn't been honest with me and that he would consider what I'd said. I'd been hoping to slam the car door and click away on those horrible heels but then I lost my balance and my nerve!"

"What happened?" Petroula asked.

"Actually, I stumbled and dropped my handbag! Then, I apologized for talking so bluntly and told him that I wasn't exactly what my profile said either! Then, we started laughing and I said that my age was a bit different and it was a secret anyway and that my hair was hardly honey blonde!"

"Then?" Everyone was leaning forward engrossed.

"Then, he looked relieved, took one of my hands and kissed it, all very French, and told me he'd had a wonderful evening and that he would like to meet up soon and so we parted company."

"That is amazing!" said Julia.

"I'm not holding my breath! and I'll think twice about meeting someone from a dating site again."

Suddenly, Alexi stood up and looked at the clock. "I've got to get ready, Julia can you help me?" Within moments, they were back, Alexi was now heavily disguised as Santa Claus! He gave a bow amidst cheering.

"I need a cushion for his tummy," said Julia, so Betty took one off the settee and stuffed it down his jacket. "You look perfect."

"The beard tickles," Alexi said, in a muffled voice.

"What's the occasion?" inquired Lt Mavromatis. "You'll get stuck if you try climbing onto roofs or down chimneys!"

"Ho, ho, ho," replied Alexi. "Actually, I'm going to a party at the children's home." He turned to Tom and Petroula and asked them, "Would you like to come with me?"

"We'd love to," she said. Tom had now finished making his 'something.' It was a big sign with 'L' on it, as in 'Learner Driver', with a Santa Claus sticker on it and he presented it to Matthew.

"You can p-p-put it onto your new walking frame so everyone will see you are a learner!"

"Thank you so much, Tom. It's a great idea."

"Come on, we'd better leave, get your jackets," said Alexi and they trotted off down the lane with Caesar padding alongside his tail waving. Calypso was covered in a red rug and there was red tinsel around the cart. Tom turned and waved goodbye.

"That looks fun," said Matthew, a little sadly.

"Cheer up," said Andy encouragingly. "Next year, you'll be walking and swimming again, you'll see. It just takes time."

As the sun was shining, giving an illusion of warmth, Nikos, Julia, Bartholomew, Kitso, Andy and Jacob all decided to have their swim, once there and back from the buoy, for practice. Inside the cafe, things were quietening down: Marina was clearing up, Lt Mavromatis and Dimitris were watching TV and Louli was asleep under the Christmas tree.

"Ah, I've got something for you."

"For Christmas?"

"Sort of." Lt Mavromatis produced a stick. It was obviously quite old, decorated with a gilt ring and a carved sheep's head on top as the handle.

"Whose was this?" Dimitris examined it carefully. "It's very well made."

"It belonged to my uncle; you can use it to help you get about."

"Thanks … or I can use it to bang on the floor if I need anything!" Their attention was drawn to the window by the sight of a police car pulling up.

"Oh, oh, now what? That policeman doesn't look old enough to drive!" They laughed together. However, it was an older man who entered the café and removed his hat. The regulars glanced up, feigning indifference.

Brimming with self-importance, he began, "Good afternoon all, I'm Sergeant Dimitrakis. We've had a report of a cart and horse driven by a Santa Claus going down the main road. This is all very irregular. I hope the driver has a licence. I was wondering if any of you were aware of this." They all shook their heads solemnly! Marina was just about choking with laughter. "I just want to check up on that incorrigible old man, Alexi ... come on, I know he comes here every Sunday... You know the one who shot up the storks' nest last year and blew out the village fuse box?"

"Really, I never heard a word about that," said Lt Mavromatis seriously.

The policeman narrowed his eyes and looked around. "This place looks familiar ... Isn't this the place where the man left his clothes ... the one who committed suicide?"

Betty saved the day. "You know fine well it is. We had the police here last year and we know nothing about it."

"Strange case that ... everything was in place, except there was no cash on him ... and how did he get here ... by bus?"

"Who knows?" said Betty refusing to be drawn.

Undeterred, the Sergeant continued, "Now, one more thing, a complaint has been made about a red sports car that has been seen in the vicinity recently and the driver was reportedly using binoculars ... Does anyone know anything about that?"

"Absolutely nothing," said Betty emphatically and they all shook their heads blankly.

Matthew now decided to pull rank and introduced himself. "Sir ..." the sergeant clicked his heels.

"I'll keep an eye on things here for you, shall I?" The sergeant nodded. "By the way, I want all charges against a local farmer called Manolis, who was involved in a motor bike accident a few months ago, dropped. Trust me," he touched his leg, "It was a pure accident, the potholes in the road need fixing as soon as possible though ... I could have been killed." With a smart salute, the sergeant marched out.

The others returned from their swim, cold but pleased that they had made the effort to go and they sat around the stove eating and drinking and warming up.

"Did I see a police car?" asked Nikos.

"Yes, Matthew grinned." Nothing to worry about! Just Sergeant Dimitrakis snooping about, asking about a Santa Claus on the loose!" They all laughed uproariously. "And about the owner of a certain red sports car ... I forgot to tell him you'd given him a good knock and sent him on his way."

"I hate violence," he muttered.

"Then, he was on about those clothes that were left on the beach here a year ago," added Betty. Jacob froze. "It's strange, he said that there was no money found on them."

"Let it be, Betty. The man is long gone, whoever he was or whatever trouble he was in," said Lt Mavromatis. If only you knew, thought Jacob, and glanced at Antigoni who was quietly making Christmas cards in a corner with Poppy.

There was a clip clop outside and Santa Claus returned in all his glory ... tinsel streaming out behind the cart, Calypso now wearing the red cap with a white pompom and Santa with a cigarette in his mouth, rather the worse for a glass or two of Metaxa. When Calypso was unhitched and fed, Julia helped Alexi out of his costume. "Let me give you a kiss!" said Alexi, pulling her close.

"You're all tickly ... get off!" She pulled the cushion out of his jacket. "Was it fun?"

"Fantastic! The kids loved Calypso and Tom helped give out the presents from the church and Father Efthemias was there to organize the games." Tom was looking a bit sad, though. "Didn't you enjoy yourself"?

"Yes, but ... t-t-those little kids, do they have m-m-mummies or d-d-daddies?"

"I don't know, probably ... maybe, don't you think it's better for them to be living in that nice house with food and toys ... Some folk just can't afford to give their kids what they need when they have no work." Petroula was looking tearful.

"They seemed h-h-happy but it's not the same as b-b-being in your own home, is it?"

"No, but we did what we could to brighten things up a bit, didn't we?"

"You certainly did Alexi, well done." But he wasn't listening.

"Where's Caesar?"

"I saw him when we left the Children's Home, I'm sure he was behind the cart!"

"Hey, Santa, Sergeant Dimitrakis was here asking after you, he said something about a license. Have you got one?" asked Lt Mavromatis.

"Not yet, the bureaucracy takes forever, the office said it would take months."

Bartholomew suddenly sprung to life, keen to exercise his new bureaucratic position. "Excuse me, which office did you apply to? I'll see what I can do to hurry the proceedings along."

"Thanks, but I really must find my dog now, I'll be back soon." He winked at Tom and went off down the lane calling for Caesar.

Bartholomew continued to anyone listening, "Since I got elected to the local council, I have access to all kinds of things. Mostly, it's a nightmare of paperwork and tapping on a computer all day. I wanted to put up some Christmas lights in all the local villages around, a simple idea you'd think! Ha, turns out they have to be of an approved design and safety standard, a certain colour so as not to upset drivers or residents, bought from a certain supplier, set up by so and so, blah, blah ... and paid for by the taxpayer and accounted for ..."

"Wow, just for some lights," said Kitso, hoping he'd stop.

But Bartholomew was getting carried away, "And next year, I want to tackle the problem of the rubbish dump. It's a disgrace: heavy lorries day and night ruining the roads, the noise, the smell, the seagulls. If nothing is done soon, the ground water used by the farmers will become polluted."

"Really, that's awful." Nikos was now paying attention.

"It must be serious because some medical research boys came around asking for statistics on the number of people suffering from leukaemia and cancer in a twenty-kilometre radius of the dump."

As the evening drew in, Alexi returned looking downcast without Caesar. "Maybe the kids in the home have got him?" he said. Tom gave everyone a home-made card as they begun to leave. When he got to Alexi, he took the boy to one side and from his pocket produced a black and white kitten like a magician.

"Ohh!"

"Do you like him?"

"Yes, yes, t-t-thank you."

"Happy Christmas, boy," he said gruffly.

Petroula nodded reluctantly. "Okay, but he's your responsibility." Nikos was standing behind her. "You'll be able to join us for Christmas, won't you?"

"For sure, then slightly embarrassed. "I've something to show you," and he opened an envelope and held up his Third School Certificate.

"Wonderful, well done!" She reached up and kissed him. "That's quite an achievement."

When everyone had gone home, Betty, Jacob, Marina, Andy, and Dimitris remained sitting around the stove. The TV was buzzing on. It briefly mentioned that African soccer superstar Kalim and his wife were considering moving to France … a wise career move … Jacob turned the T.V. down. They sat and enjoyed the warmth and the Christmas tree twinkling when there was a knock on the door. It opened slowly and standing there, was a slim man dressed in a checked shirt and jeans.

"Good Lord! Come in Thanasis!" Betty jumped up, patted her hair, and straightened her clothes, then found a chair for him. "What are you doing here?"

He acknowledged all present rather stiffly. "If I may have a word with you, Betty" and he sat down. "You certainly gave me a lot to think about the other day." She looked down in some embarrassment and opened her mouth to speak. "Please, just let me talk. Don't be fooled by the posh clothes or the expensive car. They're just trappings of the job, for show."

He paused, as if he'd prepared what he wanted to say with a lot of thought." Every day, I live by following my agenda, which is divided up into fifteen-minute slots, organised by my secretary. Then, there is the endless paperwork, the meetings, and the reports. Then, just when you've got home, the phone will ring and there is some minor crisis, so it's back to the office and work until three, sleep on the office settee, shower in the men's room, grab a clean shirt and start another day."

"I had no idea it was so demanding," she interrupted.

"Yes, it can be ruthless. I used to enjoy the rough and tumble of politics but now it's become a dirty, cut-throat, back-stabbing game where someone is waiting for you to stumble and the media is always there to dog you."

Betty looked out of the window quite alarmed. "Will they come here?"

"I doubt it, as you can see that I'm incognito. Today, I'm Thanasis the butcher, my lucky brother! Betty, my life may seem glamorous but it's rather lonely. Yes, I do get sent to interesting places, eat out in nice restaurants, stay in amazing, ridiculously expensive hotels, and make small talk with countless over-dressed women caked in make up with false smiles. Trust me, they are so boring.

Then, I spend hours negotiating with stubborn, narrow-minded egotists and hypocrites who have the attention span of a toddler, who'll believe everything except the truth! I'm high on caffeine half the time and pray that my translator has got it right. So, you see, I never get the time to go out and meet someone nice and normal, with their own opinions." He smiled broadly, "Someone who says what they think openly without any intention of hurting anyone."

"Didn't you ever marry?" Betty asked awkwardly. Thanasis didn't flinch.

"Yes, I've been married twice and divorced twice! They couldn't put up with me being married to the job. I have a daughter, but she lives in Sweden now. I wasn't around much when she was growing up and I regret that."

"In short, you really screwed up your life," said Jacob passing an unkind judgement.

"Jacob, that wasn't necessary," Betty reprimanded him sharply.

"He's right though," confirmed Thanasis.

"I have an idea," Betty said suddenly, "Why don't you come over and spend Christmas Day with us? Marina and I cook dinner and the men usually take the dogs for a walk on the beach."

"It sounds great!" Then his phone rang. "Damn, I have a conference call to Brussels in ten minutes and then I have to find someone in Washington before they leave work ... sorry ... but now do you see what I mean? I'll see you all on Christmas Day, 'Bye," and then he was gone.

"This should be an interesting Christmas," thought Betty as she lit the lantern in the window and gazed out at the dark sky and sea.

Sunday 7

Happy New Year

The New Year had come and gone. Now was traditionally a time when hardy men would brave the dark and often none too clean waters of a harbour to dive for a cross which had been thrown in by the local priest. The one who retrieved it would be blessed accordingly. However, there was often a bit of a competitive punch up between the swimmers, so now the church had taken the precaution of attaching a line to their property to ensure it didn't get lost in the melee and sink into the debris in the murky depths.

Those following the older Georgian calendar had now exchanged presents and eaten themselves to a standstill. Resolutions had been made and doubtless ignored, broken, or conveniently forgotten about in the sober light of day. This year, the weather was hardly conducive to swimming. Most would have looked outside, closed the shutters, switched up the heating, if they had any, or made a hot water bottle and gone back to bed. Many Greek houses were just not made for the cold and today, the chill crept in through wooden window frames and under doors. At the beach, however, Jacob had already set up the lines and buoys for the race, but the wind was chilly, and snow was beginning to fall, flecking the sand, and sticking to the mountain tops around the city.

At this time of year, the scenery could be lovely with white-topped mountains and pine trees laden with snow, a pristine, silent landscape where only months before, the heat shimmered, and fires raged. Once every ten years or so, the city really got hit by a blizzard and as the snow started to pile up on the balconies, forcing those who wanted their plants to survive, to rush out and wrap them lovingly in plastic bags or drag them inside. If the wind was bone-cold, thick blankets would be nailed up across the window frames to make life inside tolerable. For a few glorious days, children would be free to make snowmen, have snowball fights and slide down the rocks on Philopappou Hill. Schools would be closed, work postponed, and the traffic would disappear, leaving a strange muffled silence cocooning the city. Anyone with a real wood fire in their apartment would find that the entire family had moved in for a while, happy to bed down on any flokati rugs available. But at night, the acrid smell of burning rubbish reminded residents of those less fortunate, the broken or outcast who lay in shop doorways wrapped in blankets and cardboard or the refugees stranded in the transit camps, crouched in the mud around feeble fires. While others waited, wide-eyed, peering out from flimsy tents, waiting for a lift to the border, the traffickers sat sweating in the stifling warmth of a nearby hotel lobby, counting their cash. Such was life. So, Happy New Year.

By midday, the café was full in anticipation of the race. The Russian stove was on and the smell of baking wafted through from the kitchen. Most of the regulars were drinking their morning coffee and talking about the weather. A handmade notice had been pinned to the tree. This time, it read, 'New Year Swim Race, All Welcome. Medals to be won. Good Luck'. Tom had been busy! Oblivious to the cold, Alexi was sitting alone outside on the bench. He held his head in his hands, obviously heartbroken. Caesar had been missing since the children's party. Julia had spent most of Christmas phoning around to see if he had turned up, but so far, to no avail. They had even put out an alert from the animal shelter with his description and chip number. Naturally, Alexi was very upset. Lt Mavromatis looked at him through the window and asked, "Any news about Caesar, Julia?"

"No, nothing."

"He looks awful. He'll get ill if he stays outside all day."

"Well, he had a bit too much to drink last night."

"That won't help, will it?" he replied, disapprovingly, clicking his beads around.

"Let's leave him alone for a while. He'll come in when he's ready," she advised. Calypso was tethered close by, covered in the red rug, sensing that something was wrong. She nuzzled him, and he stroked her neck absentmindedly.

"Horses are amazing," said Kitso. "She knows that he is upset," he continued. Most people stopped talking as another flurry of snow swept down. Alexi just ignored it. "How was your Christmas, Betty?" he asked.

"Different! We had an unexpected guest. Thanasis turned up in his brother's' butcher's van, wearing a checked shirt and jeans."

"The real Thanasis?"

"Yes, and he brought a couple of bottles of excellent wine, some caviar and a French cheese. Marina and I cooked the turkey Nikos had prepared for us, which was delicious, and Dimitris and Andy had a good talk, courtesy of Thanasis' translating skills. Jacob and Antigoni ate with us, then went off to visit friends. What about you?"

"Poppy and I had to be at the club working but Nikos and Petroula came for a while, then Lt Mavromatis and Valerie arrived and showed everyone how to dance! Then, Petroula spotted Kosti in the crowd with his cameraman friend, Manos. Those boys certainly know how to party. They stayed until dawn!"

"Wow. Sounds like a good night to me," said Antonis wistfully, "I went to Matthew's mum's house."

"And it was dead boring," said Matthew. "I can hardly dance in this chair, can I?"

Sensing tension, Bartholomew spoke up, "I spent most of the day singing in church. Then, my wife and son and I had dinner together in the evening. It was all very pleasant."

Kalim and Nadeen each holding a child bundled up against the cold in matching fleecy outfits, were now trying to get at the stars which were suspended from the ceiling by tinsel. They joined in. "We went to the team's Christmas party," Kalim announced.

"In a very posh hotel restaurant," added Nadeen. "I'd expected most of the wives to be models or divas. In fact, many were girlfriends from school days and had young children to care for. Of course, there were a few who just complained and criticized everything. She imitated them, 'my manicurist ruined my nails', you know, the long false ones encrusted with strass or 'my cleaning lady left streaks on the bathroom mirror' or 'my nanny was late again'. Nothing seems to satisfy them … I hope I never become like that." She lowered her voice, "I've seen so much poverty, desperation, senseless violence, genocide and abuse of women and children …" Her voice cracked. "Sorry, I don't know what's got into me." She wiped her hand over her face, as if to wash away the painful memories.

Julia put her arm around her, "That was another time and place. Don't feel guilty about being rich, just enjoy it and think about what kind of life you can offer to the twins. They'll never have to suffer like you did."

"I know, but the bad things that happen aren't talked about and the men are not punished. War is used as an excuse for rape ... young girls, toddlers even babies ... it's a mercy if they die." Her voice was very quiet. "Even if you survive, your own people will treat you as an outcast. It's terrible ... and all those women can only see as far as their next visit to the spa ..." There is a moment's silence as the regulars tried to understand what kind of life she once had.

Bartholomew tried to draw her away from the darkness of her thoughts. "What do the other players think about your move to France?"

"Most of them say 'go for it'. There's nothing to lose, I suppose," replied Kalim. "We both speak French, so that's not a problem. It's just that I've got to think of Greece as my home and I wonder if we will fit in. It's a very big decision, actually."

The Christmas talk continued. Jacob was watching Antigoni carefully. She seemed a bit withdrawn and weepy. "Are you okay? Did what Nadeen say upset you?"

"Yes ... but it's just that I miss my dad. He's been gone over a year or so already. I love this café and the beach, like he did ... I feel he's here in a way ..." She wiped away a tear and smiled. "He wouldn't want me to cry."

"Is there something else then?"

"Yes, its Maria. She now thinks that she got married too soon. Vangeli has started coming in very late and is being a bit vague about where he's been. She thinks he's messing around with another girl."

"That's a pity but we shouldn't jump to wrong conclusions."

"Dad would be very upset, as he moved heaven and earth to give her that fairy-tale wedding. He won some money on the lottery you know and spent it all on the wedding."

"Oh! Did he?" Jacob gulped. If only she knew the truth, he thought.

"Dad had such bad luck at work, a horrible boss, an injury that never healed properly, another job but the place closed down and he was made unemployed again. Then, the job in the warehouse with the forklift truck, which was a bit better, but they only paid by the day. How mum and dad managed with Maria and me I don't know. We rarely had new clothes, but mum seemed to find us decent stuff, God knows where from, but we were always quite fashionable. I remember Maria being teased at school because her trainers weren't a famous brand name; Mum was in tears, and dad was furious. I remember him shouting, "It shouldn't matter what kind of trainers you wear, as long as you've got shoes on your feet; there are plenty of kids who have none!" Maria never mentioned clothes again even though the bitches at school were nasty to her ... always talking about what they'd bought, the boys they dated, the clubs they went to, their summer houses, making Maria feel like crap.

Luckily, Maria had Vangeli; they've been together since high school. He's always treated her well and is a hard worker. He helps his dad run a petrol station. Then, I wanted art lessons and somehow, dad managed to find the money and paid the school fees off in instalments."

"I had no idea that things were so tight."

"Yes, they were, after dad died, I had to give up the art lessons but one teacher phoned my mum and said I had talent and persuaded me to return for a couple of hours a week for free."

"That was very generous of him."

"Her actually, Mrs. Katherina, she's the one who teaches us how to draw and paint icons." She picked up the picture from the windowsill. "Do you think it's any good?"

"It looks good to me. Let's ask Bartholomew. He has connections with the church. He'll know."

"What happened to your dad? You've never told me." He looked into the distance as the memories came flooding back.

"He got cancer and refused treatment. He used to play with my brother Yannis and me on this beach."

"Your brother?"

"Yes, Yannis died in a canoe accident, the canoe was found but we never got him back from the sea. Mum lights that lantern every night for him ... we know he'll never come back but ..." She put her hands over his and squeezed them.

"How our lives are so mixed up!"

"Umm ..." He avoided her eyes and thought about what had happened at the beach. If only Antigoni knew how George had stolen the cash from his dead boss's jacket when his clothes had been left on the beach after the man had died of a heart attack when visiting Nadeen in the brothel once run by Kalim and that Kalim had swum out to sea to leave the man's body there because he didn't want to be accused of murder, making the whole incident look like a suicide. He sighed. Yet, if it hadn't been for George's persistence when giving him Maria's wedding invitation, he would not have shaken off the fog of depression and dope which had enveloped him since finishing his army service. Suffice to say, he just shrugged. "Yes, we've both got a lot to thank George for."

Bartholomew picked up the icon, "Is this your work, my dear?"

"Yes, it is."

"I think it's excellent. Would you like me to show it to the Archbishop of the Cathedral? I believe there are some icons in desperate need of restoration, I'm sure he'll pay quite well."

"Oh! That would be great!" She reached out excitedly to hug Bartholomew, once again, a happy girl. Jacob breathed a sigh of relief.

Suddenly, Lt Mavromatis blew a whistle. "All winter swimmers who wish to race, please get ready!"

This was followed by a flurry of activity, while there was general noise and activity, Nadeen took Poppy aside to talk privately, "Guess who I met at that football party"? Poppy was intrigued.

"I've no idea."

"Remember the coloured girl with the white ribbons in her braids, the one who was going to work when you were finishing yours?"

"Of course."

"I met her at the party! She's called Violet."

"Is she dating one of the footballers?"

"No, she was working as a waitress for the catering firm and doing very well."

"Wow! That's made my day!"

"Everyone to the beach!" announced Lt Mavromatis with another blow of the whistle. He looked up at the sky anxiously as the sun disappeared behind grey clouds and a chill wind blew. As they were just about to leave, an old car drew up and a young priest got out in his full Sunday attire.

"It's Father Efthemias from St, Augustine's. That's the church where Alexi shot up the storks' nest last year, now what? Maybe he's come to swim in the race?" The priest entered the café, pulled off his black hat and demanded unceremoniously to see Alexi. Sensing impending trouble, Julia came forward. "You'll find him sitting on the bench at the back. He's very upset because his dog has gone missing," she said gently.

Efthemias wrapped on the window and beckoned Alexi to come in. Like a child in trouble, Alexi approached looking wretched. "Cheer up man, it's New Year and I have something of yours!"

"Oh! Really?" he perked up immediately.

"We had an unexpected guest over Christmas. When you were busy at the kid's party, which was a marvellous success, by the way, Caesar found his way to my house and let himself in and made himself at home. It could have been that my collie dog Bella was in heat" He coughed, "I hope you'll help find good homes for the puppies!" Alexi reddened and nodded." Of course, my dear mother fell in love with him and she's been feeding him all sorts of Christmas treats."

"Where is he?"

"In the back of my car ... asleep." They opened the boot and there was Caesar with a very full tummy sound asleep. He opened his eyes slowly, thumped his tail, jumped out and up at Alexi.

"Come here you old rascal, I thought you'd run off with the gypsies or been knocked over and left to die in a ditch." He patted him vigorously.

The priest returned to the café. "Is it race time?"

"Yes, we're just about to start," said Lt Mavromatis.

"Can I come along?"

"The more the merrier."

Father Efthemias jammed his hat on his head against the cold wind and they set off for the beach followed by the troop of brave winter swimmers. When everyone was lined up, he waved a sprig of basil about, held up his cross and quickly blessed the proceedings. Lt Mavromatis fired the starting gun and the race was on! The snow was falling gently now, and snowflakes flecked their clothes. A few hardy and well-wrapped-up spectators watched from the beach. Valerie was holding one of Tom's hands whilst in the other, he clutched his home-made medals. This year, he had used small paper plates and covered them in silver foil, each with a number in the middle to show their position. But due to the unpleasant weather, there were far fewer swimmers than usual this year to get their rewards.

"I hate swimming in cold water," Themias looked dismayed, "I don't know why they do it?" Those now thrashing their way down to the buoy were probably asking themselves the same question. Once again, Jacob and Antonis were in the lead, with a group of villagers plus Kalim, Nikos and Bartholomew not far behind.

Andy had dropped back to swim with Julia, but halfway there, she stopped.

"I can't go on," she gasped, so Andy guided her back to the beach.

"She's got cramp," he said to the onlookers.

"What did he say?" Julia translated and they wrapped her in a blanket, then she started to shake.

"I can't feel my foot."

Caesar bounded up to comfort her. "Not now, boy." Alexi and Andy helped her back to the warmth of the café. Marina organized a chair in front of the stove for her. "That was good of you Andy. I know you wanted to complete the race."

"Och, there'll be others, I'm sure." Caesar instinctively snuggled into Julia to keep her warm and she cuddled him.

"Didn't you find it cold"? She asked.

"Cold? A wee bit." He laughed. "Where I come from, this is a fine day in May!" A flurry of snow hit the window as the wind picked up again. The other swimmers were now swimming hard towards the beach, and this time, it was Antonis who just beat Jacob. The swimmers collected their new medals and ran back to get changed as fast as possible.

Father Themias returned to his car accompanied by Alexi and Caesar. "Your horse and cart combination is a brilliant idea, you know. We've had a few enquiries; one from the local agricultural society, another from the tourist office and some shops were wondering if you'd do some promotions. Ah, before I forget, the school was asking if you'd let some special needs kids visit the animal shelter to help out. What do you think?"

"I don't think there will be a problem ... and thanks for bringing Caesar home. "Alexi gave the priest a little bow of deference.

"My pleasure, I've had a lovely time ... I don't suppose I'll be seeing you in church though?"

"Err..."

"Just joking!" Alexi looked visibly relieved. "Be a good dog, boy." He patted the dog fondly, "and come and see your puppies." His car disappeared in a whirl of snow and wind.

Back inside, Poppy was helping Julia recover from the cramp. "Remember what happened to me last year? I could hardly move. Then, I felt so sleepy." She rubbed her feet.

"Thanks, how is work going at the club?"

"Oh, I hate it! The noise, the smoke, the chit-chat, the smell of alcohol is disgusting, even the music gives me a headache. I'm going to have to leave soon because I'm not happy at all. I miss school life. Can you keep a secret?" Julia nodded; her eyes wide with interest. "It's top secret for now, but I've found a suitable place in the village and I'm planning to open a small private English school. There must be plenty of kids in the surrounding villages who could attend, and I can use Kitso's name for the business."

"What does he think about it?"

"He says it's up to me, but I think he's getting a bit tired of the club too. It's time for a change."

"Sounds like a good idea to me." Nadeen joined them.

"Talking of changes, it seems like we are off to France at the end of the season. Kalim decided to take up the offer with Marseilles, so we'll both get a fresh start."

"Congratulations!" said Poppy. "You lucky girl, I hope you'll be happy there."

"I'll be okay but Kalim really likes Greece." Antigoni sat down with them.

"No harm in trying is there?" added Julia.

"I'd like to try and get into an art school in England." Antigoni announced suddenly.

"Really?" said Marina. "You do know you'll have to pay fees unless you do an Erasmus programme or get a scholarship."

"Is it expensive?" she asked naively.

"I don't know. London will cost a fortune, you'll have to look it up on the internet."

"Is it true that most students have debts in the UK?"

"Very true, imagine being twenty-three years old and owing over thirty thousand pounds! If you find work, you then spend the next few years paying off your university fees, unless your parents are rich enough to help you.

Forget about saving up to buy a car or a house, never mind getting married or having kids."

"It's true," added Poppy. Antigoni looked a bit shocked and disheartened.

"That's awful. I didn't realize how lucky we are here." Marina still felt the need to reinforce the message.

"Indeed, have you heard of the Sugar Babes?" Nadeen rolled her eyes in warning.

"No. Wait, aren't they a Russian punk group?"

"No, that's *Pussy Riot*. I'm not talking about them. In England, a lot … a lot of girls work their way through university. There are many sites for Sugar Daddies looking for Sugar Babes. The girls post their photo online, the typical sophisticated royal look, long hair in loose curls, slim figure in a tube dress and heels to match. It's a buyers' market, so to speak. So, they meet and come to an arrangement, say dinner and sex three times a week and that will help pay thousands off your debt."

"I'd rather be in debt!" she replied indignantly.

"Don't be too hard. Everyone has their own way to survive, you know," Nadeen said softly, talking from experience.

Dimitris, who had been listening quietly, shook his head sadly and cuddled Louli, who had found a warm place to curl up in. He was just about to doze off when Tom pulled his sleeve.

"P-p-pappou." Dimitris smiled at the child and waited patiently. "Remember telling me about h-h-horrid kids wearing p-p-pink pyjamas?"

"Something like that, why?"

"Look, I've got a b-b-black eye!" Dimitris puts on his glasses and examined the child. Sure enough, there was a small bruise at the side of his eye.

"Yes, you have. How did that happen?"

"One boy called Demos kept on poking me in the back in maths class, then he c-c-called my mum a p-p-prostitute, so I p-p-punched him hard and told him he had a f-f-fat muffin arse with s-s-spots on and that he was a waste of space and that he wore p-p-pink pyjamas. Then, he hit me here." He pointed to his eye. "Then, I hit him again and we fell down and rolled over and over. Then, Mr Brakachello came up and grabbed us by the ears and p-p-pulled us apart."

"Well done, son. He'll not bother you again, I'm sure." Tom stroked Louli.

"W-w-what shall I call my kitten?"

"Is it a boy or a girl?"

"A boy," Dimitris called across the room to Alexi, interrupting his game of cards with Lt Mavromatis. "Where did you find the kid's kitten?"

"A farmer found him in among his vegetables when he got to market, why?"

"We're trying to find a name for the animal."

"That's easy, Spinach. He was found under a pile of the stuff!"

"Do you like that name Tom?"

"Yes, S-s-spinach he is."

On the wall, the TV flickered, showing a ghastly rubbish dump. Piles of plastic bags and debris were scattered around. Large dumper trucks came and went while others crushed the waste down. Overhead, the seagulls wheeled and dived, scavenging for food. Nikos and Bartholomew were watching intently.

"It's a bit too close for comfort," said Nikos. "When the wind blows in the wrong direction, I can smell it at home."

"It's disgraceful. If I was on the committee, I'd try to get it closed down. Think of the pollution of the land, not to mention the contamination of the ground water and the amount of plastic in the sea and on the beaches. It's shameful. I heard that a whale was found in Norway and the poor creature had starved to death because his stomach was full of plastic bags."

"That's awful, but I'm concerned about my farm."

"It's dangerous for everyone. What did that reporter say? Something about a marked increase in leukaemia cases. Maybe, Betty's friend Thanasis knows the right people and has some influence."

"It's worth a try. I'll ask him."

Evening was now approaching, and the winter swimmers wanted to get home before the roads became slippery or blocked up, as one decent snow fall could bring Athens to a standstill in a few hours. As they were rising to leave, Marina stood up and tapped a spoon against a glass. When everyone was listening, she took a deep breath and announced, "On Sunday, in the next month or two Andy and I are getting married and you're all welcome." She blushed and Andy beamed at her. She had her hair piled high in a bundle on the top of her head and she was wearing a collection of jumpers and leggings and looked radiant. The room erupted in jubilant whistles, applause, and shouts of congratulations.

Left alone in the café, Betty sat with Jacob and Antigoni. The candle was flickering in the lantern and there was a moment's peace before the washing up had to be done. They all stared out at the black sea and the white patterns left by the snowflakes which were sticking to the windowpanes.

"Have you any idea what to do with your reward money, dear?" Betty asked.

"Do you need some money, Mum?" he inquired, immediately.

"No, but thanks for asking."

"Well, I was thinking about opening a one-room bike garage, maybe next to Vangelis' father's petrol station, so I should get plenty of work."

"Sounds like a good idea. You've always been practical, and you'll be able to work for yourself." Betty walked across to the window and touched it with her fingertips. It was icy cold, and as the candle flickered, it made the snow crystals encrusted on the window frame sparkle. "I'm so thankful to be here. Those poor refugees, it must be freezing in those camps," she whispered and crossed herself automatically.

Sunday 8

No Place Like Home

Spring was in the air, but March could be a treacherous month; the sun seemed warm, then the wind could chill you to the bone. So, many children wore woven bracelets for protection against illness. In the city, the orange trees had dark green leaves and sweet white blossom. Sadly, their glorious fruit was left to fall and rot or be kicked about by kids after school. At weekends, people had started to walk about again so the street sellers had set up shop. Displays of intricately made jewellery glinted in the sunshine attracting the early tourists or passing walkers. Behind the stalls, when trade was slow, the men played endless games of chess or listened to the African buskers playing their drums. Occasionally, an old man turned up and played an ancient santouri which sounded like water running over pebbles.

At dusk, the street-sellers gathered around small fires lit in old square olive tins to keep warm whilst the owls hooted melancholically from the trees in the park. When everyone had packed up and left and the night was at its darkest, a lone nightingale performed from deep inside a forgotten yard thick with lemon and pomegranate trees. Then, before the din of the traffic broke like the surf of a distant sea, a blackbird took a stance and heralded the start of a new day.

Out near the beach, new grass had sprouted along the verges of the lane and around the swings of the park. The trees had an aura of green around them and yellow jasmine poured down the cliff face. Geraniums were starting to bloom, and the 'Easter' trees shimmered with purple petals. Higher up, splashes of yellow broom swayed in the breeze. Overhead, early swallows flitted around whilst on the ground, grey wagtails strutted, much to the interest of Louli who watched them from the café window, all hunched up, tail swinging, ready to pounce! High in the pine trees, new candles seemed to have grown overnight, from where the magpies continually flapped from branch to branch, squabbling over their housing allocation and tax, no doubt!

The surrounding farmland was rapidly shaking off the apathy of winter. Nikos' allotments had been freshly turned, thanks to his reward money which had purchased a new mechanical hand-plough. A neighbour had given him some goats, but they were proving to be a playful bunch of miscreants who seemed to escape at any opportunity, only to be found eating their way through someone's garden. Nikos knew they would be trouble.

However, it was now carnival time, an excuse to go out and be crazy after the confines of winter. In every village, town or city, squads of children wandered about self-consciously waving guns or swords or wands, all trussed up in fancy dress, chaperoned by elderly relatives eager to show them off as princesses or super-heroes while big kids waited until dark to then throw away all restrictions of gender or decorum! Hairy, inhibited men now paraded about happily in tight school-girl or nurses' outfits complete with wigs, false nails and eyelashes, stockings, suspenders and heels, feeling free to flirt with black clad vampires, dripping with ketchup on their false teeth or Egyptian mummies swathed in bandages or toilet paper, if it had been a last minute act of desperation. A ripple of applause preceded a truly original number. Every café or bar seemed to have a party going on, the music blared, drinks were swallowed, and strangers danced with one other. A ghost whisked away a Venetian-masked girl in a ball gown or a Tsolias in traditional outfit hung out with a Jack Sparrow pirate chatting to a Marilyn Monroe in a sparkly dress whose blonde wig was now somewhat askew. For the revellers, Sunday would mean sleeping off the excesses of the night before, examining their 'selfies', consuming large quantities of coffee and Depon and trying to remove the vestiges of make up before the reality of Monday kicked in.

In days gone by, as the regulars of the café were fond of retelling, this time of year was heralded by the clang of cow bells and the dull thud of the tambour or the whine of the gaida. Then, a group of inebriated men, dressed in black and white hairy costumes, would make their way down the main street clanging and banging to make an appearance in the school yard, much to the delight of the children who knew that lessons would be over for the day. After much noise and organized chaos, a pole was erected with ribbons attached around the top so that the children could dance for the hairy creatures. After a while, most of the teachers and the hairy creatures would seek sanctuary in the local taverna where they spent most of the afternoon drinking! Alexi often recalled one time when a real bear was paraded down the street and a strong man called Samson dressed in his swimming trunks chopped up planks of wood and even bits of stone with his bare hands.

This particular Sunday though, was bathed in warmth but to deter swimmers, a notice had been pinned to the door saying, 'Cafe closed to the public. Wedding guests only. No swimmers'. However, as nothing was happening until later in the afternoon, most of the regulars disregarded this request. As it was such a nice day, the temptation to swim before the wedding was too great. Nikos, Kitso and Jacob were hovering about near to some plant pots at the side of the hut while the dogs snuffled about happily. The back wall had been freshly painted over except for the Owl by 'LOAF', Nikos paused to look. "I've often wondered who did that."

"A friend of mine, who would rather remain anonymous," said Jacob.

"I see, what does 'LOAF' mean then?"

"Umm, I think it stands for 'Love Over and Above Fear'." Nikos nodded, "Nice one," then, they turned their attention to the seedlings.

"Aren't they beautiful?" said Jacob, cooing like a proud father.

"Humm," said Nikos. "They'll need re-potting soon and some fertilizer."

"Then, by midsummer they'll be over two metres high," added Kitso. "You will have to keep them out of sight of nosy parkers!"

"Don't worry, if mum asks about them, I'll tell her they're exotic ferns! Top secret." They shook hands and giggled like school kids. Betty, ever vigilant, tapped on the window and called out to them.

"Hey, what are you boys up to? I need some help in here."

"Oops, I'd forgotten. I've got to move the tables and chairs. Give me a hand, will you?" The men returned and started moving the tables and chairs into long lines across the room. The stove and the settee and other bits and pieces had already been pushed out of the way. They counted the chairs." There're about thirty," concluded Jacob. "That should be enough." Poppy, Julia and Antigoni started putting on white clothes and Lt Mavromatis, who was in charge of the glasses, followed behind them placing the glasses in strict order. Meanwhile, Dimitris was carefully polishing and placing the cutlery into a box. Outside, Alexi was grooming Calypso and preparing the cart when the beeping of horns announced the arrival of Bartholomew with Petroula and Tom, followed by Kosti and Manos in a bright yellow jeep!

Nikos looked up and groaned, "Here comes the frilly character. He'll be tweaking and twerking all over the place … Who's that with him?"

Kitso glanced up, "Don't worry, the man festooned with cameras is his friend Manos." Petroula greeted everyone and introduced Kosti and Manos.

"I've brought my mastermind wedding planner and a crack photographer to help." The regulars acknowledged them warily.

Kosti was pushing along an enormous suitcase full of wedding decorations to transform the café interior. Sensing a captive audience, he couldn't resist starting his act. "Darlings!" He waved his arms about, "What a glorious day to get married! Are we all ready to make this place into a wonderland? Let's start by getting rid of this carnival stuff." He began to take down an assortment of paper streamers, garlands, and plastic clowns. "That's better." The regulars mumbled assent, not quite sure what they were letting themselves in for. He unzipped the suitcase and pulled out reams of white lace, ribbons, garlands of artificial flowers and white candles.

Meanwhile, Manos had made himself at home in a corner and started to assemble his gear assisted by Antigoni who was keen to look at his equipment. In contrast to Kosti, Manos was a stocky, introverted, shy type, dressed in casual, stylish clothes, wearing rather old fashioned dark-framed 'nerd' glasses, behind which were large thoughtful grey eyes with none of the loud flamboyance of his friend. He took time to admire Antigoni's icons and showed her how to put the cameras together. Kosti was now giving instructions to everyone, "Hold on to this ... take that over there ... pin it up a bit higher," and so on.

Dimitris, who was still laboriously polishing the cutlery, shook his head. "I thought I'd come here for a bit of peace and quiet!"

Within no time at all, the café had been tastefully transformed. Kosti stood back, hands on his hips, and surveyed it all. The tables had real flowers on them and large white candles in glass vases had been placed around the room. The ceiling was now draped with white netting and the artificial flowers and ribbons were woven in and out. He collected the cutlery from Dimitris and started to lay the tables, then he hit his forehead dramatically. "The cake! Manos, be a dear and fetch the cake out of the back of the car please!" Without any fuss, his friend obliged. Unfortunately, as he returned carrying it carefully, Caesar, keen to be part of the action, bounded across and jumped up.

"Down boy, down!" said Manos turning his back on Caesar, only to catch his foot on a chair, toppling backwards! There was a stunned silence, as if in slow motion, Manos fell over Caesar and the cake rose high in the air. Just as it was about to fall to earth and be smashed up, from nowhere, Jacob did a kind of rugby tackle lunge and landed on the floor with the cake in his arms above his chest.

"Got it!" he gasped.

"Well held!" said Lt Mavromatis, taking the cake from him. "Alexi, get Caesar out of here, will you?"

Alexi grabbed Caesar by the collar. "One more trick like that and I'll tie you up mate!"

Antigoni started to gently rub Jacob's shoulder. "That was quite a catch. I bet it hurts a bit."

He winced. "Tell me! At least the cake isn't ruined. By the way, how are Maria and Vangeli getting on?"

Antigoni looked pensive. "I can't tell. They are being polite to each other and carrying on as if nothing is wrong. They should come clean and talk about things. The problem isn't going to go away on its own, is it?"

"No, it won't. I suspect that he was just working overtime to get some extra money for the summer holidays."

"I just don't know," she said flatly. "She told me that she can't trust him anymore."

Kosti interrupted them. "Ah, Alexi, just the man I want!" He emerged with an armful of flowers. "These are for Calypso."

"Bravo, will you help me arrange them? I'm not very artistic."

"My pleasure" and they went off together like old friends. Lt Mavromatis and Dimitris raised their eyebrows in surprise. Soon, the horse and cart had been transformed into a wedding carriage and everyone crowded outside to inspect it.

"What a good idea!" said Poppy, admiring Calypso's headdress of white feathers.

"Thank Kosti," said Alexi immediately. "I would have tied a bow around her neck. Look here, there are new seat covers in white velvet. Now, I've got a red one for Christmas and a green one for coastal trips with the tourists. Clever, eh?"

"Brilliant," said Julia who was holding Calypsos' bridle and stroking her head.

"It's nothing," Kosti waved his hand but looked pleased with himself. The arrangements were nearly complete. Betty had done some cooking and supervised the caterers' delivery of the main dishes. There was a moment's peace, and everyone stood around looking at the results.

"It's lovely," said Dimitris simply. There was a crunch on the stones in the car park and several cars had drawn up, one was a butcher's van, another was Pavlos' taxi and the third was Kalim and Nadeen with the twins. Betty became rather flustered and fiddled with her hair in the mirror!

"Relax Mum, you're fine," said Jacob, "Come in Thanasis."

The dapper, grey-haired man in smart, casual clothes staggered in, carrying three cases of champagne. "I hope these are suitable. They've been collecting dust in the office for nearly a year now. They were a gift from a visiting Saudi dignitary."

"Let's put them in the kitchen fridge to get cool." They disappeared with the boxes. The three regulars looked at each other quizzically, and then gave the thumbs-up!

"That was generous," said Dimitris.

"He didn't exactly pay for them himself, did he?" Lt Mavromatis noted quietly.

"Give the man a chance," said Alexi," and if he doesn't play fair with Betty, he'll answer to us, eh?" The three regulars nodded conspiratorially.

As it was such a nice day and now that things were organised, some of the winter swimmers prepared to have a quick swim. Before they left, Matthew and Antonis arrived. Matthew was now using a Zimmer walking frame and was taking slow, measured steps.

"Are you guys going swimming today?" He took a big breath and made a decision. "Then I'd like to come too." "Are you sure?" Bartholomew fussed. "Have all your wounds healed up? You don't want to get any infection."

"Relax, where's Andy? He'll know," said Antonis.

"Andy has been working in a city hospital for a month now, replacing a doctor who is away on sabbatical," said Betty.

Kalim came inside to say hello. "Alexi, can Nadeen let the little ones touch Calypso?"

"Sure, I'll just come outside though."

Petroula, Kosti and Manos decided to have a cappuccino and a rest, so the remaining winter swimmers slowly made their way down to the sea. Betty called after them, "Hey boys, don't you dare bring any sand inside!" Jacob and Nikos helped Matthew down the beach and into the sea. The others follow carrying a plastic chair, Zimmer frame and towels. Once in the water, he floated and moved his arms and legs.

"This is perfect!" The light danced on the water. He was buoyant and free, so he tried a few strokes.

"Hey, take it easy!" shouted Antonis. After a while, they helped him out and he sat in the chair to watch the others swim.

I'm going to make it, he thought. Then, he reached out for his walking frame and tried to stand but his leg gave way and he fell sideways on to the sand. Tom, who had been playing with Caesar, raced towards him.

"I'll get the f-f-frame; don't m-m-move." He tried to lift him but couldn't, so he sat on the sand with him. Kitso was next to arrive and helped him back into the chair.

"There you go, steady now. Have you done any damage?"

"No, I just feel stupid. I wonder if I'll ever walk properly again?"

"As Andy said, it will take time." With the help of the other men, they returned to the cafe to get changed and ready for the wedding. The wedding planners were beginning to watch the clock now. Valerie arrived in a floaty cocktail dress and heels with a shawl for the evening. She caught Julia's attention and beckoned her over. Julia, not to be outdone, was also glammed up in a patterned outfit with an enormous hat, matching beads, and gloves.

"I've done it!" she said mysteriously, picking up Louli and cuddling her to stop the cat from pulling at the white ribbons and decorations.

"Done what?"

"Found you an ideal place to live."

"Really? What's it like? Where and how much?"

"Not too far from your original place. Do you remember one of the side streets leading off the square, about halfway down, there was an old classical building in need of renovation?"

"Of course, it's a nice street with lots of orange trees; the smell of blossom is lovely."

"Well, it's been turned into flats and there is a ground floor apartment for rent. It's not very big, one bedroom, a lounge, small kitchen, a bathroom but best of all, there is a secluded back yard with a door onto the street."

"It sounds perfect. When can I see it?"

"Next week or whenever you can."

"Thank you so much Valerie, you've made my day." She looked tearful.

"Come on girl, don't cry, you'll make a mess of your make-up, one more off the bucket list eh?" said Lt Mavromatis.

Valerie looked puzzled. "What's all this, Michael?"

"Last year, we sat on the swings and said what we'd like to do before we ..."

"I've got my wish," said Dimitris. "Now, I can die a happy man."

"Don't say that, you've got a long way to go yet and you'll be babysitting before you know it!"

"Talking of dreams coming true, did Michael tell you about our plans for summer?"

"No." They all leant forward to listen.

"Ah, yes, we've planned to take a trip to Russia! We plan to visit St. Petersburg and Moscow, then catch the Trans-Siberian Express across to Vladivostok."

"Then, we thought we'd carry on and see something of Japan too, as I've got some business friends there," added Valerie.

"Wow!" said Julia, feeling a little envious.

"How long will it take?" asked Poppy.

"About three months."

"That's great! Oh well, I suppose I'll be busy grooming Calypso and organizing the tourist trips!" She laughed.

Petroula was getting nervous. "Half an hour to go everyone. Please get ready for the church." She looked at Tom, who had chosen today to become awkward. He was insisting on wearing his fancy dress to the wedding, which was a policeman's outfit, along with those trainers that had battery lights which flashed on and off when you walked. The jacket was a bit big for him and the sleeves were turned over and the hat kept falling over his eyes, and he kept 'arresting' people with the pistol and handcuffs.

"Tom, you must change your clothes now," she ordered, glaring at the boy.

"No-n-n-no." He looked tearful. "He's in f-f-fancy dress" and pointed to Alexi who was now sporting top hat and tails. Nikos looked over at her and mouthed silently, "Never mind, it doesn't matter." For once, she gave in. Alexi and Dimitris, both in fancy dress, climbed into the cart and drove off to pick up Marina. Meanwhile, Pavlos was picking Andy and his family up from the infamous Aqua Palace, where they had complained about the legendary awful plumbing three times already! And Marina's parents had decided that they'd rather fly back to Greece from Canada when the baby was due.

The regulars prepared to leave, the men in an array of suits, jackets, ties, and best trousers. Antigoni wore a simple printed dress while Nadeen looked stunning in a shimmering designer dress. Petroula had chosen a plain straight dress with a few bits of chunky jewellery. So far, everything was going according to plan except for Tom, who seemed to be getting over-excited. But Nikos had now taken him by the hand and was talking quietly to him. Kosti and Manos went off first to check that the flowers and candles had been properly arranged in the church. The others would leave a little later, as it wouldn't take long to get to the church by car and traditionally, the guests usually had time to hang about outside the church chatting and eyeing up each other's outfits discreetly before the ceremony started, as the bride would often arrive a little late!

Thanasis had volunteered to stay behind to keep an eye on things. Before Bartholomew left, Thanasis drew him aside. "A word with you," he said with authority. Bartholomew straightened up. "I read your report on the local rubbish dump. I gather it has become a health hazard." Bartholomew nodded. "I read the statistics about leukaemia and contaminated ground water. Unfortunately, unless half the village contracts food poisoning from eating vegetables grown locally, the media won't hype it up enough for anyone to take notice. However, politics work in strange ways … and I happen to know that the president's wife has some land out this way and there is a large hotel, the Aqua Palace I believe, which makes its money from tourists from Eastern Europe … so big business doesn't want any association with a dirty environment. In short …"

"Yes?" Bartholomew interrupted him eagerly.

"In short, don't get your hopes up but I know that a prominent member of your council has a little tax problem which he wouldn't want the public to know about, so I think he can be persuaded to vote in favour of closing it down. However, …"

"Yes?"

"Rubbish has to be recycled, burnt or buried, then the land has to be reclaimed, so an alternative site has to be found. Perhaps you could give this some thought?"

"I'll try." Bartholomew was beginning to feel out of his depth and mumbled, "Thank you."

Thanasis waved them all goodbye, looked at the clock and calculated how much free time he had. He then opened his brief case and pulled out a wad of files and documents. 'I've got about two hours to finish this lot,' he sighed and opened his computer. 'No rest for the wicked,' he thought as he poured himself a whiskey and ginger, plopped in a few ice cubes and moved Louli off his papers where she was just about to curl up, threw Caesar a ham sandwich, who then slumped down for a sleep. "Lucky dog!" he muttered, as he rubbed his face to keep awake. Suddenly, his phone rang, he listened for a moment. "As I was saying earlier Minister, we have two options available to us, neither of which are particularly beneficial. Yes, I'm well aware that the lawyers have been paid off by the corporation boys ... blah ... blah ... blah ... what's new? Yes, I'm well aware of what the Turks are up to. No, I'm not at home. No, I'm not in the office. No, I can't come in today. I'm at a wedding actually ... Yes sir, tomorrow first thing ..." He clicked his phone off." Pompous, incompetent idiot ... Get a life!" He downed his drink and started to read though his files.

The blaring of car-horns announced the arrival of the bride and groom. Slowly, the cart and horse plodded into sight. Thanasis quickly packed up his things and opened the café door. Andy got down first and then lifted his heavily pregnant bride down gently. She had chosen a simple, if voluminous, lace dress with a circle of flowers around her head. "Congratulations!" said Thanasis as he showered them with some rice. The cafe quickly filled up with the guests for the reception; Tom had made place-names for every seat. Marina gazed at the decorations, "This is wonderful!" Andy, who was still recovering from the rigors of a Greek wedding, just nodded. As everyone was getting seated a strange noise could be heard from outside ... bagpipes! Andy dressed in his kilt, sporran, and black jacket, went to open the door and there were his relatives with a piper. When the applause had died down, the piper stood in the middle of the café and played a song by Robbie Burns, "My love is like a red, red rose," which Andy sang quietly to Marina.

When everyone was seated, Andy's' father got up and tapped his glass. He was dressed in full highland costume and had an air of quiet authority about him which impressed Lt Mavromatis. "Ladies and gentlemen," he said in Greek with a heavy Scots accent, "Forgive my Greek; it's a long time since I did classics." All eyes were on him, listening expectantly. "So, here is my wife Margaret, who was always better at classics than me." He was a gaunt man with grey hair and the same sea-blue eyes as his son. He then extended a hand and helped his wife to stand up.

She was dressed in a long, dark green brocade dress with a tartan plaid which was held in place on the shoulder by large silver and emerald brooch. She had long greying hair done up in a simple French plait and for her age, she had remarkably smooth skin. She smiled at everyone with the ease of a no-nonsense, experienced teacher surveying a room full of rowdy fourth years. She then opened a paper and spoke in passable Greek. "As Stewart was saying, my classics were a bit better, but I've forgotten a lot, so when I learnt that Andy and Marina were getting married, I started going to modern Greek lessons to polish up a bit."

There was a murmur of appreciation. "First of all, let me say a big thank you to you all for taking my boy into your hearts and making him feel welcome in your community. Marina is a lovely girl and we are blessed to have her in our family." She turned to Dimitris, "She will have a home in Scotland with us at any time." He nodded at this. "And thank you to Betty and Petroula and everyone who helped to make this day so special. So, on behalf of my husband, my son Cameron and me, we wish the children all the best in life." She raised her glass and they all toasted the couple. "Cheers!" The party could now begin!

When Betty signalled the catering company girls to start serving the food, she noticed a few empty places then the door opened and Father Efthemias appeared proudly with Foffie. "Greetings. Look who I found stranded on the road with a flat tyre."

Dimitris stood up using his stick, "Come in, my dear, sit down," but fate had placed them at different tables, the young priest was sitting close to Alexi and Julia. For a moment, he glanced wistfully at Foffie, wishing he'd had the chance to keep her company! But now, she was between Dimitris and Cameron, to help with translation. Foffie, of course, caught everyone's eye dressed in a rather deliberately innocent-looking short frilly dress and heels.

"Mercy me!" said Nadeen quietly. "She's out to make an impression!"

"What, don't you approve?" Kalim teased her. When the food and drinks had been served and consumed, some of the tables were moved back and Kitso started to play his clarinet and to everyone's surprise, Andy led Marina sedately around in the wedding dance.

When it was over, he said, "I had lessons, for weeks! It was one of the most difficult things I've ever done!"

"Bravo!" Lt Mavromatis praised him. "You carried it off well."

"You wait, how about this then?" He waved to the piper who warmed up his bagpipes. The noise sent Caesar under the settee and Louli into the kitchen! Andy then borrowed Dimitris' stick and took the poker for the fireplace and laid them on the ground criss-cross. "These are my swords!" Then, he proceeded to do the sword dance, hopping and swirling in among and over the swords. The noise was deafening! People were clapping, shouting, and whistling.

Amidst the festivities, no one noticed a police car crawling up to the café and when the door opened, Sergeant Dimitrakis was standing there. It took several moments for the room to fall silent. The floor was littered with bits of broken plates and the air was hot.

"What do you want?" asked Lt Mavromatis.

"I want a word with your charioteer, here." He pointed to Alexi who had a forkful of food halfway to his mouth and his other hand around a glass of wine. "I warned you, no gallivanting around the streets in that horse and cart without a license. Now, I'll have to put them into a compound and arrest you." Alexi went pale.

"Excuse me," said Bartholomew raising himself up as tall as possible, "I think this is what you require." With a flourish, he produced an official looking document. "If you notice, it is back dated to November of last year." The policeman adjusted his reading glasses and studied the paper.

"Everything seems to be in order. However," he smiled slyly, "there is the small matter of a raki distillery which was found behind the animal shelter. You don't know anything about that, I suppose?" Alexis' eyes widened as Julia glared at him.

"Err ..." Father Efthemias stood up. "If I may intercede here, Sergeant, now come along, this is neither the time nor the place. We are celebrating the marriage of this young couple. Will you join us for a drink, perhaps?" The policeman was under the gaze of thirty pairs of annoyed eyes, so he gave in, took off his hat, undid his jacket and loosened his tie.

"Just one then," he said and sat down.

"Wise man." The priest said quietly. When the noise and music had resumed, he leant across and told him, "That little cooking stove you were referring to is mine actually, we use it for medicinal purposes only, to give to the poor in need ... do we have an understanding?" The Sergeant just nodded. Who could argue with the power of the church anyway? After another few drinks, he found himself dancing happily in a circle with Poppy on one side and Kitso on the other. The dancers followed each other's steps in unison, reinforcing the bonds of generations; a dance which surpassed time, surrendering all to the power of the wine and its magic.

Foffie and Cameron seemed to be engrossed in each other's company. He was studying archaeology and was fascinated by some broken bits of pottery he had found under the tree near the café and had laid them out on the tablecloth for her to see. She, in turn, told him all about the reward for rescuing the Italian tourist and how she planned to do a midwifery course.

"You could always do your training at Glasgow University," he smiled at her winningly. He too, had the same blue eyes as his brother and father.

"I'll give it a thought," she said coyly. "Then, I could check out the rest of your collection!" With that, their plans were made!

The men were now dancing zeibekiko, where one dances whilst the other kneels and claps. Kalim and Nadeen indicated that they had to go, as the twins were lying on their shoulders half asleep, still beautifully dressed although their faces and hands were covered with chocolate cake. They said their goodbyes and they were wished good luck in France.

Dimitris looked around the room trying to focus. The champagne had made him feel sleepy. As he dozed off, Marina put a cushion under the side of his head. Nadeen was at the door struggling with the double pushchair. Without thinking, Matthew got up and walked across the room to open it for her, Antonis just waited and when he returned, he just said, "Well done."

Matthew was puzzled for a moment, then surprised. "I did it! I did it! Hey, this is better than Holland any day, isn't it?"

Antonis agreed, "Yes, there's no place like home."

Manos was going around taking more photos and Kosti, glass in hand, was soaking up the atmosphere. "Oh! I do love church weddings," he announced, getting misty-eyed. "Why do they have to make it so difficult for us to get married properly? It's cruel. I want it all, the whole palaver, Elton John, eat your heart out." The other boys looked nonplussed! Manos returned. He had taken one last photo, one that would eventually be framed and displayed in the café for many years to come and they started to take the camera equipment out to the car. Suddenly, there was a shriek and a commotion outside. Kosti and Manos ran back into the café looking flustered and pushed their backs against the door.

"Help!" squawked Kosti, "There's a herd of goats outside and they're eating everything! They're pulling the garlands off the cart and chewing your top hat, Alexi!" Everyone was laughing uproariously except for Nikos, who rolled up his sleeves and accompanied by Petroula with a sweeping brush, and the sergeant, went outside to round them up.

"Can't you arrest this lot?" he asked Dimitrakis, hopefully.

"Afraid not. I can give them a verbal warning, if you think they'd listen." As he'd had a bit to drink, he tripped up and giggled at his own joke. With much shouting and waving of arms, they drove them along the lane.

The night was still young. The Winter Swimmers' Club was in full swing and it would be a night to be remembered for a long time. Betty glanced across the room. Everyone was talking and laughing. She caught her son's eye for a moment, and he smiled across at her and she beckoned him over. "I wish George was here. He would have had so much fun. He was such a generous man. Did you know he spent the money he won on the lottery on his daughter's wedding?"

Jacob examined his glass, pretending to be indifferent. "Yes, I heard". His voice trailed off. "Mum ..."

"Mmm ..." Betty sipped her champagne and waved across the room at Thanasis who was talking to Andy's parents. He blew her a kiss back!

"Mum, that's not quite true, you know."

"Go on." Betty put down her glass and paid full attention to her son.

"Remember the man's clothes that were left on the beach a while ago and the body washed up further down the coast?"

"Yes, the police said it was suicide."

"Well, it wasn't exactly that. The man was George's ex-boss, the nasty one, and he died while visiting a call girl and the body was disposed of to make it look like suicide."

"Dear God! What are you saying?"

"It was Kalim and Nadeen who staged the suicide and left the clothes on the beach. George saw it all and found the money when he examined the clothes. I was watching from the hut window."

"Did George know all this?" She looked stunned.

"Yes, and he asked me not to say anything and what's done is done! I was a bit spaced out at the time and he was having a hard time financially, so there's no harm done eh?" He moved across the room to stand with Antigoni who was giggling at something Bartholomew had said. Jacob looked knowingly back at his mother and puts his finger to his lips and said "shh."

"No harm done?" she wanted to yell at him, but she just stood still clenching her glass, oblivious to all the noise around her, collecting her thoughts and calm a sudden rush of mixed emotions. She felt she'd somehow been deceived by those she'd grown to love and trust. But this was neither the time nor place to make sense of it all.

So, she turned away to light the candle in the lantern on the windowsill and picked up Louli who had been lying behind it out of harm's way and gazed out at the darkening sky and the gentle swell of the sea. In the dusk, a bat flitted back and forth, chasing insects. For a moment, pain and happiness burned her eyes. Out at sea, she saw a small red canoe and a young boy waving to her, without thinking, she raised her hand in reply. Then, the sea was empty again and the rising moon glinted on the waves. "Well, as they say, you can't cross the same river twice," she said to herself, quietly. She took a deep breath and with a smile on her face, turned to face a room full of people again.